Advance praise for

SILVER BEACH

"A gorgeous and heartbreaking fugue of unforgettable lives—three women bound by loss and family, addiction and pleasure, class and the longing to escape. Claire Cox inhabits the women of this family and their landscapes—all their grief, humor, and desire—with a vital brilliance, and a stunningly humane eye. Cox shines a brave and generous light on life as it is lived in the margins of every heart and every family. This novel is nothing short of pure gift."

   —Sunil Yapa, author of *Your Heart Is a Muscle the Size of a Fist*

"*Silver Beach* speaks with candor and compassion to the sometimes overwhelming weight of the family romance, revealing the courage, doubt, tenderness, cruelty, frailty, and resilience of human nature. The people in Silver Beach are real, their stories artfully, painfully true."

   —Sam Michel, author of *Strange Cowboy: Lincoln Dahl Turns Five*

"An indelible debut. This incisive, darkly funny novel asks the question: What do you owe a parent in crisis, when that parent is the crisis of your life? Claire Cox is brilliant at chronicling the indignities of the ordinary, the unbearable awkwardness of being alive: there is recognizable despair here, as well as tenderness and grace. San Diego, that postcard place, is rendered in mordant, skeptical detail as the scene of tragedy on both a personal and local scale."

   —Colum McCann, author of *Apeirogon: A Novel*

SILVER
BEACH

SILVER BEACH

a novel

CLAIRE COX

UNIVERSITY OF MASSACHUSETTS PRESS
Amherst and Boston

Copyright © 2021 by University of Massachusetts Press
All rights reserved
Printed in the United States of America

ISBN 978-1-62534-564-6 (paper)

Designed by Sally Nichols
Set in Minion Pro and ITC Franklin Gothic
Printed and bound by Books International, Inc.

Cover art by © Jodielee / Dreamstime.com

Library of Congress Cataloging-in-Publication Data
A catalog record for this book is available from the Library of Congress.

British Library Cataloguing-in-Publication Data
A catalog record for this book is available from the British Library.

Excerpt from Jorie Graham, "Mirror Prayer," 1983. Reprinted by permission.

for CJM

But what is it
        I'm looking for
for you? That you
        could finally break free,
arrive? A shape for
        that?

—Jorie Graham, "Mirror Prayer

SILVER
BEACH

Chapter One

The waiting room in cardiology is fancier than the emergency room, with potted plants and abstract paintings that match the carpet. Responsible adults, people who've showered, stare into their smartphones. Shannon, whose dead phone is not smart, smells the sour whiffs coming off her jeans and t-shirt, pulls her stomach in, and inspects her chipped toenail polish, her flip-flop feet.

She has to call her sister in Massachusetts. Half-sister.

Would there even be a pay phone? She walks down the hall to the elevators and wanders back to reception, where a man is peering into a computer screen.

"Excuse me?"

The man's eyes scan the display, his lips fluttering. "Yes," he says to the computer.

"Is there, like—a pay phone?"

"Downstairs, fifth floor."

"Do you know how much it is? To another state?"

He stares at her.

She has three dimes, a nickel, two pennies. She can't call collect again. She wanders back to the waiting room and chooses a seat in the corner where she can see everyone. The woman across from her stands up and finds another seat.

"Shannon?"

A doctor is looking around the room. She is older than Shannon but still young, beautiful in a nailed-down professional way, with a hundred-dollar haircut. Shannon's cheeks are hot. The doctor strides toward her.

The doctor is talking to her, and Shannon is looking at the woman, the face, the name badge, the skinny wrists, the watch, the diamond ring. She doesn't understand anything the woman is saying.

"Shannon?" The doctor pauses.

"Sorry."

"If she makes some lifestyle changes," the doctor begins again, "she could make a full recovery. A lot of people do after a heart attack."

"She's not going to quit smoking."

The doctor blinks.

"She's not going to quit drinking, either, just so you know."

"We've actually got a great rehab program—"

"Did you ask her?"

The doctor closes her eyes, waits, opens them again. "You can be a really important part of her recovery."

Shannon's face doesn't change.

"You know Al-Anon?" the doctor asks. Shannon went once in high school. After the fourth or fifth person told her it wasn't her fault, she had to leave.

"I go to Al-Anon myself, actually," the doctor says.

Shannon raises her eyebrows at her feet.

"At this point," the doctor says, running a hand through her shiny brown hair, "you should go home and get some sleep."

"Can I see her? Can I drive her home?"

"Plan on coming back tomorrow. We'll call you if anything changes."

"What if I hadn't found her?" Shannon swallows.

A thoughtful, practiced look comes over the doctor's face. "It's very good you found her when you did. She's lucky."

If you're anywhere near the Pacific, the dawn sky in San Diego is low and grey like sleep. Shannon rolls the windows down, and the cool, damp air blows at her eyelids. Even with the breeze, she stinks.

The concrete of Washington Street ribbons ahead of her, the same color as the opaque sky. Everything is closed except for twenty-four-hour taco shops, twenty-four-hour Rite Aids, gas stations. A familiar drunk from Silver Beach trudges up the sidewalk, pushing a shopping cart. The freeway is empty and, as she merges, an airplane tears over it to land in Lindbergh Field like a giant insect coming to rest.

Her mother is going to live.

She exits the freeway and drives west, past the idiotic sign in the median: *Welcome to Silver Beach Where the Sand Meets the Surf.* She pulls into the parking lot of the Denny's on Marina Boulevard, empty except for some trampy seagulls. The pigeons prefer the defunct transit depot across the street, an incredible ruin coated with layers of their shit.

Her first stop is the lonely high-fee ATM, where she'll withdraw a single, expensive twenty. She could get back in the car and drive to her own bank's ATM, skipping the fee, but how much would that be in gas? She pushes the button to check her balance, her stomach plunging.

Over a hundred, more than she thought.

From the serenity of her booth, she scans the color photos of pancakes and bacon. A waitress pours coffee, wincing through the steam. Shannon orders oatmeal, and the waitress takes her menu and shuffles off.

Alone with her coffee, she looks out the window at her life. The old depot: back in the fifties, in the tuna cannery days, you could catch a bus or a train from here; now you have to get on a freeway and go to the station downtown. She can see herself doing it, parking her car in the lot, boarding a bus, leaving forever.

She can almost see the ocean at the end of an alley, just on the other side of a cinder-block wall. It could have been the same path Mara and Allison took to the beach the day Allison drowned. It wasn't the most direct route, but her sisters wouldn't have done the practical thing that day. They would have done the fun thing, and this entrance has the winding stairs with the sea-lion fountain.

She thinks about this all the time.

Her sisters—half-sisters—were strong swimmers, but they were small. There was no lifeguard—it was early, a fall morning. There was a rip current.

Is this true?

She doesn't know how she knows the story. Mara was seven, Allison almost nine, and Shannon was a baby. Their mother had taken Shannon to the doctor—she was a fussy baby, their mother thought there was something wrong with her—and the girls were home by themselves. They decided to walk to the beach.

Mara's father took her back to Boston with him after it happened, leaving Shannon with their mother. Is that when she turned into a drunk, or had it already started? For as long as Shannon can basically remember, her mother was a drunk. You can't get disability for alcoholism anymore, but when she applied for benefits you still could, and Linda had been a pretty, pitiable, young white woman whose kid had drowned. Her caseworker liked her.

Sitting in Denny's, Shannon sees the checks arriving into the future, sees her mother trundling home with her little paper sack.

She buys a fifth every afternoon, never more, though it would save her a thousand dollars a year if she would just buy the jug.

Shannon could save herself: drive to the station downtown, get on a Greyhound, ride as far as it will take her. When she gets there, she could get on a boat. From the boat, maybe a train.

The waitress sets a bowl of oatmeal in front of her, refills her coffee, and sets a side plate of sausage next to it. Shannon looks up.

"On the house," the waitress whispers, and she's gone.

Shannon tears into the sausage, thinking, Who does she know outside San Diego, that she actually likes? Mara lives back east, which, not. She pictures sitting with Mara on what would be her perfect living-room couch, candles, classical music playing, passing her a pipe. She smiles and covers the sausage with syrup.

She leaves a 50 percent tip for the waitress. Afraid of falling asleep at the wheel, she walks home on the boardwalk. The marine layer is thicker, the air warmer. The drunks are up now, the beach foragers, the dogwalkers, everyone moving at the same pace as the fog itself, even the joggers, floating over the hard-packed sand below the cliffs.

She doesn't remember Allison, but she imagines her drowning all the time, pictures her floating away from the shore, the noise of the beach fading. There's a long pier to the south, near the city line, and when you walk to the end of it, you notice how quiet the water is without the waves crashing. The ocean swells and foams, sleepy and regular, hypnotizing you if you stare down at it. Sometimes, she thinks she would like to be there in the waves, in the quiet, under the water. When she gets super-stoned, she feels like she's already there.

The door to the apartment is unlocked. She fishes the cordless out of a pile and replaces it in the cradle to charge. She walks down the hall to her room and settles onto her bed, takes out a Ziploc, and packs what's left of its contents into her gummy pipe. She leans against the pillows, and finally, finally, inhales the vacant-lot taste of Mexi dirt weed. When it's cashed, she'll have to wait till next Friday, seven whole days from now, for her final paycheck. Her dealer is an asshole.

Later, she drifts into the living room to watch TV and falls asleep on the couch in her mother's spot.

When she wakes, bombs are exploding in her brain. She blinks in the nonspecific light: it could be any hour, any planet. The downstairs neighbor is playing video games that rattle the cups and saucers in the sink. She turns up the volume on the TV.

The cordless rings. She stumbles toward it. "Hello?" she coughs and mutes the TV. "This is her," she says.

The voice on the other end softens. "Your mother's taken a turn." A weird phrase: the caller has an accent Shannon can't place.

"She had a small stroke," the voice says. "It's called a minor stroke, but it's fairly serious. We're going to need to keep her a while longer. Can you come in today?"

"Is she going to need a bedpan?"

"Beg pardon?"

"Is she going to need a bedpan when I bring her home?"

"... No, I don't think so—but please come in as soon as possible." Shannon is quiet.

"Hello? Miss?"

She sets the phone on the counter and observes it. The phone's voice is tiny, a bug's voice. She creeps backward. She crouches at the coffee table.

The voice goes quiet. After half a minute, Shannon hears a recording: *If you'd like to make a call, please hang up and try again. If you need help, hang up, and then dial your operator.* Then an accusatory, stuttering tone fills the room. She walks back to her bedroom.

6

She yanks her sheets and makes the bed, something she can't remember ever doing. She jogs back to the kitchen and hangs up the handset. She dials her friend Brandy's number: Brandy's dad pays her gas-card bills, among other things.

"Hey, girl," Shannon says, purpose creeping into her voice. "Wanna go for a drive?" Her free hand crumples a receipt on the counter into a little ball.

"I don't know," she says. "How about New Mexico?"

Chapter Two

Mara's phone vibrates again, the same California number, no voicemail.

Two minutes. She thumbs the number, puts the phone to her ear, and calculates the walk to the library.

"Mara?" Her sister's voice. Half-sister.

"Where are you calling from?" Mara asks.

A very small girl in overalls: "Miss MEADE!" Mara dips to squeeze the girl's shoulder and walks past the first graders, down the hall to the double doors.

"I'm on my friend's phone," Shannon says, muffled. Mara switches ears, pushes the door open to the quad, and steps into sunshine. "Something happened with Mom," Shannon is saying.

Even as she speed-walks to the library, Mara is holding her breath, which she is very good at. "She's in the hospital." Mara's eyes take in too much light, and everything goes mercury for a second. "It's like—I guess it's a heart attack—"

Mara hurries down the stone path across the quad, a reedy figure in bright linen, floating.

"'Cardiac event,' I guess that's like a heart attack, right?"

Has Mara spoken? Is she supposed to speak? The fourth-grade teacher is behind her, leading her class. Their library hour is about to begin. Mara fumbles for her keys.

"Mara?" Shannon's voice. Mara hasn't seen her in years. Shannon, a chubby, yellow-haired kid, though now, Mara supposes, she's what, almost thirty? Behind her, the fourth graders are waiting, their teacher waving goodbye. They're filing in after her, swirling into the library, collapsing into beanbag chairs.

"How is she?" Mara hears herself say. The fourth graders open their notebooks and begin scribbling, following the instructions she has printed on the board. Her handwriting is lovely, a small part of her fame at the Amherst Friends School. Her half-sister is demanding she fly to California.

"I can't do that," Mara says.

"She had a stroke, too," says the voice at her ear.

Suddenly the room is freezing. The ten-year-olds are bent over their composition books, bangs falling into their eyes. A long-haired skateboarder raises his hand, signaling for the bathroom pass.

"She's gonna need someone to be there."

Mara's hands give the skateboarder what he needs, and she turns her back to her students.

"But you're there," Mara says.

"I'm in jail."

Mara wraps her arms around herself. "You're—I'm sorry?"

"I got a D.U.I. It's my third one, I have to serve thirty days. I'm at Las Colinas."

"Las what?"

"It's a correctional facility."

"But you're calling from your friend's phone."

"It's the jail phone."

• • •

Mara feels the children's eyes on her and turns around. They've finished their task, they're waiting for her. She stands there, long-boned, suspicious, like an egret.

"I'll call you back," Mara murmurs, and drops the phone into her pocket.

By 3:00, the teachers are in their cars, racing each other to happy hour at the bar on Route 116, where a dozen craft beers are on tap. Two weeks left in the semester, the air buoyant with grass cuttings and dogwood blossoms. Friday. The May sun high in the daisy-bright sky.

Mara is alone at a picnic table at the edge of campus, on the phone to California. A nurse is saying her mother can come home Monday.

"She'll need to be picked up," he says.

"I'm in Massachusetts." She's already told him this.

"Do you have family here?"

"I don't know where my sister is."

"There's a shelter near here, Hope House, they have a recuperative care unit. I can see if they have any beds." The man's voice is gentle.

Mara's body is weightless, levitating off the picnic table. "My mother has her own bed. She has an apartment in Silver Beach."

"She's going to need care, is the thing. We set her up at the RCU, she gets a caseworker to do the paperwork, schedule a home-health aide, get her into rehab . . ."

"My sister needs to pick her up. They live together."

"Miss Meade, no one is picking up that phone where your mother lives."

Mara ends the call and drops her phone on the table like a dead thing. The sun pulls a tuft of dandelion into the air. She gazes at the glowing afterimage against her eyelids.

Mara's building is a ramshackle triple-decker with peeling white paint in Northampton. The foyer is dim and cool, the carpet thin, the wallpaper ancient, the curtains old lace. Her mailbox is empty: there isn't any mail, or Nell already got it. If Nell is upstairs in Mara's apartment, she has forgotten to text. Again. Nell would like them to move in together, but Mara doesn't want to give up her apartment, or share it. She certainly doesn't want to get married, now that it's an option. She prefers to spend weeknights by herself, reading or at the movies or working on . . . whatever. A quilt, a pie, a time machine. When she has company, she wants to be texted.

She ascends the stairs, listening to each one squeak under her foot, the stairwell otherwise quiet as a coffin. At her door on the third floor, she sticks the key in. Locked. Mara shoves open the door, and the apartment that greets her is stuffy, inert, the only pulse a red light flashing on the handset: Shannon. Mara's shoulders droop.

Shannon doesn't really exist, or if she does, they aren't related. It was just her and Allison; then she lost Allison, and Shannon was the replacement, a disconsolate baby for a magic sister. This is how she orders it in her head, though Shannon was a year old, maybe two, when Allison drowned.

She remembers when Shannon was born. The day of the baby's birth, Shannon's father drove the girls to the hospital. Things had been weird for more than a year—their father in Boston, their mother in love with a brooding, mustached man who was always on the verge of making a scene. He talked like he was in a movie, punched walls, cried a lot. Linda was crazy about him.

At the hospital, their pretty mother looked frightening, hair plastered to her face, broken blood vessels around her eyes. She held a red gopher to her breast.

The gopher, Shannon, turned out to be an annoying infant, a projectile vomiter, a wailer, a flailer, a farter. Allison, whom everybody loved on sight, tried to win her affection, but Shannon threw fits when Allison held her. Oddly, she took to Mara. "Here," their mother would say, handing her over as she screamed, "she likes you." The baby's father left soon after, never to be heard from again, which was probably better.

The last time Mara saw Shannon was two years ago, in L.A., where she had gone for a librarians' conference. There was something raw and unformed, almost petulant about Shannon's face. She was blond, like their mother, but otherwise didn't resemble anyone in Mara's family; at twenty-five, she was still thick in a pubescent way, as though she hadn't shed the husk of babyhood. She had an impatient, out-of-breath way of talking, like she had to explain everything but had already decided you didn't care or wouldn't understand.

Mara's clothes are hot against her skin in the airless apartment, and she crosses the living room to yank open the sliding-glass door to the balcony. She pads across the plank floor to her bedroom, opening windows, propping the door open to get a cross-breeze. She pulls a bottle of wine from the refrigerator and presses it to her forehead to cool herself.

The lock turns, and the apartment door opens. Nell peeks her broad face around it, her eyes smiling.

"Hey, you," she says.

Mara discovers she is very grateful.

Nell crosses the threshold in her athletic way. She walks out of her flip-flops and bends over at the waist, pulling her mass of hair into a topknot. She stands upright, triumphant.

"Hi," she announces. In the kitchen, she kisses Mara's neck, and Mara feels a heat thread down her body, from her face to her knees, a live current. It's a feeling she forgets, but here it is again, savory, unruly. She places the bottle on the countertop and grips Nell's waist with her hand, pulling her close. She breathes for a beat before releasing her.

Nell goes to the fridge and squats in front of it, contemplating the afternoon's aperitifs. When she emerges, she plunks her finds next to a cutting board and produces a chef's knife, a paring knife, fingerbowls, and ramekins, and sets to work. She presents it all on a tray on the coffee table in the living room, beckoning with her head for Mara to join her. Unlike Mara, who grew up alone with her father in a hushed house full of dark wood, Nell does things with a flourish, like a good host. She comes from a big, noisy family and resembles her own father, who died right after they graduated: square-jawed, green-eyed, freckled, with thick, wavy hair the color of dark ash. She's beautiful in a hardy way, beauty being the absolute least of her concerns. It took Mara years to fall in love with her, years she can't quite remember.

"Hi," Nell says again. "Are you sharing that?"

Mara, who hasn't moved from the kitchen, rests her chin on the bottle.

"Are you talking to me today?" Nell asks.

Mara raises her eyebrows and smiles, pulling two stemmed glasses from the cabinet. She empties what's left of the bottle into the glasses and carries them into the living room, handing one to Nell, tucking her feet under her on the sofa. She surveys the olives, tapenades, nuts, crackers.

"Try the one with the fig," instructs Nell, who cannot always wait out Mara's interminable silences.

"It's date paste." Mara smiles. "I made it last night."

"Are you hungry?"

"No."

"More for me, then," Nell says, reaching for a handful of almonds. "Guess what?"

Mara waits.

"My mother is getting married."

"To whom?" Mara blinks.

"He was friends with my parents in high school. I say good luck to him."

"Is there going to be a wedding?"

"Oh, that's the best part. I'm supposed to be her maid of honor."

"*You?*" Nell comes from a flock of sisters. And you don't ask your daughter to be your maid of honor, you ask your friend. Nell's mother might not have friends.

"Anna has children," Nell says, "whereas *my* life is frivolous and interruptible. And Sarah's moving to Montana with her kids, and nobody wants to deal with Nikki's whatever, so . . ." Nell sweeps a strand of hair off her face. There is at least one more sister, but Mara doesn't ask.

"I was like, 'I'm bringing my *girlfriend*,' I hope that's all right with you," Nell says. Mara has met Nell's mother a hundred times, but now that they're together, Nell always says "my girlfriend," which drives her mother nuts.

"And?"

"She changed the subject." Nell picks at a piece of walnut bread, pretending not to look at Mara. "You aren't getting out of this."

"When is it?"

"August. Maybe she's pregnant." Nell laughs.

"I actually might have to go to California," Mara says, not believing herself.

"What?" Nell yelps.

"My mom had a heart attack." Did she say it out loud, in English? It doesn't feel true, it feels like she's in a play, saying lines. "And a stroke," Mara adds.

"Oh, my God."

"A minor stroke. Which is apparently not minor at all."

"Shannon's there?"

"Apparently she's in jail."

"She's—excuse me?"

"That's what she said, but I think she was lying. They want to put my mom in a shelter because no one's there to watch her."

"Jesus Christ."

"I don't have a choice. Right? I have to go."

Nell sets her glass on the table.

"You would go. If you were me."

Nell is quiet, staring at a ramekin of almonds.

"I can't leave her there *on a cot somewhere.*" Couldn't she leave her mother on a cot somewhere? Mara feels her body shift, like her joints are loosening. "She almost died; they said it was a miracle she made it," she says. "My mother's going to die, and it's going to be my fault."

"You've said that before," Nell says.

Mara tips her head back and empties her glass. She goes to the kitchen, pulling another bottle from the fridge. Her face is grim as she works the wine key into the cork.

"It's not like she hasn't been courting death my entire life." Mara refills her glass and takes a long gulp from it, the wine's cold heat worming down to her heart.

Nell nibbles a green olive, daintily holding the pit, working her way around to get every rag of flesh clinging to it. She renders it clean and drops it into a fingerbowl. "What do you want to do?" she finally asks.

"I don't know."

"Yes, you do." Nell fixes her eyes straight at her. "Mara."

Mara doesn't look at Nell. She regards the sweating bottle, the violated cork. She abandons them and walks across the apartment to the balcony. She stares through the sliding screen door across the street, holding her arms in an old gesture of comfort.

She doesn't turn around. After four or five minutes, the weeping beech and the tarpaper roof across the street, the telephone line stretched across it, halving the frame, are glowing shapes of negative space.

"Mara."

She doesn't answer. She hears Nell wait, gather up the tray, and take it into the kitchen. She hears the water running, the fart of the dish soap squeeze bottle, the dishes being placed in the wooden drainer. She could cry for how badly she wants to turn around, undo her silence, live inside her life instead of next to it, but she has turned to stone. She hears Nell recork the wine and return it to the fridge, hears her lover's stubborn refusal to thaw the moment and make Mara talk. Nell wipes the counter clean. Rifles through old mail. For some time, Nell waits; she might be staring at Mara's back, which burns with shame. After a long while, Mara hears Nell slip into her flip-flops. She hears Nell pause, can feel her eyes— Mara still holding her arms, her fingers tingly—and listens as Nell disappears, easing the door closed until it clicks. The stairs creak in the hall. And still Mara doesn't move.

Chapter Three

By the time Shannon was in high school, she was good at hiding, not that anyone was looking.

On a Monday in the spring of her senior year, she smoked like usual with her friends at lunch and didn't see the point of going to her afternoon classes. But instead of heading home, she went to a Rite Aid, a different Rite Aid from the one where she worked, and walked like a criminal to the aisle with the shoe polish.

A group of boys, eleven or twelve years old, had been banned from Shannon's Rite Aid because they kept stealing inhalants—shoe polish, paint markers, acetone. Shannon caught them once out back, leaning against a wall in the shade, dazed and stupid, their noses stippled with blue marker. She cursed them out, surprised at her fury.

So why had she filled a discarded gas can partway with gasoline at the Arco one night and taken it to the boardwalk, where she inhaled its fumes until her vision had holes in it? Why did she keep buying, then throwing out, bottles of Wood Stain & Finish Stripper and king-size paint markers? Was she stupid? Did she know about brain damage, about instant death? She did; she looked it up in the school library, which had dozens of books about drugs and addiction.

It was a lonely hobby. She did it at night, or in daytime shadows, pushing her sleeves over her hands to conceal the marker, never so dumb as to get it on her nose. She liked gasoline the least—too heavy, too fast, the smell impossible to get rid of—and shoe polish the best. There was something subtle about its layered smell: it made her feel safe, it made her think of reliable men in nice leather shoes, Jimmy Stewart in old movies. You could only smell it when you got close. She kept buying markers, and paint thinner, and other things—she didn't switch to using shoe polish exclusively. It was a treat, like good liquor.

She always threw the thing away after using it once. Awash in shame, she'd swear off it, cursing herself for being like those fuck-up twelve-year-olds, for wanting such a pathetic, white-trash high. Then the decision would fade, and she'd get that feeling— like her life was a stray plastic bag floating further and further from the surface of the earth, like she was headed into the ozone. A drifty panic.

She buried her purchase in a pile of incidentals—tampons, a bag of chips, a pack of gum. She smiled at the clerk, who knew her.

The final class of the day would be over by now. Shannon had an image in her head of Brandy laughing with her sophomore girlfriends in the quad, afternoon light on their shiny hair. Shannon didn't know Brandy's other friends.

She took her bag and let it dangle from her fingers, liking the medallion heft of the shoe polish. A nascent brushfire, the beginnings of shame, prickled in the distance past her ears, but she ignored it. She watched the sidewalk beneath her feet, didn't admit where she was going until she was there.

Two streets from her apartment, there was a house no one had lived in for a year. Flat-roofed, with stucco walls, bars on the windows, a chain-link fence, a scraggly brown lawn, and a short palm tree in front, dense with dead fronds. Silver Beach had only recently gotten expensive, desirable beyond the condos that lined the boardwalk. In the seventies and eighties, when they razed the cottages on her block and replaced them with dingbat apartments, it was a mix of middle class, working class, and sketchy. Drunks, bar fights, and tattoo parlors lined Obsidian Avenue; on the residential streets, there were meth labs and neighbors who had loud arguments in the street mixed in with quiet, straight-laced types who watered their lawns. Before that, in the forties, fifties, and sixties, it was regular blue collar—sailors and Convair workers and their cheap little houses, which were renamed "bungalows" when they started building things even cheaper and uglier. Now the bungalows were going for half a million, or that's what Shannon's manager at Rite Aid said. But not this one, for some reason.

Trash gathered at the seams of the property. Shannon let herself in through the gate. The windows weren't boarded up: you could see stripes of shadows and light inside. She tried the front door, the broken lock, and let herself in, ducking into the dim stillness.

There was a concrete floor, a folding chair, empty forties. In Shannon's head, Brandy left her last class, driver's ed, and walked into the sunshine with the sophomore girls. They linked arms and headed to the parking lot. Maybe they would do homework together, their honors history, their grade-level math. Brandy's mother would bring them a plate of snacks. Shannon dropped her backpack and her Rite Aid bag on the floor and sat in the folding chair.

She gasped at a stirring of movement in the corner of her eye. A cat sauntered out of the kitchen, tail switching, and stopped to inspect her. Shannon clicked her tongue and reached her hand low. The cat twitched its nose and approached her.

"Pss-pss-pss-pss-pss," Shannon whispered. "Hi, puss." It butted its head into her palm, and she ran her hand behind its ears. It began to purr. It jumped up and settled in her lap; she stroked its back, her fingers playing along its head.

She imagined Brandy and her friends on Brandy's big sofa, watching a movie, eating out of a Tupperware bowl of popcorn. She reached down to the Rite Aid bag, careful not to disturb the cat. She grasped the shoe polish tin and drew it up. She nudged the lid open and looked at the smooth perfection of it, amber-gold.

You were supposed to use plastic bags for huffing: this produced the most acute high. Just sniffing an inhalant made you feel out of it, but not *high,* unless it was something really strong, like gasoline. Her method with most things was to dip her head down and inhale. She didn't mess with plastic bags.

Today, though, Shannon emptied the Rite Aid bag, put the tin inside, and lowered her face into it, closing it around her nose and mouth. Just to try. She took a long breath, the chemical edge of the smell cutting through the fog of plastic. What you had to do next was huff. She fixed her gaze on the window and began breathing quickly, deeply, hyperventilating. She got dizzy and stopped. For a second, everything was bright, lifted off the hinges. She huffed again, faster, and stopped. She was out of it, but not fucked up. She tried again.

Again.

The floor shifted beneath her, startling the cat, and she fell off the chair. The cat ran away. A laugh—whose laugh?—someone definitely laughed. She looked around for the bag. Her hands were huge pieces of foam, her arms detached from their sockets. She was a cartoon, her extremities floating away from her.

She refocused her eyes, but everything kept moving. She crawled to the bag and plunged her face into it, breathing in and out, faster, deeper, tumbling down a loooooooooong elevator shaft. What was an elevator shaft?

She was flat on her back, staring at the ceiling. There were stars, not like the ones in the nighttime sky: five-pointed ones, and they were dancing, circling, a giant formation like the aerial view of a water musical from the forties. A what? How did she know this stuff? Then: music. Carousel melodies, violins, laughter. And still, a feeling like she was made of gas, endlessly expanding. She watched the show, her body disappearing.

Then: lead face. A terrible headache, a metallic throbbing. No more foam, just lead. Gravity stronger than she'd ever felt. She was absolutely going to barf.

A long time seemed to pass.

How long had she been smelling this smell?

How long since she moved her limbs, fingers, eyes?

The sun outside looked the same. It occurred to her she should have looked at the time first, to see how long it would last. The thought came from the distant end of a filament far away from her brain, a flicker. Where was the clock? What was this room? Was this a room in her brain?

So dark in here, so bright outside.

Her head was empty. No thoughts. Something about a clock.

She tried it again. Her body knew what to do.

She awoke in the same place, but the sky outside was dark; a shaft of streetlamp light fell into the room. A horrible sweet smell, like cat vomit, an incredible headache, and the sense of waking from the deepest sleep of her life. She sat up and wiped her mouth, looked down at herself. A damp spot on her shirt. The house was quiet as a wall.

She walked home. She eased her key into the lock and cracked the door, peeking into the gloom: the TV was on, and there was her mother, asleep on the couch, head back, mouth open, cigarette unraveling a thin stream of smoke from the ashtray. Shannon slid in and whispered the door shut behind her, keeping her eyes on her mother. She tiptoed past and tunneled into her bedroom, where she washed a handful of ibuprofen back with a swig of Crown Royal and fell asleep in her clothes.

She didn't earn all her credits by June. She graduated on a cloudy day in January and took a tin of shoe polish out to the pier, where something terrible happened, and she ended up in the emergency room. One of the fishermen out there took her in, or that's what the nurse said. The doctor got in her face: "Do you understand me? You could have *died. So stupid.*" She was eighteen and didn't let them call her mother, or anyone; she checked herself out and took the bus back to Silver Beach.

Chapter Four

Mara can't sleep. She stares at the gauze curtain in her bedroom window, flutterless in the warm, damp night. A trilling chorus of gray treefrogs sings from the marsh at the end of her block. An owl has taken up residence nearby, its eerie hoot weighing in every time she comes close to drifting off. Eventually, tiny flutes of birdsong in the darkness tell her it's almost dawn. A mourning dove coos from an eave.

At the first hint of coolness, she slips out of bed and walks naked into the kitchen. She spoons the coffee grounds into the funnel of the stovetop espresso maker, screws the top chamber tight, and turns on the flame. She stirs the computer mouse at her desk in the living room, and the screen blazes with surprised white light. She pads back into her bedroom for slippers and a bathrobe. The espresso bubbles and hisses.

Mara fills a mug and sits at her desk, peering into the screen. She opens a spreadsheet, FY_2010, and gazes at the color-coded columns of income and expenses, projections, separate tabs for spending categories and the interest on her modest investments. Her father is always admonishing her to invest more boldly because she's young.

If she bought the ticket now, a flight to San Diego would be exorbitant. It would interfere with everything. And what would she need to pay for in California? Her mother might not have a car. Her mother and sister might be on Medicaid, but she has no idea what that covers. The hospital bills could be huge, and there could be endless incidental expenses, and who knows how long she'd be there? She pictures her expense column growing and growing like the strip coming out of a cartoon adding machine.

Her mother hasn't worked in years; Shannon has some horrible minimum-wage job. Her father wants nothing to do with his ex-wife. Linda's own family—she has a brother in Orange County—hasn't spoken to her in decades. Most of them, grandparents, aunts, uncles—dead.

How do they live, her mother, her half-sister? She pictures Linda on a cot in a shelter, skinny and abject. What she feels isn't sympathy but incomprehension.

Already, she feels herself stepping back. She imagines the rupture sealing up, the way wet sand fills with seawater when you dig a hole too close to the waves. She can feel herself forgetting Shannon's call, deleting the messages from UCSD.

She closes the spreadsheet. She opens her browser and scans the headlines in the *Globe*. She finishes her coffee and tucks her feet under her, reads the Ideas section. She puts the monitor to sleep, turns on NPR, and makes another pot of coffee. The sun brightens, the air swells with moisture, and from the window, she hears the jeering peal of blue jays.

At ten o'clock, her phone buzzes with a text message: Nell.

happy birthday!! xx

Mara had forgotten. She is thirty-three today. She hopes Nell hasn't planned anything, like a surprise party. Nell wouldn't do that. Would she?

so it is, Mara texts back. *xx.* She wonders if Nell is mad about yesterday and, if so, how mad.

what are we doing? Nell texts.

come over, Mara replies. Moments later, she hears a key in the lock. The door is nudged open with a foot, and Nell steps into the apartment, carrying a plate of doughnuts, grinning.

"Happy birthday!" she squeals softly. It's as though yesterday never happened, the ocean filling everything in. Mara stands up, and her bathrobe falls open slightly. She gazes lustily at the plate.

"Just one. I'm taking you to brunch." Nell comes closer, kissing her on the neck. Maybe she is forgiven. Maybe they don't have to talk about it.

Nell steps back, studies Mara's reaction. Mara hopes Nell believes her smile; she would rather sit in the apartment in her bathrobe eating doughnuts with her girlfriend until Tuesday with her phone turned off than go to brunch and encounter other people. Before Nell can hustle them off, Mara encircles her wrist and pulls her into the bedroom.

"We've got a reservation," Nell says, but Mara can tell she doesn't mean it.

"I'll be quick," Mara says.

They are late for brunch, and when they walk into Farrell's, the sprawling restaurant on the ground floor of the old Calvin Hotel downtown, Mara discovers why there is a reservation: there are a dozen of them.

Surprise.

To Mara's horror, Nell has invited more than a few of their friends and colleagues, collected over the ten or so years they've lived in Northampton, and crowded them into a circular booth in a sunny corner of the restaurant under a fleet of hanging ferns, their cocktail glasses half-empty, coated in fruit pulp. A busgirl sweeps past them.

"What the fuck?" Mara whispers as they approach the table, but she's drowned out by a fusillade of greetings and happy birthdays and an eruption of laughter at a joke they've just missed. The warm looseness Mara was feeling, lingering post-orgasmic waves in her hips and knees, contracts into a small, cold feeling between her joints.

She likes these people. She loves some of them. But she doesn't want to see them all at once, certainly not today.

Maybe this will make it easier to forget. She smiles and settles into the booth next to an old roommate, a red-haired, unpretentious woman whose wife just had a baby. The woman squeezes Mara's shoulder and explains her wife's absence, looking relieved to be out of the house with a mimosa in her hand. Nell seats herself across from Mara, far away on the other side of the gigantic round table, and immediately begins chatting with two young men who have become omnipresent since they arrived in Northampton from New York and opened a bookstore on Main Street. One of them, whom Mara privately thinks of as the smart one, shellacs his dark hair into two halves separated by a severe, ruler-straight part. As he rattles on, his boyfriend—the dull one, the blond—listens impassively behind tortoiseshell glasses. Mara suspects an independent source of income, because who could pay commercial rent downtown with a *bookstore?* Nell loves them, finds them witty and energizing, a solution to her perennial complaint that Northampton has a glut of lesbians and no gay men.

Mara surveys the rest of the chorus: Anh, an older, hip, bisexual architect who graduated ahead of them at Smith, on whom Mara has always had a secret crush. Jen and Mark, a grave, earnest, straight couple they know from the co-op. David, an old, funny friend Mara keeps reminding herself to make more time for. Raina, a high-pitched vegan Nell has some kind of loyalty to because they worked together years ago on a union campaign at

UMass. Sheila and Tasha, a couple who run a performance space and bar in a converted foundry in Easthampton and seem to find Mara deathly boring, something Nell assures her isn't true.

If it weren't for Nell, Mara would have only three or four friends, people she's known forever. Maybe that would be fine.

Mara's old roommate is giggling in her ear, pulling her phone from her purse to show Mara a video of the baby hiccupping, and the video is surprisingly funny and sweet. Would Mara ever have children? She gets this question more and more, and usually says no. Nell has stopped bringing it up, not that she wants children herself necessarily, but she's more open to being talked into it.

"I work at an elementary school," Mara says to her friend. "I have a hundred children." Of course it isn't the same; it isn't even like being a classroom teacher, because the librarian gets to hand them back after an hour, like a grandparent. But it's sufficient to end the line of inquiry.

As the woman leans away to join the conversation between Raina and the co-op couple, Mara glances at Anh, who is listening wryly as Nell tells a story. Anh leans back into the booth, arms crossed, half-smiling. She doesn't look forty.

Nell has assembled a rapt gay audience around herself, as usual. Sheila and Tasha are cracking up as she relates some local political outrage, putting a lacerating, sardonic spin on the story that seems out of place here in Northampton, "in the irony-free zone, behind the Tofu Curtain" (Nell's phrase).

Mara suspects Nell would be happier in New York, more aerated. She's the kind of person who gets whatever job she's after; she's currently in charge of cultivating major donors at a teensy liberal arts college nearby, but she could do anything. Nell is always ragging on Northampton, but they can't walk down Main Street without running into a dozen of her acquaintances. She has plans nearly every night of the week.

Here's the thing: they are mysteries to each other. Everyone thinks only Mara is mysterious, but it's mutual. They've been friends since college and have dated for a year (two? is that even possible?), a transition that felt seamless, if only because they always behaved a little like a married couple: intimate but respectful of each other's autonomy. The main difference is the sex, which was fraught and disorienting when they were friends, and is now . . . predictable but much better. Maybe it works because they still don't understand each other.

"Okay," Nell says after the waiter has taken their orders. She taps a fork on her glass and pulls everyone in with her eyes. When they are quiet, she waits a beat longer than they expect, sitting on the bubble of their silence. She takes a breath.

"As you know, the love of my life is another year older today," she grins.

Love of my life?

"And everyone here loves Mara, too," Nell continues.

"Word," Anh says. The bookstore owner whoops.

"Let's go around the table and say something we love about Mara on her birthday," Nell instructs.

"I'll start," David says, holding his fork like a microphone.

Mara is on record as being deeply chagrined by moments like this, but there's something tender about this one, a pomegranate seed of sincerity.

"Here's my favorite Mara story," David begins. He's an impish man, curly-haired, with laughing eyes. He's now an assistant professor of philosophy, but he and Mara met when they were undergraduates working on a farm one summer and discovered their respective colleges were a few miles apart. "It was Jan term, the one when we got nine hundred feet of snow. We were holed up in her dorm at Smith one night, super-late—"

"I remember that Jan term," Nell says.

"And we've just finished a cheap bottle of wine—" David looks pointedly at Mara. "But for Mara, the night is not over. Problem is, we're snowbound. And at this hour, nothing is open for miles."

"Where was I?" Nell interjects.

"You were dating that horrible girl," Mara replies.

"Snap," Anh says. Nell raises her eyebrows at the memory.

"So I'm like, *Mara,* what are we going to do? Put on our snow-shoes and break into a liquor store? And Mara's like, *Little boy.* She fishes around in some drawer and produces a set of keys." He pauses. "There is a *cabinet full of wine* in the basement of this dormitory, this being Smith College, I guess they're saving it for their, like . . ." David searches for the word.

"Fêtes?" Anh offers.

"Fêtes! *Fêtes.* And Mara, of course, has the keys to it because the dorm matron or whoever has entrusted responsibilities and keys and secret codes to her, because—well—wouldn't you? And Mara's calm as you please, taking me into this *dark* basement at God knows what time of night—"

"I turned on the lights," Mara says.

"It was full of old lady ghosts. I saw one floating near the chandelier." The table laughs. "Mara pops open this cabinet—and she knows the best bottles to take, she has the inventory memorized—"

"I did not," Mara protests. It was a cardboard box, not a cabinet.

"She locks the room back up, drops the key into her little pocket, and *voila,* two underage virgins proceed to get trashed on some really excellent Bordeaux in Mara's room."

"I didn't get trashed," Mara clarifies. "And I wasn't a virgin."

"We had a bottle each, but only *I* got trashed, now I remember. I passed out under your bed. You had to dress me up like a girl and sneak me out the next morning."

Mara shakes her head.

"I have one," Raina pipes up. Mara hardly knows Raina; how could Raina have a story about her?

"Remember when we graduated?" Raina says knowingly.

Mara cocks her head. She doesn't know where Raina went to school.

"In '99?" Raina prompts.

"You went to Smith?"

"I lived in Sessions. Remember?"

Mara nods, but she doesn't remember. "It's graduation weekend, everybody's parents are there," she says. "My mother looks ridiculous, with like, multiple diamonds and some kind of beaded blouse, and I'm like, Mom, *it's hot out,* you look ridiculous, and she's like, What?" Raina does an impression of her mother. "I'm dying of embarrassment. And meanwhile my *father* is talking to the dean as though he's some kind of neuroscience expert, and I'm just, *gone.* I leave them at this cocktail *lawn* party thing, and I go downtown." Raina is probably referring to one of the fêtes (!) the development department at Smith hosts for parents who are either major donors or prospective donors—Nell organizes parties like this all the time. They're for very rich people. "And, you know, I'm kind of upset, and I decide to have lunch at that Italian place on the corner near City Hall, and who do I see, but *Mara and her mother!* Eating lunch!"

An icy shame sluices through Mara's body.

"And I'm like, hey, guys, mind if I join? And—this is classic—Mara's mother leans in, and she's all, *What are you drinking?* And I'm like, this is my kind of lady!"

Nell shoots Mara a look. Mara can't remember running into Raina that day, but an oily nausea begins to brew in her stomach.

"So basically . . ." Raina sighs. "I got *completely* smashed with Mara's mom over the course of a *very* long lunch. The waitresses kicked us out so they could serve dinner."

"What did we talk about?" Mara asks. "I can't remember." She wonders if Raina is making it up.

"God, let me see . . . your mom was hilarious. I guess we talked about boys? We definitely made fun of the waitresses . . . I know I was hammered afterward. Mara's mother likes dirty martinis," she explains to the table.

"Do you like dirty martinis, Mara?" asks one of the bookstore boys. Everyone but Nell is smiling; they think the story is funny. "I was thinking of throwing a dirty martini party, no joke, where the theme is martinis and filth."

"No," Mara says.

"She's more of a wine snob," David says. He turns to Mara. "Your mom came to graduation? I thought she was afraid of flying."

"She is," Mara lies. "But she took a Valium and came anyway." Which is true, except it was more than one Valium. Mara's mother was on pills—Valium, Vicodin, and various uppers—for most of her visit, which she combined with copious amounts of booze, like Keith Richards. The astounding thing was how much it took for her to get truly fucked up. When she finally did, Mara spent graduation night in the emergency room with her, something she told no one, not even Nell. Her father had gone home that afternoon and knew nothing about it. She remembers the weekend in disconnected flashes, as though she, too, had gotten so wasted she blacked out.

The table falls quiet. Mara fingers her mimosa flute, warmed by the greenhouse effect of the windows and skylights around them, and stares at the sidewalk traffic behind Raina's head.

She doesn't know how Nell or David stands it. Everyone else at the table came to this brunch for Nell, because she asked them and she's excellent company, while she, Mara, is a dark absence, a collapsed star, dense with brooding gravity.

"Excuse me," Mara says, getting up. "I'll be right back."

In the bathroom stall, Mara squats at the toilet, staring at the water. The bowl is cold with condensation; the smell of dried blood from the trash wafts up.

Will Nell forgive her if she doesn't return to the table? It would serve her right, throwing a surprise party.

Nothing comes. Mara wipes the thin spittle from her mouth and rises, rubbing her nose to get the smell out. She washes her hands, avoiding her reflection. She composes her face and marches back to the table, gracious, pleasant, smiling. She eats, has another mimosa, listens, or looks like she's listening, laughs, hugs, says they should get together soon, someone should throw a dinner party. Summer's coming, she says, they could take a picnic somewhere. Go swim in a lake.

On the ride home, Nell is quiet. Mara parks the car in front of her apartment, and Nell follows her in.

"I'm sorry," Nell says softly.

"For what?"

Nell shakes her head. "You hate surprises." She hesitates. "I shouldn't—"

"No—"

"I just thought it would be fun, to celebrate, and—"

"And I never want to celebrate anything."

"I wasn't going to say that."

"It's true," Mara says.

"It's not true." Nell pauses. "I should have canceled after you told me about your mom."

"That's silly." Mara unlocks the door and walks into the apartment. For once, it brings no comfort.

"Are you okay?" Nell asks. She stands in the doorway.

"I'm fine," Mara says lightly, filling two glasses with ice water. "Tired. I couldn't sleep last night."

"I guess I didn't want to—"

"I'm fine, let's not talk about it." Mara hands Nell a glass and clinks it. She crosses the living room and sits on the sofa.

"About what?"

Mara cocks her head. "Huh?"

"What aren't we talking about?" Nell is still standing. She closes the door behind her.

Mara glares at the air for a moment. She scans the room, her eyes finally landing on a copy of *Dwell* on the coffee table. She picks it up. She stretches her feet out on the sofa, settles into a pillow, and begins reading.

"Mara," Nell says. Mara's face is placid. Nell stands over her. "What is wrong with you?" she whispers.

Mara lifts her eyes from the magazine. "Excuse me?"

"What are you going to do?"

"About what?"

"*Mara.*"

Mara wills a long sigh into submission. She closes the magazine and sets it on her thigh. She shuts her eyes.

"No," Nell says. "You get one of those every other month, max."

Mara pops one eye open. Nell scoops up her girlfriend's legs and seats herself beneath them.

"What are you going to do?" she asks again. "Uh-uh! Eyes open!"

Mara glowers at Nell. "I don't know," she says after a long pause.

"Have you heard from Shannon?"

"No."

"What about the hospital?"

"I don't know."

"What do you mean you don't know?"

"I deleted their last message."

"You can't just make it disappear."

"I don't want to be rude," Mara says carefully, "but this whole thing is actually none of your business."

Nell shakes her head. "What are you going to do?"

"I don't know!" Mara's voice rises. She flings the magazine off her lap, pulls her legs toward herself, and wraps her arms around them. "I don't know." She sighs. "I don't have to explain it."

"Can I call the hospital? Let me help you."

Mara shakes her head. "I'm not letting you get tangled with that woman," she says quickly, wishing she hadn't.

Nell studies her. "So what, you're estranging yourself from her, basically?"

"How long have you known me?" Mara asks.

"Rhetorical question."

"And what do you know about my mother?"

"I met her at graduation, for, like, a minute. Is that story true, by the way, that Raina told?"

"Why did you invite her?"

"She's our friend! She's been our friend for ten years!"

"She's *your* friend. I don't remember seeing her at Smith."

"We hung out all the time."

Mara squints past Nell at the scene out her balcony, the image transformed by yesterday's vigil.

"So is that story true?" Nell asks.

"I don't remember."

"How can you not remember something like that?"

"There's a reason you don't know much about my mother."

"Okay."

Mara slumps against the arm of the sofa, the words in her mouth giving up. She closes her eyes again.

Nell nudges her. "What do you mean?"

"I don't like talking about her. Obviously."

"Why not?"

"She's a fucking mess, that's why."

"Lots of people's mothers are a fucking mess. *My* mother is a fucking mess."

"My mother makes your mother look like Michelle Obama."

"How?"

Mara sighs and sets her mouth in a line.

"You hate this conversation," Nell says. "We've never had this conversation."

"Yes, we have."

"We literally haven't." Nell gives Mara the same baffled look she's been giving her for years. "It would take a lot to make my mother look like Michelle Obama," Nell says. "Figuratively, not literally."

"Well. My mother's a drunk."

"My mother's a drunk."

"Your mother drinks a glass of wine every night. So do I."

"Tell me you are not sitting here saying my mother doesn't have at least a *small* problem with alcohol. You were at my sisters' weddings."

"*My* mother," Mara says, stretching her legs out again, "is basically on a liquid diet. Of vodka. And pills, when she can get her hands on them, for fiber."

"How does she live on that?"

"I have no idea."

"How does a person like that end up with your *father*?"

"I have no idea."

"Seriously."

"I seriously have no idea. It didn't last."

"They had you."

Mara says nothing.

"And then what? Your mom got together with Shannon's dad?"

"Something like that." Mara shifts and resettles her ankles on Nell's lap.

"She cheated on your father? She cheated on *Charlie Meade*?"

"They split up first. He moved to Boston."

"*Charlie Meade* left you *behind* with your *drunk mother in California*?"

"It wasn't supposed to be permanent. We were all supposed to move to Boston. It's a long story."

"You've never told me any of this."

"Yes, I have."

"You have not."

Mara retreats again into silence.

"So you were all going to move to Boston. From San Diego?"

Mara nods.

"Where in San Diego?"

"Silver Beach."

"Where is that?"

"By the beach."

"*Where* by the beach."

"Near the airport."

"Okay," Nell says. "Why were you going to move to Boston?"

"My father," Mara says slowly, "had this thing about moving east. He'd never been to the east coast; he was born in the desert, near Palm Springs. His parents had never been anywhere. He had a job at a firm in San Diego, and then out of nowhere, he's like, I got a job in Boston. And we're like, *Boston?* I'm in kindergarten, first grade. I don't even know what Boston is."

"What did your mom say?"

"She thought he was nuts."

"What was the deal with Boston?"

"I mean: if I was married to my mother, I'd be looking for a way out."

"But you were all going to go out there."

"That was the plan, but the writing was on the wall. They started fighting about it. They fought all the time anyway, but this was worse, we used to hide behind the sofa and listen to them."

"You and Shannon?"

"No, Shannon wasn't born yet."

"You and who?"

"Allison."

"Allison?"

"My sister."

Nell stares at Mara. She stares and stares, drawing her chin back, then leaning in and peering more closely. She opens her mouth, then closes it again. After a long time, she says, "Who is Allison?"

"My older sister."

"You have an older sister."

"Yes."

"Where does she live?" Nell's voice is a whisper.

Mara gives her a funny look. "She died." There is a long pause. "She drowned in a rip current when I was seven. After that, my father came and took me to Boston."

"You had a sister. An older sister. Named Allison."

Mara nods.

Nell shifts Mara's legs off her lap and gets up. She stands, hovering over the coffee table. She paces carefully to the sliding-glass door at the balcony. She turns around.

"You had a sister. An older sister. Named Allison. Who died when you were seven."

"Yes." Mara cocks her head. "You knew that."

"No," Nell says. "I didn't."

Mara stares at Nell.

"You never told me that. Not ever." Nell's hands flit in the air for a moment. "You never told me that." She paces again, then turns to face Mara.

"How could I not know that?" she squeaks. "That you had a *sister*? And she *drowned*?" She shakes her head. "Now it all makes sense!" She goes to the door and slips back into her sandals.

"Where are you going?"

Nell crosses the room to Mara, who is glued to the sofa cushion. She bends down and kisses Mara on the neck. Her eyes are shiny.

"That's crazy." Her voice is tender, hitching on her words. "I'm sorry you lost your sister." She bites her lip. "I gotta go."

"Where are you going?" Mara asks. Nell leaves without glancing behind her, closing the door. A lawnmower across the street doesn't cut the silence in her wake, and the oscillating fan barely seems to push the air around. The apartment feels dead.

Mara pulls her knees to her chest. She tries to picture Allison but can't. The scenes she's retained are so worn she doesn't trust them anymore. A swinging ponytail, an eight-year-old neck browned in the sun, covered in downy blond hair. Hands stained with Kool-Aid. Bathing suits on the porch railing. They could be anyone's memories.

Mara goes to her computer, wakes it with a wiggle of the mouse. She opens the page she bookmarked that morning and skims the flight times and ticket prices. She clicks through, purchasing a ticket for two days from now, a Monday, Memorial Day, an early flight from Bradley, arriving at Lindbergh Field at ten in the morning. No refunds. She opens Excel and enters the amount into her spreadsheet.

She puts the computer to sleep and returns to the sofa. It's Saturday. She is thirty-three. She closes her eyes and finally sleeps as the sun climbs higher in the sky.

Chapter Five

These people are finally letting Linda go home. She hasn't had a moment to herself, to *relax,* since they brought her in and, sure, the Vicodin drip is lovely—like floating in a square of pure light, like being suspended in a diamond—but what she would really *prefer,* if you don't mind, is a small cigarette. Just one, the fine, crisp edge of it. And a cup of tea, straight out of the freezer.

The indignities are ghastly. The cotton *sack* that ties in back, the needle pokes every two hours, the moaner next door, silent now, God help her.

The pain is manageable. She'd been scared it would be awful, but it isn't. There'll be a scar. She can't say she feels like a *stroke victim.* A *heart attack survivor.* She feels like she always felt: like a young girl. There's a fog behind her eyes, nothing more. A weakness. They carded her at bars when she was thirty-five. Her license picture looked like Ann-Margret. Everyone said so, until they forgot who Ann-Margret was.

A young nurse's aide, sweet and brown-skinned and clumsy, comes into Linda's almost-room and helps her get dressed. Her real clothes, finally: pink tennies, white slacks, a floral-print blouse that shows off her collarbones and hides the bandage. She was lucky she was dressed that night, or she'd have a muumuu to put on now.

Her hair is tragic.

She needs a cigarette, a cup of tea, a shower.

The clumsy aide stands up, and a man appears.

"This is Vincent, he's a social worker," the aide says, trading places with a white man in his forties. He is slim, short, with tousled grey hair, wire-rimmed glasses, and a silver wedding band. He smiles. Linda lifts her chin and sits up straight, the hostess of her pathetic little room. The man waves, and she lifts her hand, charmed, but he doesn't take it. Maybe he's gay. The poor wife.

"Hi, Linda, how are you?"

What was his name?

"Fabulous," Linda smiles. Her throat is sore. "Is my daughter here? I mean, did you see her? Blond, chubby, looks about sixteen?" The pain in her chest is sudden and mean. She fingers the bandage, and it passes.

"That's what I'm here to talk about, actually." The man smiles again. "The hospital was unable to contact either of your daughters."

She leans forward. "Shannon's at home. She *lives* with me. Just *call her,* I have the number—" She gropes for her purse.

"She's not answering, and no one came to the door," the man says.

"Well, where did she *go?*"

"I can have them file a missing-person report, if that's what you want."

"Shannon isn't *missing.* She's just irresponsible. Have them call that friend of hers, Brianna-something. Brenda."

"Do you have Brenda's number?"

"Of course. I don't know." She thrusts her purse at him. "Here, have a look."

The man gingerly paws through her purse's contents. She refuses to be embarrassed. He sets the purse on the table.

"They're discharging you today," he says. "I'm going to take you to a shelter, it's not far from here—"

"Excuse me, a what?"

"I'm going to take you to a shelter, it's not far from here—"

"I live in Silver Beach. In an *apartment*."

"Linda, you're going to need some help for a little while."

"What sort of help?"

"Medication. Physical therapy. There are things you'll need assistance with, at least for now, like bathing and getting dressed."

"I don't need help getting *dressed*," Linda sniffs. "That little Chinese girl who helped me? She's about as coordinated as a lampshade." She razors her eyes around the curtains. "If someone would just take me home, I would be *fine*." She glowers at the man. "I have another daughter, you know."

"We couldn't reach her."

"She's done very well for herself."

The man says nothing.

"What do you mean, you couldn't *reach* her?" Linda presses. "How hard is it? Did you dial the right number? Give me that," she says, pointing to her purse. He gives it to her, and she stabs her hands into it, but they won't obey her commands. "Well," she says, "if you take me to my apartment, I can get you the number. The *correct* number."

"I don't know what number they used. I can look into that if you want. But right now, I'm going to take you to a place called Lantern House. You'll get your own bed, you may even get your own room. It's temporary. I'm going to make sure you get everything you need, Linda. That's my job."

Linda stares at him. She tightens her knuckles around the strap of her purse.

"May I smoke?"

The man hesitates.

"Is one allowed to *smoke* there."

"It's not a great idea to smoke right after a heart attack."

"I asked if it's allowed."

"I believe so, yes."

Linda looks off. "Good." She returns her face to him, cleansed of animosity. "Do people tell you you resemble Peter Fonda?" she asks.

"No," he says.

The nurses say hello to him in the elevator. His name is Vincent. They make her wait an eternity in the waiting room while Vincent signs forms and has conversations with aides, nurses, doctors, secretaries, telephones. For a man who lacks height, he seems well built; his forearms look strong. Frankly, she prefers tall men. She comes from a family of tall people, though she herself is only five foot two. But she doesn't see any point in meeting a man, in *considering* him, if he isn't tall. All her exes: tall.

Vincent strides toward her, confident and hale despite his stature.

"Ready?" he says.

Linda shakes her hair as if it were still long and lustrous, not limp and L'Oréal blond with the roots showing. "Sure," she says.

They put her in a wheelchair, which makes her feel both special and preposterous. As Vincent pushes her to his car in the underground parking garage, he explains that social workers don't usually drive patients to shelters, but there's no one to pick her up, and they're understaffed at Lantern House. Linda decides this, too, makes her special; they could have just kicked her out and left her on the sidewalk.

"You know, I have an apartment." She grips the armrests.

"This is more like a halfway house than a shelter."

"For *drug addicts*? And *ex-cons*?" She twists her face toward him.

"That isn't—that's not the only function of a halfway house."

Linda sticks her foot on the brake and pulls them up short, Vincent almost tripping over the wheelchair.

"Take me home."

"Linda, I'm sorry, I can't. It's that simple." A hatchback eases around them on its way to the exit. "Listen." He walks around to face her. His demeanor shifts. "If you refuse to come with me—if that's what you're doing—I can call you a cab to take you home, and you'll be on your own. You'll have to pay the driver." He crosses his arms. There's something touching about his attempt at being firm. Linda thinks of her empty wallet, the pennies in her purse. Shannon has her credit cards. Vincent walks around behind her, flips the brake, and keeps pushing. Linda allows him to be a gentleman and help her into the car.

She is quiet as they pull out of the garage and drive toward the freeway. "I live right over there," Linda says, pointing. "I won't tell," she says coyly.

Vincent shakes his head. His impassive sunglasses betray nothing.

"You really do," she says.

He glances at her. "What?"

"Look like Peter Fonda."

"I never heard that one before."

"I knew him," she says. They're on the freeway now.

"You knew Peter Fonda?"

"That's my exit," she says, pointing. "Obsidian."

"How did you know him?"

"Right lane." Linda squints into the sun. "I have *medication,* you know."

"All your medication's here."

"I don't have any panties!"

"There's plenty of clothes at Lantern House you can use. Remember, this is temporary."

"Vincent, turn this car around!" Linda shrieks. "I said turn *around,* for God's sake!" She pauses, watching him. "Vincent! Do as I ask!" She unclicks her seatbelt.

He darts his eyes at her lap, glances over his shoulder, changes lanes, and takes the next exit.

Linda sighs. "See?"

Vincent is quiet as he drives down the off-ramp and pulls into a gas station. He silences the engine. Linda could be this man's mother.

"You can't do that," he says.

"We're both adults here, Vincent."

"You know what?" His face is colder than before. "I can call a cab. Or you can just get out of the car."

"No," Linda says softly, enjoying the anger in his voice.

"Then I need you to work with me."

Linda nods.

"I need you to keep your seatbelt on." She complies, fumbling until it clicks. As he turns the key, she steals a glance: he's angry, shaken.

They arrive at Lantern House without incident. Lantern House is in the barrio. It's a fat pink snake of a building with depressing metal awnings over the windows, and no landscaping, just gravel. A freeway interchange roars overhead. Short, dark-haired people mill around a storefront next door, the sign in Spanish. She glares at it through the windshield. Vincent helps her out of the car.

"Is it safe?" she whispers. He doesn't answer and walks ahead of her up the walkway. "Vincent?" she calls.

He turns around.

"I didn't tell you how I knew Peter Fonda." She catches up to him. "I used to be an actress," she explains. "I didn't pursue it much after I got married, but I should have, and I always . . . well, I spent some time in Hollywood."

They enter through the automatic doors, and Vincent leaves her to approach the desk.

Linda finds an ugly chair and sits down, cradling her purse. The room reminds her of the welfare office. She spent eons in rooms like this one, waiting to meet with social workers after Charlie took Mara with him to Boston—drab, miserable spaces that made her feel poor, Shannon crying inconsolably on her knee, Linda afraid to give up her place in line. In those days, you could smoke. When her name was called, her caseworker greeted her from behind stacks of paperwork, his own fort. But when he finally looked at her, everything changed: he gave her everything she asked for.

Linda *was* pretty. After she "blossomed," in high school, she got used to second and third glances from men, to the clumsy, hungry way they responded to her. It was the first time she felt any kind of power—she, whose mother couldn't stand her, whose father was so henpecked he could hardly speak, whose origins were tragic and secret, whose favorite great-aunt, the only one who understood her, died when she was twelve—she, Linda, could make people— men—do what she wanted. Boyfriends, friends who were boys, teachers, cashiers, businessmen, Hollywood people. She stopped having so many girlfriends, preferring men's company instead.

Charlie still pays the rent, too, after all these years. There was never an alimony agreement; he sent a short letter, *I've got the rent,* after Allison died, after he took Mara with him, as though payment, somehow, for the loss. Of course, Linda told him about the rent increases over the years, numbers that sounded realistic enough for Charlie to send more money. He didn't ask for details. This was how they lived.

Shannon still doesn't know.

"Linda?" Vincent is all smiles again, gesturing for her to join him. Linda attempts to rise from her seat with a semblance of grace, but her center of gravity is elusive. She stumbles, catches herself, glances hotly at Vincent, but he's talking again to the man at the front desk, leaning to him confidentially. She walks unsteadily to him.

"Yes?" she says.

"You're all set. These guys are going to take care of you, okay?"

Linda nods stiffly. Maybe her pain meds are wearing off.

She won't be here a day. Shannon is probably on her way; she'll be a babbling mess of apologies when she shows up.

They give her a blank speck of a room, a nun's room. She isn't there five minutes, testing the mattress, when another woman is shoved in, white like her, but definitely from the wrong side of the tracks. Her teeth are atrocious. Her face is collapsed on itself, like her skull has shrunk. She was thin once; her fatness has that inflated quality. Linda figures she's about twenty years younger than she looks.

"Hi," the woman says from the doorway.

"Hi," Linda replies, sitting primly at the edge of her bed.

"First time?" the woman asks. Her voice is smoother than Linda expected.

"I'm sorry?"

"First time at the Lantern? What do you do? Wait, lemme guess." The woman studies her. "Pills. Right?"

"Excuse me?"

The woman waits for Linda's reply.

"I'm only here because my daughter is out of town," Linda says.

"You have a place," the woman says, nodding.

"Yes."

"Everybody says that. Hey, I have a place, too."

"Why don't you go there?"

"Why don't you go to your place?"

"I asked you first." Linda crosses her arms.

"I can't stay at my place." The woman picks something off her t-shirt. "They want to evict me. My landlord's a criminal." She stares at Linda, waiting for a rejoinder. "Crystal," she finally says. "What about you?"

"Linda."

"No—that's not my name." She laughs.

"Oh." Linda is flustered.

"Crystal *meth*."

"Oh. I don't—I don't have a drug problem. I had a heart attack," Linda says.

"Right," the woman says. "Pills?"

"Why do you keep saying that?"

The woman looks at her thoughtfully. "It's usually the house-wives who do pills." She squints at Linda. "Or you could just be a drunk."

"I am not a *drunk*."

"A-ha. You know what I say about drunks?"

Linda regards her with contempt.

"Who isn't?" The woman laughs. "Irene," she says, "by the way." She comes closer and extends her hand. Linda shakes it, and Irene's hand feels like a wan balloon. Irene steps back, surveys the room, and flops down next to Linda on the bed, grinning hideously, bouncing Linda with the impact.

"Married?" she asks. She looks at Linda's left hand.

"Divorced."

"Me, too." She cocks her head. "Don't look at me like that! I was married once!"

"I didn't say anything," Linda sniffs.

"He's the one who started this whole thing," she says. "I was a goody-two-shoes before I met him. What about you, was your ex a drunk?"

"No."

"Are you from here?"

"No."

"So . . . where are you from?"

"Orange County. Tustin."

"Aren't you going to ask me where I'm from?"

"Sure," Linda sighs.

"La Jolla." Irene watches Linda's face. "I know, right?" she says, nodding. "How did *that* happen? Well: don't believe what they say about nice girls from good families."

Linda looks out the window through the horizontal blinds.

"What about you?" Irene presses. "Were you a nice girl from a good family?"

Linda stands up. "Where are your things?" she asks absently. Irene points to a duffel she shoved under the bed. "You've been here before, right?" Linda asks her.

The woman nods.

"How does it work?"

"What do you mean?"

"This isn't rehab," Linda clarifies.

Irene shakes her head. "They ship you out for that in the druggie buggy. It's in La Mesa."

"How hard is it to get out of here?"

"You can check yourself out. It's not a psych ward." Irene's tone becomes protective. "If you don't want to be here, let someone else have that bed."

"No, I just want to go and get something," Linda says airily. "And come back." No one is home in her apartment. No one to drive and get groceries, cigarettes . . . she can see herself falling up the stairs to the apartment. Falling in the shower and lying there until she drowns, the water pelting her face.

"Oh," Irene says, nodding. "They look through your bags when you come back. You can't bring anything in. Unless, you know, you put it up your . . ." She gestures with her finger.

"That's disgusting."

"With pills, though, it's the easiest—"

"I don't take *pills*!"

"I forgot, you're a drunk. Did they put you on Librium? You shouldn't drink if you're on Librium."

"They gave me a tray of medications this morning, and I took them."

"Fancy."

Linda crosses her arms, agitated. The only pill bottles and drips she'd paid attention to were the painkillers, but there were other drugs, maybe Librium, which she's never heard of but sounds intriguing. The pain meds are definitely wearing off.

"Do you smoke?" she asks.

"I quit." Irene smiles her tragic smile. Linda leaves the room, listing slightly, reaching to the wall for balance.

She finds a long hallway that opens onto a concrete patio crowded with chairs, chilly in the shade of tall, mournful eucalyptus trees on the other side of the fence. Their gummy-sweet smell reminds Linda unpleasantly of the yard of her elementary school. A chain-link fence, obscured by pink privacy slats, separates the patio from the alley beyond. It occurs to her that everything here is pink: the stucco, the smudgy walls, the linoleum, the carpet, the patio furniture, the scrubs the aides wear. It isn't a nice pink, like her shoes, or the floral print on her blouse; it's vomit pink, she can almost taste it. She opens the sliding-glass door to the patio and finds a Black man, her age perhaps, with a dancer's figure, seated—draped—on a chair, basking in a stripe of sunshine, a cigarette floating in his fingers. His hair is short and grey, his eyes closed in the sun. When he was young, he might have been very good-looking.

Linda sits two chairs away. He doesn't stir. She watches his cigarette, the ash extending as it burns. She crosses one leg over the other and leans back, closing her eyes, a cat angling for a bit of sun. She is always cold, even in the summer. She inhales the smell of the man's smoke: American Spirit, she thinks. Fancy. She feels him move the cigarette to his lips and inhale. She pops one eye open and looks at him. He returns the sidelong stare.

"Good afternoon," he says, and closes his eyes again.

"Good afternoon," Linda says. Linda has no idea what she's supposed to do in this place, what happens here. Vincent said someone would "coordinate her care," but so far, no one's talked to her except other inmates. She waits for the man to initiate a conversation; men usually do.

A minute passes. In her head, Linda counts to a hundred. The man's cigarette dies—he hardly inhaled, she notices—and he lights another, from a fresh pack, the uniform white cylinders glowing in two neat rows.

"Pardon me," she says softly, leaning toward him. He opens his eyes and looks at her skeptically. "I was wondering—would you mind—?" She gestures toward the cigarette pack. He exhales through his nostrils, two plumes of synchronized smoke plunging and fading.

"Here," he says, handing it to her. He closes his eyes again.

Linda takes one. "I'm sorry, do you—?" The man gives the sky an irritated look. With effort, he digs in his pocket and tosses her a little purple Bic. He doesn't offer to light it for her. Men these days rarely do, unless they have excellent manners.

"Ah," Linda finally says, her voice full of postcoital pleasure. "Ah." She takes the cigarette and examines it, turning it over in the sun.

"Those things'll kill you," the man murmurs.

"Life kills you," Linda says. "Why not enjoy yourself?"

"I'm an addict," the man says flatly. "Everything I do . . . has some addictive element. Filthy habits." He flicks an invisible thing away with his hand.

"What are your filthy habits?" she asks.

"None of your business," he replies. "What are your filthy habits?"

She looks at him. "If you aren't going to tell me *your*—"

"I asked you what are your filthy habits." The man settles back into his chair and returns his attention to the middle distance, gazing past the fence. She wants to tell him everything.

"Well. Cigarettes, obviously."

"Obviously." He takes a drag, blowing the smoke up this time. "What else?" he asks, not looking at her.

"I enjoy a cocktail. But who doesn't?"

"I don't."

"It was a rhetorical question."

"But I can't seem to stop myself," he continues, as though she hadn't spoken.

"Oh," Linda says. "Well, neither can I, I suppose." She's never said this out loud.

"Are you in the program?" he asks, turning to her.

"What program?"

"Are you a friend of Bill?"

"Who's Bill?"

He resettles himself. "Never mind." The sun widens the stripe of light on the cramped patio to include them both. "What else?" he asks.

"Cigarettes, cocktails . . ." she recites.

"When you say 'cocktails,' what do you mean?"

"You don't know what a cocktail is?"

"Do you use mixers?" he asks. "Do you add ice?"

"Sure," she says.

"Or do you just pour cheap vodka into a coffee mug and sip at it all day?"

She stares at him. "I probably watch too much television," she says, and concentrates on the end of her cigarette.

"Mmm."

"What?"

"That's not an addiction."

"Sure it is."

"I'm talking about controlled substances."

"Who doesn't like a painkiller?" she says. "I just got back from the hospital. Vicodin *and* Percocet."

"Pill-popper. I should have guessed."

"Why does everyone keep *saying* that?" she asks.

The man smiles mirthlessly into the sun. "You should try it."

"Popping pills?"

"The program."

"Linda?" A heavyset young blonde sticks her head out of the sliding-glass door. "Linda?" she says again. "I need you to come with me, darlin', okay?"

Linda dislikes her immediately—only gay men can call her darling—but she rises from the chair, not without difficulty, that tricky center of gravity again. She attempts to move in as dignified a manner as possible from the patio to the door, aware that her smoking companion might be watching her. She wants him to be her friend. Linda glances over her shoulder to see if he's turned around, but she only sees his regal back, his hand and arm aloft as he brings the cigarette again to his mouth in slow motion.

"Follow me," the woman says in her cotton voice. She introduces herself as Tara and leads Linda into a tiny, windowless room with a desk and two chairs. Linda seats herself and crosses one knee over the other, her back high and straight. She used to be a ballet dancer. She was the best dancer her teachers had seen in years.

"Has anyone gone over the house rules with you?" Tara asks, tunneling through the papers on the desk.

"No."

"Okay," Tara says, placing her fingertips on the desk's surface. "Number one: this is a sober house. No drugs, no booze, no pills."

"Can you people stop with the *pills*?"

Tara rifles through a pile of folders. "If you're caught with drugs or alcohol of any kind, we discharge you and give the bed to someone else. Yes?" She's all business now, Tara, her honeyed affect gone. "And smoking is outdoors only, in the back, not out front."

"That's where I was," Linda says.

"I know."

"Where can I get cigarettes?" she asks.

"There's a store around the corner. But they're not cheap. He won't sell cartons." It's either an admonishment or a gripe. "Number two," Tara continues. "There's a mandatory meeting every night at 7:30, after dinner."

"A meeting?"

"Have you been to A.A. before?"

Linda shakes her head dismissively.

"Really? Never?"

"Yes, really."

"*Really?*" Tara says. "At your age?"

"I *beg* your pardon?"

"No, I just—huh." Tara shakes her head. "Number three, no fighting. That includes verbal fighting, profanity, et cetera. That'll get you discharged, too. Any questions?"

"What am I supposed to do here?"

"What do you mean?"

"My daughter was supposed to pick me up from UCSD, and instead that man Vincent drove me here. My daughter is coming, but I don't know when."

"They didn't tell you . . . ?"

"Tell me what?"

"Vincent's usually really good about that." Tara resumes her search through the files strewn across the desk. "This is a recuperative care unit; do you understand what that means?"

"Of course," Linda says.

"Have you been to a place like this before?"

"Of course not."

"Okay. The goal here is to get you back on your feet. On the one hand, I'm talking about—a-ha, here we go." She seizes a folder and opens it. "Your . . . heart attack . . . and your stroke, but it also means"—she looks meaningfully at Linda—"recovery from your addictions."

Linda leans forward in her chair. "I'm not addicted to anything."

"It says here that you're a heavy drinker. Would you say that's accurate?"

"Not precisely, no. I enjoy a cocktail every now and again. Do you enjoy a cocktail every now and again?"

"I do, but I'm in recovery, so I stay away from them." Tara smiles.

"But you're—" Linda pulls back and studies the woman. "You must be twenty-five years old."

"I've been in recovery since I was sixteen. Trust me, it was the right thing to do." Tara smiles again. "I'm thirty-six," she adds. "How do you feel about entering an addiction recovery program, Linda?"

Linda leans forward again. "*I don't have an addiction,*" she stage-whispers.

"Everyone comes to the program in her own time," Tara says, closing the folder. "But the nightly meetings are mandatory. You don't have to say anything, just show up." She narrows her eyes. "Don't be late." She rises from her swivel chair and squeezes a narrow path out of the little office, swishing down the hall, leaving Linda in the overbright fluorescence.

Linda returns to the patio, but her friend is gone. The chill of her solitude is starting to tickle the edges of everything, like a draft swirling around her ankles. She stares at the sky through the eucalyptus leaves, a lattice against the sun-pale blue, and thinks of her other daughter, the one who seemed to turn into a ghost after the oldest daughter drowned: Mara. It's like she lost them both at once, and her husband too, the bungalow, the whole life: it was a movie she'd been watching, and then it was over, the credits rolling, leaving Linda in a velvet seat with broken springs, smelling like popcorn as the lights came on.

She loved going to the movies as a girl. *That* was life: heroic, gorgeous, composed. Her actual life was only ever a boring disappointment.

Mara was her mystery child. Allison was charming; Linda saw herself in the girl's game, dimpled smile and determined affection. Allison was everyone's favorite: Linda's, Charlie's, the mailman's, her teachers'; the sweet old widows at both ends of the block, the man at Thrifty who scooped ice cream. Mara flickered in Allison's shadow.

Allison was athletic and golden, an almond of a girl who looked like she had on a white bathing suit when she ran naked through the backyard sprinklers. At the beach, she skipped from the sand to the water to the sand, turning an ever-more-gentle brown all summer, her chestnut hair shot through with streaks of gold, like corn silk. Linda had been meaning to get her into modeling and commercials.

Mara was thin and pale, freckled, prone to sunburn. She reminded Linda to slather more sunscreen on her, always. Her brown hair was dull, dun-colored, frizzy. Mara insisted on boring details: hunger, thirst, discomfort, the threat of bad boys at school. Linda couldn't see herself in Mara, couldn't find the familiar dancing light in her eyes. Both her girls' eyes were the same color, though Allison's were somehow brighter. Neither of them inherited Linda's ridiculous azure eyes, which were so blue people asked if she wore contacts. They got Charlie's grey-green eyes instead. Tidepool eyes.

When Mara was a toddler, she spoke in an incomprehensible babble, and Allison, not quite two years older, translated. When the bad boys picked on Mara at school, Allison's intervention—talking to them on the playground, explaining they needed to stop bothering her sister—was more successful than Linda's and Charlie's pleading with teachers, or Charlie's stern, lawyerly call to the boys' parents. Allison loved Mara. She loved everyone, but Mara especially. She forgave her seriousness, her accusatory silence.

After Allison died, and Charlie took Mara to Boston, Linda would have brief, horrid phone conversations with her. She was seven, then eight, and you could say she was only a child and didn't know how to converse with adults, but it never got better, not even when she grew up. Mara's infrequent visits were also awful, in their way, and after she graduated from high school, they stopped altogether. Linda, terrified of flying, never went to Boston. She did fly, once, to see Mara graduate from college. She did do that.

Linda lets the sunlight make her vision go metallic. She closes her eyes, and the afterimage is the silhouette in reverse.

Mara *blamed* Linda. That grave little girl. She could hear it in Mara's voice as soon as it happened.

She was probably better off: Charlie gave her the best of everything, a beautiful home, a stepmother (eventually), good schools; he paid for that expensive girls' college she went to, probably paid for her graduate degree in Montreal.

Linda lost them all at once. Allison was the worst. Then Charlie, then Mara, then Stan. One by one, things were taken from her, as they always had been and always would.

"Linda?" Some nurse's voice again, aide, porter, whatever: a woman in pink scrubs. "Time for meeting," she says. No "the," just "meeting." The sun has fallen below the building across the alley, but an orange orb glows between the slats in the chain link, and Linda holds it.

The nurse won't leave. "Linda?" she says again. How do they all know her name?

Linda doesn't give her the satisfaction of a response but begins, slowly, to lift herself from the chair.

Chapter Six

"I'm on the jail phone," Shannon says, Brandy's cell phone greasing her cheek. The plane of Arizona desert flashes in front of her, a giant sheet of tinfoil. She inhales the purity of it, the sage, the sand, sunlight itself. What even grows out here? Did she learn it in school? Cactus. Scrub brush. Which is, what?

She could run into the sand, run and run, take her shirt off, not care what her stomach looks like, run until she can't see the highway. It's another planet here. She heard somewhere that deserts were formed millions of years ago from the bottoms of ancient oceans and seas.

Mara says something about calling her back and hangs up.

Shannon hasn't told Brandy about her mother. She said they should drive to Las Cruces, stay in a motel, then go to Roswell, where the UFO crashed. Brandy thinks they're turning around after that; she thinks it's a three-day trip.

Shannon weighs the pros and cons of the possibility that Brandy is snorting coke in the rest-stop bathroom. She herself has already smoked a significant portion of the excellent weed Brandy brought, but Brandy said she was saving herself for uppers.

"Dude." Brandy's voice at Shannon's shoulder is not her coke voice. Brandy has reapplied her eyeliner and powdered her face: she seems not to know how attractive she is, how darling, like an illustration of a person, the saucer eyes, the flushed satiny skin, the flawless teeth. She's like the fantasy you had when you were little that your doll would come to life.

"All this sand used to be at the bottom of the ocean," Shannon murmurs.

"Everybody says that." Brandy guides Shannon back to the car, a red Del Sol her father bought her when it looked like she was going to get her associate's. She didn't, but he let her keep it. She says she's going back in the fall.

Brandy keys the ignition. The music roars back on, and icy air sprays from the vents. She pulls onto the highway, which stretches forever, like they're driving on a bridge to another dimension. Shannon digs for the Pixy Stix in a bag at her feet and upends one into her mouth.

"Do you have more of that Lowryder?" she asks.

"It's not Lowryder, it's Blueberry," Brandy replies.

"Whatever."

"Save some for me, dude."

"I thought you were saving yourself. You don't even like downers."

"I wouldn't have bought it if I didn't want to smoke it."

"Don't get mad."

"I'm not mad."

Shannon folds the Pixy Stix wrapper into a tiny accordion. "So do you have more?"

Brandy turns up the volume on the stereo.

Outside Las Cruces, the sky drains its color. The Del Sol rolls down a wide boulevard lined with parking lots, video stores,

Arby's, an EBT grocery, a fabric store, a Rent-A-Center, an alc bar.

"Let's get dinner," Shannon announces, spying a Taco Bell glowing in the distance.

"We have to find a motel."

"I'm *starving*. Aren't you starving?"

"No."

Shannon peers at her. "You *did* do coke. You just didn't tell me."

Brandy rolls her eyes.

"That place has a motel behind it," Shannon says, pointing to a Mexican restaurant the size of a warehouse. It has a giant sign on the roof, a woman with a neon hibiscus in her hair, holding a margarita. "We can get those margaritas with Coronas in them," Shannon says. Brandy pulls in. Shannon's minimart trash falls out as she opens the passenger door. Heat radiates from the asphalt.

The restaurant's interior is dark and inviting, the booths separated by stained glass. A woman in an off-the-shoulder peasant blouse hands them enormous menus.

"I want what that guy's having," Shannon tells her, eyeing a long table in the middle, birthday balloons floating above the fray.

"A Mexican Bulldog?"

"What's it called when there's two Coronas?"

"A double Mexican Bulldog."

"Yeah."

"Me, too," Brandy echoes.

"Can I see some I.D., ladies?"

Shannon digs for her wallet. Brandy shows the waitress her driver's license, and the woman stares at it, stares at Brandy, and stares at it again.

"It's real," Shannon says. "She just looks sixteen."

The woman holds it up to the light, turning it over. "Wow," she finally says. She glances at Shannon's license and disappears with her tray.

Brandy sighs.

"What?"

"Casey was a dick about letting me take the weekend."

"You're his favorite; it's not like he's gonna fire you."

"I cursed him out. I was like, Anthony's is right across the street, they probably don't abuse their servers like you do."

"What did he say?"

"He told me to fuck myself. Then he gave me the weekend." She scratches her nose. "If I'm late on Monday, he's going to flay me alive."

"He's in love with you."

"He's disgusting. He's, like, forty years old. He has kids." Casey is one of the biggest drunks at the restaurant. "I don't think he sees them," Brandy clarifies. "He has their names tattooed on his arm."

Their drinks arrive, Flintstone huge, in heavy glasses dense with frost. Shannon peeks through the glassware and catches Brandy's eye.

"Jesus Christ," Brandy whispers.

"It's my birthday," Shannon says, grinning at the waitress. Brandy kicks her under the table.

"She saw your license, retard."

At some point, the manager brightens the lights and turns off the music. The funk of enchilada sauce hovers over muddy smears of refried beans somewhere beneath Shannon's nose. The red casino glow of the lamp over their table throbs brighter, dims, throbs again. Their eyes meet: Shannon can't read her friend's expression. Brandy reaches over and nudges her.

"Hey," she murmurs.

"Hey."

"We gotta go."

"Lemme finish this," Shannon says, indicating the rest of her third double Mexican Bulldog. "Plus," she says, and trails off.

"Plus what?"

Shannon looks at the air in front of her. "Plus, they're probably closing soon, and maybe they do shots."

"Every restaurant doesn't do that. And it's the *staff* that does shots, not the staff plus whichever drunks are still there trying to finish their fifth margarita."

"This is not my *fifth* margarita."

"Shannon, yes it is, I just paid the bill." Brandy's eyes are half-closed.

"Brandy." Shannon tries to focus her vision. "Hey."

"Yeah."

"You're my best friend. We're best friends."

Someone in the distance bobs with a mop.

"Yeah, dude."

"So, question. *Why* am I your best friend?"

Brandy drops her forehead into her hand.

"I'm serious."

The kitchen thrums with clanging metal and charging dishwashers. A radio in back plays that Mexican oom-pah music. No one is at the bar doing shots; maybe they do them in the kitchen. Why doesn't Shannon get a job at a fancy restaurant, like Brandy, and make actual money? Do you have to be cute to get hired at a place like The Cove? They have ugly waiters, but the waitresses are all cute. She could get a haircut.

Brandy holds her face serenely above her fingertips, eyes closed.

"Because, number one," Shannon says, "I'm broke all the time. You're always paying."

"Dude," Brandy says, and Shannon cuts her off.

"Number two, you drive, I never drive, and I never pitch in for gas. Ever. Number three, I'm a bad influence."

"I'm a bad influence," Brandy asserts.

"Number four, you're hot, I'm not."

"No." Brandy opens her eyes. "Don't do that." The Corona bottles roll toward one another in their red bath. "Girls don't like me, did you ever notice that? They see my face and think I'm a bitch. And guys just want to fuck me, or they get, like, obsessed." She leans back. "I don't have a lot of friends. *You're* my friend." She looks around the dining room. "Can we go?"

"Is that true?"

"You never remember these conversations the next day." Brandy comes around to Shannon's side and gets under her shoulder. "Come on." They hobble like old ladies across the parking lot to their motel.

Shannon wakes up freezing beneath a thin, stiff coverlet. Thousands of bodies have lain on these sheets. The blackout curtain is drawn; the air conditioner wheezes rhythmically. An alarm clock beeps on the other side of the wall. She gets up to pee. Their own clock flashes 12:00.

On the toilet, she sifts through the sand in her head. Why was she in a waiting room in the middle of the night? Which night?

It materializes as she rinses her face: her mother, light as a Kleenex, carried out by the EMTs. The pretty doctor. Off-the-hook signal. Arizona highway, Mexican restaurant, margaritas the size of small cars—unconnected flashes, no story. A motel room with gummy carpet, Brandy asleep: they could be anywhere. Her mother is in a hospital bed, or wherever.

Back in their room, Brandy is face up, snoring. Shannon peeks through the curtain: a tiny circle of swimming pool surrounded by chain link, surrounded by parking lot, surrounded by brown desert, and in the distance, jagged mountains. Bottom of the ocean.

Shannon crawls under the coverlet next to Brandy. They have all the time in the world. They're never going back to California.

Water pounds the acrylic shower stall, and the room fills with the smell of Brandy's shampoo, Brandy who had the foresight to pack her own travel shampoo. Shannon gets out of bed and notices there's still a pitch in her walk. Her hangover will be terrible when she finally wakes up.

"Hey," she says into the steam. The mirror fogs, and her face disappears. "Do they have Denny's in New Mexico?"

"I fucking hope so."

Shannon makes her way to her duffel bag, nauseous but not enough to throw up. She hates her clothes. Everything she brought is smelly, pulled from the depths of her hamper. From across the room, she half-watches Brandy step out of the shower and grab a towel, her torso and shoulders childishly narrow, nipping in further at her waist, then widening into her improbably round butt, smooth as a hazelnut. An accident of genetics.

Shannon's mother acts like beauty is a sign of divine favor, or a person's own virtue, or both. When she was little, Shannon went whole hog for her mother's doting beauty routine, the curlers, the hair crap, the necklaces and bangle bracelets and cubic zirconium, the pink lip gloss and blush Linda would dab on her seven-year-old face before sending her to school. She probably looked like JonBenét Ramsey.

As Linda aged, she soured. Around the time Shannon started fifth grade, her mania faded. She was irritated all the time. Later, she let her appearance go, which was shocking. The bouncy blond hair, her golden halo: dull and oily. She wore too much makeup, like she couldn't tell the difference between the face for a drag queen and the face for an older woman. She retreated into a uniform of slippers, a muumuu if she was in the house, polyester pants for going out, a fake pearl necklace. She gave advice: "Just *eat less,* dear. Drink a cup of coffee, have a cigarette." Or, "You have to pick one or the other, eyes or lips, never both, unless you've got a certain kind of face, like I have." She made friends with an actual drag queen who met her most afternoons in the Denny's on Marina Boulevard, a fellow drunk who shared her sense of having just missed a life of fame and fortune.

Brandy walks out of the bathroom in a towel, her short hair messy and damp, and begins fussing with lotions.

"When does Roswell open?" she asks Shannon.

"I don't know."

"It was your idea."

Shannon was so busy crafting her escape she forgot to arrange anything for Roswell.

"Why don't you find us a diner?" Brandy suggests.

Shannon picks up Brandy's smartphone in its bright case and paws an app open. "There's one down the street," she says. "And we can get a fifth on the way." Their old hangover cure: pancakes and coffee spiked with Crown Royal.

"I just need food," Brandy says, smoothing something into her calves.

"Come on! Our tradition."

"We haven't done that since high school."

Shannon turns the phone sideways. "Oh, shit."

"What?"

"Tickets to see that UFO place are a *hundred bucks.*"

"Whatever," Brandy says, after a pause. "We're already here."

"No, you have to call forty-eight hours in advance," Shannon says, scrolling, "and they're booked all weekend." She sits on the bed. "*Fuck.*"

Brandy moves to her arms, and then, switching lotions, does her face and neck. She squeezes something from another tiny bottle into the palm of her hand and rubs it into her hair.

"Did you know there's a place in Texas that's, like, the Roswell of Texas?" Shannon asks.

Brandy gathers her toiletries and zips them back into her travel pouch. She takes the phone from Shannon and studies it.

"It's not that far," Shannon adds.

"What's it called?"

"Aurora."

Brandy types it in and watches the screen. She sighs. "Eight hours. Try again."

"Let's go! We can make it!"

"And get trashed at another restaurant, stay the night somewhere, go to the, whatever it is, and get back to San Diego on *Tuesday*? It took us ten hours to get here."

"I'm not the only one who got trashed last night."

"Didn't say you were."

"We can still *go* to Roswell."

"And hang out at the gift shop."

"It's not like the UFO is *still there*."

Brandy sits down on the other bed. "Let's go home. If we drive back now, I can work Sunday."

Shannon shakes her head. "No. No way."

"This trip is starting to feel lame." Brandy folds her tawny arms across her chest.

"You want to go? Go. I'm staying." Shannon stands up.

"Where? Where are you 'staying'?"

"Here."

"In the outer Las Cruces Super 8."

Shannon stalks into the bathroom, slams the door, and sits on the toilet, glaring at the floor tile. Brandy's blow dryer starts. Shannon reaches behind herself and flushes.

There is a long silence after the blow dryer finishes. Brandy's knuckles rap the door. "Breakfast. Shan. C'mon."

Brandy is like Clark Kent in her partying: she can change in and out of it, leave it hanging in the closet for next time. The first thing Shannon does after the waitress seats them is go to the bathroom with her duffel bag and emergency stash of twin fifths. It occurs to her if she ever had twins, she could name them Crown and Jack. She locks herself in the stall and remembers the ritual requires coffee.

In high school, they would pour the Crown into the coffee under the table when they thought the waitresses weren't looking. She digs around in her bag, unscrews the cap on the palm-sized bottle, and takes a sip, the heat sliding down into her chest.

Someone enters the bathroom, and Shannon freezes. The woman washes her hands, tugs at the stuck lever on the paper-towel dispenser. She rustles in her purse, clicks open a lipstick case. Shannon's fifth is frozen in the air. The woman walks out, the door swishing shut behind her. Shannon lets out a long breath and gulps at the bottle.

Coffee is on the table when she returns, and Brandy is pensive, staring into her phone.

"I ordered for you. Pancakes and hash browns, extra well done."

Shannon flops into the booth. "Thanks."

"Listen, if we leave after this, we can get back to San Diego in time to start my shift."

"You want to work a Sunday?"

"I like money." Brandy sniffs. "My parents will get weird if we're late."

"That's not late, it's early." Shannon stares into her coffee reflection, the dark eyes gazing back at her. "I'm not going," she finally says.

"Where?"

"I'm not going back to San Diego."

"You *live* there."

The food lands swiftly on their table, trailing steam. Shannon orchestrates the ketchup, syrup, butter, salt, pepper. She takes a bite. "Do you want to stay there the rest of your life?" she asks, chewing.

"I don't know." Brandy flicks Tabasco sauce on her eggs. "No."

"Why don't we keep driving? Texas, Arkansas, Tennessee . . . We can find a cheap place to live and get jobs and be on our own."

Brandy's fork pauses on its way to her mouth. "What . . . are you smoking?"

"I'm serious."

Brandy leans forward and sniffs. "You smell like booze."

"Never mind." Shannon stabs a forkful of pancakes. "Drop me off at the bus station. I'll figure it out."

"What are you talking about?"

"Don't you want to leave your parents' house? Don't you want your dad to stop breathing down your neck?"

Brandy looks out the window. "My dad's not that bad."

"What about your *mom?*"

"What about my mom?"

Brandy's mother is basically out of a movie. Literally and figuratively blond, spray-tanned *and* actually tanned, feathered with jewelry, prone to hissy rages. Brandy's impression of her brings Shannon to her knees.

"Whatever. My parents are whatever."

"You hate them!"

"I don't *hate* them."

"You don't hate their bank account."

A terrible pause.

"I'm sorry," Shannon whispers. "I'm sorry. That's not what I meant."

A song comes over the speakers, a Police song from the eighties, and it reminds Shannon, clear as a bell, of driving somewhere with her mother when she was little, a pretty road in North County, yellow flowers in bloom along the shoulder. A feeling of safety. It would have been the beauty years; she remembers the sensation of curled hair on her neck, a ribbon brushing her skin. Where were they going? Were those years kind of not bad? How far back does she have to go to remember it not being bad?

Behind Brandy, an old couple finishes their coffee and folds their newspaper. They rise slowly out of their booth. Shannon has never been able to imagine growing old.

"I'm sorry," Shannon says again.

Brandy shakes her head. She gets up and walks away from their table. Another old couple, two men, seat themselves in the next booth. Shannon finishes her breakfast.

When she returns, Brandy smells like cigarettes. It's Shannon's fault she's smoking again, Brandy whose life is basically fine, who will be fine, who will, eventually, get her associate's, get a bachelor's in hotel/restaurant management, take over for Casey, make a life for herself, marry a guy, buy a house.

"I'm almost twenty-five," Brandy finally says.

Shannon opens her mouth but doesn't say anything.

"I know it's pathetic. I'm their little princess," she says, like she's making an argument. "I thought you didn't judge me, dude. But you do."

"No—"

"I don't hate their bank account." The repetition of Shannon's words hangs in the greased air. "As long as my brother's relapsing, or calling them from jail, I can do whatever I want." She leans back against the booth. She really is beautiful; it's annoying how Shannon notices it out of nowhere. She has to remind herself it isn't Brandy's fault.

"I didn't know how rich my dad was until, like, last month. Can you believe that?"

Shannon just listens, for once.

"I'm in his office poking around, I don't know why. I notice this piece of paper on the desk, from his accountant." She leans in. "My dad makes *so much money.* Like, we could have gotten a *much* nicer house. He probably bought in Silver Beach because he thought property values were going up." She shakes her head. "Money makes you stupid. He's stupid, my mother's stupid, my brother's obviously stupid."

"I shouldn't have—"

"Stop talking. Let it stand." Brandy finishes her food in silence.

When Shannon thinks *home,* she pictures a diner booth. A bank of windows washed in morning light. Waitress-mothers, indifferent and predictable. The heft of warm ceramic, the clatter of plates. Like a dining hall at camp—she never went to camp—you come, they give you a seat, they feed you. The pleasure of shaking a Sweet'n Low back and forth and ripping it open. She became a regular at the Marina Boulevard Denny's in high school, feeling like the first teenager in America to discover diners, only to find that her mother had been a regular there for years. Crowded into a corner booth with her drag queen friend and his squad from the piano bar, nursing cups of tea, yelping with laughter. Shannon staked her mother out, learned their schedule, and avoided going between one and three forever after.

In the parking lot, Brandy speaks again. They face each other over the roof of the Del Sol in the straight-down sun, wary of touching the door handles.

"Where do you want to go?" she asks.

"Tennessee?" Shannon says, tentative and thrilled.

"Where in Tennessee?"

"Pick a place," Shannon says.

"It was your idea."

"If you're coming with me, it's both our idea."

"Is Nashville in Tennessee?" Brandy asks.

"I think so."

"All right." Brandy lets her sunglasses drop over her eyes. "Let's do it, tweaker." She pops the locks, and they climb inside.

West Texas is sun-scoured and flat. The speed limit is seventy-five, and Brandy drives ninety, her eye on the rearview. A hundred miles away, a train crawls across the horizon, slow as a cloud.

"Do you really want to see Aurora?" Brandy asks.

"No." Shannon sniffs. "Maybe."

"I know, right? I don't want it to be lame."

Texas looks like New Mexico, Arizona, and eastern California. Her first big trip, and the entire southwestern United States is dry and cactusy, which she could have guessed. Maybe Tennessee will be different.

"You wanna smoke?" Whenever Shannon tries to be subtle, she ends up blurting out exactly what she's thinking.

"Not really."

"A little?"

"Didn't we just say we should save our money?"

"But you already bought it."

"We smoke it, we have to buy *more*."

Shannon should train herself to think like an adult.

"Maybe we should think about quitting," Brandy says.

"Quitting what?" Shannon laughs. "No way."

"You're almost thirty," Brandy says.

"So?"

"People grow out of it." Brandy turns the volume down on the radio. "Unless they don't," she says, eyeing Shannon. Her phone explodes suddenly, dancing in the cupholder. Shannon grabs it: a Massachusetts number. She silences it.

"Who is it?" Brandy asks.

"It said 'unknown.' Probably a telemarketer." Shannon's heart punches her chest. Mara will do the right thing. Right? Shannon can call her when they get to Tennessee, when they have a land line. She tries to think of her mother, to make herself feel the guilty stab of what she's done, what she's doing. Every time, her mind goes white with static. Old memories keep floating up instead.

The phone rings again, same number. Shannon quiets it and turns the radio back up.

They stop for gas outside a nothing town. Shannon chomps on a piece of gum and holds the gas pump, watching the numbers turn. Brandy comes out of the minimart talking on her phone, a plastic bag hanging from her wrist, the contents of which Shannon hopes very much are ranch-flavored.

"She's right here," Brandy says.

Shannon replaces the gas nozzle. Junction, Texas, reminds her of El Cajon in East County, which she and her friends always called Kentucky, because of the rodeos and rednecks. They should have just called it Texas.

Brandy covers the mouthpiece on the phone. "Shannon, what the *fuck?*" She thrusts the phone at her. "Here."

Shannon takes it and stares at the screen, the clock on the call advancing by the second. She pictures Mara at the other end, testy and full of authority. She presses her thumb to end the call and hands it back.

"Do you want to *walk?*" Brandy hisses.

It seems so long ago. Her mother, her life, the state of California, receding into the distance like a stray balloon, dancing above the power lines.

"What did she say?" Shannon finally asks.

"I want to hear it from you."

"I'm not in jail."

Brandy's face twitches.

"I told her to come out here and deal with her mother."

"Who is in the *hospital*."

"I know."

"She's your *mom!* She could die!"

"She's pretty hardy."

"You *left* her there; what if she did that to you?"

"That's, like, my entire life."

"How do you know she's going to be okay? It's not like you called to ask."

"The doctor told me she could make a full recovery if she quit drinking and smoking, and I was, like, well." The gas pump beeps and spits out a receipt. "Then what? She'll come home, pick up where she left off, and I'm her ambulance-dialing service? She doesn't listen to me."

"She's your *mom*."

"You keep saying that." Shannon shakes the nozzle out of the gas tank, and fuel drips onto her toes. She thunks the nozzle back into the holder.

"Mara is a grown woman with a life. She has an actual job. In Massachusetts," Brandy says.

"So?"

"So, you can blame your mom for whatever you want, but that doesn't mean you just *leave her there*. I mean, *fuck*. Get her home from the hospital and *move out*. I've been telling you that for years."

"She needs someone to be there."

"To do what?"

"She had a stroke, too."

"Jesus Christ!"

"*I* have an actual job. *I'm* a grown woman with a life."

"You don't have a job anymore, which was not an actual job. And you're not a grown woman with a life. Neither am I."

"That's why we need to move to Tennessee."

"You can't be an adult in San Diego? You can't be an adult at the one moment it's super important to *be an adult*?"

"You know how much either one of them cares about me?" Shannon's eyes curtain with moisture. "They can take care of each other."

"Mara didn't say she was coming."

"She didn't?"

"She was like—she was more hung up on whether you were in jail."

"I'm not going back," Shannon says again. Her cheeks are damp.

"So, what?"

"We're gonna go to Tennessee." She tries to see into Brandy's sunglasses. "Now you don't want to."

"I do," Brandy says.

"Maybe I should go by myself."

"Yeah, right."

"That's my whole problem. I need to go by myself."

"How much money is in your checking account? Which of your credit cards work? Whose car are you going to drive?"

"People more broke than me figure it out."

"Yeah, but like, you want to avoid that, if possible."

"I'll find a job."

"What job? Can you pay rent and buy groceries and pay for a car on a minimum-wage job, *by yourself*?"

"I do that now! My mom's checks don't even help, she spends it all on booze and cigarettes."

"Mara's father's checks don't hurt."

"What are you talking about?"

Brandy's eyebrows float above the frames of her sunglasses.

"What are you talking about, 'Mara's father's checks'? I fucking wish he sent checks."

"Your mom pays the rent with them."

"*I* pay the rent." She gives her mother cash in an envelope, the same oddly formal ritual every month. She'd been putting off thinking about what would happen when her paychecks stopped. "*My mother told you she pays the rent with checks from her ex-husband? Why would she tell you that? Why would you believe her?*"

"I don't know. I can't remember. I thought you knew." Brandy's face betrays nothing. "It's harder than you think to go out on your own."

"How would you know?" Shannon wipes her face. "You don't think I can do it."

Brandy stares at the asphalt.

"See?"

"I don't want to fight with you."

"You want to go back to Silver Beach?"

Brandy raises her face to the pink sunset. "I don't know."

Shannon opens the car door, reaches in, and pulls her duffel out. She digs around the seat and grabs the minimart bag, slams the door, and hoists the duffel over her shoulder. She stalks across the gas station to the road and turns toward the traffic, squinting at the horizon, wishing she'd asked Brandy to buy her a pair of sunglasses. She thrusts her arm out, thumb up. She walks backward, scanning the road. An SUV barges into view and thunders past. A pickup truck slows down, honks, but doesn't stop. A minivan cruises by. The sun drops a quarter-inch.

She glances at the gas station and watches Brandy climb back into the car. Another pickup clatters past, chopping the wind. She picks the hair out of her eyes.

She looks again. Brandy's car is gone.

The thing about feeling alone in the world is that when you're *actually* alone, for real, you realize what a pussy you were, feeling sorry for yourself all that time.

The sun goes red, painting the sky a tawdry pink that fades up to purple, then blue. A star blinks in the dark overhead. The cars turn on their headlights.

When she can't see the gas station anymore, she sings to herself from *Dark Side of the Moon*. She walks backward at the same slow, careful pace. Someone will stop, or morning will come.

When Brandy pulls up an eternity later, she doesn't get out of the car. Shannon climbs in and says nothing.

As the Arizona sky fades into dawn ten hours later, Shannon pulls to the side of the road. She tells herself, if Brandy wakes up, she won't do it: Brandy's porcelain sleep is the sleep of a child. Shannon doesn't feel guilty as she removes what's left of her friend's weed and zips it into her duffel. Ditto as she unsnaps Brandy's wallet and slips two twenties and the emergency credit card out from behind the debit card. Another seven hours to San Diego.

The apartment in Silver Beach is empty when Brandy drops her off. Shannon locks the door behind her and decides to smoke the weed as quickly as possible.

Chapter Seven

The hanging lamp over her dining table shines a bright circle on Mara's letter in the predawn dark. She is a person who writes letters, but the habit has faded. Her stationery, creamy yellow, is a gift from her stepmother.

Hey, Mara writes at the top. *Not much to say except the obvious. I'm sorry.*

I decided to go. Not sure for how long, results tbd. Do you mind checking the mail, watering the plants while I'm gone? Pretty please?

Forgive me?

I'll call you from the other side–

xx

m.

She folds the paper in half, slides it into the matching envelope, and writes Nell's address across the front in her neat typeset handwriting.

She pulls the Amherst Friends employee handbook from a file drawer and rereads the sick-leave policy. There are only two weeks left in the semester, she can't imagine it will be a problem—this time of year, most teachers eschew library hour for end-of-year portfolio presentations and celebrations anyway. She'll call the head of school when she lands.

Her suitcase and a carryon are by the door. The return flight will be quicker because of the jet stream, then the airport shuttle from Hartford, then home. She'll shove her door open and find Nell on the sofa, glass in hand. Forgiven.

The tiny-throated vernal choir chirps from the trees around the marsh; are there treefrogs in San Diego? She hears the rubbery *glunk* of green frogs and the gloomy interval moan of bullfrogs, imagines their mirror eyes shining in the faint glow from the moon. She thinks of the new leaves on the river birch, the yellow confetti of the forsythia tangle out front. The daffodils on the sunny side are in full bloom; peonies are on their way. The children next door call her the Flower Lady.

She glances at her watch as the van rolls onto the gravel, hears the brief toot of its horn. She slides the glass door shut, locks it, and slips into her clogs. Grabs the letter, hoists her bag onto her shoulder, and pulls the apartment door closed.

In the airplane over Pennsylvania, she sleeps heavily. She wakes up over the plains, her eyes alighting on a thin smear of cloud, geometric farmland below. She stirs again over Colorado. She orders coffee and burns her tongue. Out the window, the snow-tipped peaks of the Rockies flatten into the deserts of New Mexico and Arizona: rust-colored, sulfuric, windswept.

A panic tingles in her ear. They're too free, too fast up here. Hurtling.

When Arizona fades into California, the plane begins its dreamy descent, so subtle no one seems to notice the nose tipping gently downward. Mara peers through the dense little window at Yuma, El Centro, the Anza Borrego desert, the dry, light-scoured terrain oddly familiar, though she shouldn't remember it. As the plane tilts, her panic spreads.

San Diego looms into view, carpeted with houses, sprawling for infinite miles, everything the same one- or two-story height, flattened by the sun.

She is shocked at how low the planes fly as they approach Lindbergh Field. People are on the ground, milling around Balboa Park, joggers, picnickers. She sees someone wave, and her hand flickers involuntarily in her lap. She blinks, and the plane is slicing down the tarmac, fighting the wind to pull to a stop. Through the porthole, she catches sight of San Diego's little downtown, a cluster of prisms reflecting sunlight.

The airport has expanded and upgraded in the years since she's set foot in it, but it still feels provincial, unserious. People's sunglasses pushed up on their foreheads, faces unguarded and eager. She glides down an escalator in an atrium with enormous mobiles of seabirds floating from the ceiling. At the bottom, strangers scan the crowd for their relatives, and Mara floats through them.

As she pilots the rental car onto Harbor Drive, the scene doesn't look real. It's noon; springtime; high postcard weather. Every surface reflects the unrelenting light: windshields and car bumpers, billboards, low-slung rooftops, the water in the harbor, the swerving concrete of the freeway. That two-dimensionality again, every texture ironed by the glare. A city sealed in fiberglass.

As she makes her way to the hospital, Silver Beach and the Pacific Ocean behind her, she compresses her panic, turns it to stone, buries it at the base of her spine. The GPS voice, female and British, delivers impassive commands, and Mara follows them.

The hospital isn't far. The surrounding neighborhood, which she remembers as edgy and cool—whatever that meant to a seven-year-old in the eighties—has become precious and manicured, flower shops and salons, sushi restaurants, highly specific boutiques.

The nurses on the phone were imprecise in their instructions. One of them told her Linda would be discharged Sunday; another said today, Monday; a third said Tuesday. She was on hold for a half-hour; another time, they hung up on her.

She is in no hurry.

It's late afternoon in Massachusetts, and she hasn't eaten anything since the cheap snack on the plane, the salty film lingering in her mouth. She spies a fussy little café and pulls into a parking spot on Washington Street. Standing on the sidewalk, she remembers it's a holiday. She peers inside, and a solicitous young man opens the door and ushers her into the empty restaurant, seating her at a linen-covered table by the window, where she consults a menu and orders a glass of Riesling. The only sounds are metallic dings from the kitchen, and then soft jazz comes through the speakers.

A memory she hasn't thought about in years:

After Allison drowned, Linda sent Mara and Shannon, a toddler then, to Mara's paternal grandparents in Indio, way out in the desert by Palm Springs. They stayed a month. Her grandfather drove them home in his old Chevy Malibu and turned around immediately, saying he wanted to get back before the sun set— his eyes were bad and in Indio, once the sun sank behind the San Jacinto Mountains, he said, the valley was dark as pitch.

Early the next morning, Mara woke up furtive. The house was a grotto. The blinds were closed, the windows tight, a smell like skin and old clothes, a banana-ish sweetness at nose level. Allison's bed was still unmade. By then it must have been October, or nearly, and the room looked the way it had all summer: naked Barbies and bruised My Little Ponies strewn across the carpet, the bedsheets funky with sand and whatever else their bare feet had picked up outside. The bed made Mara's legs itch, and she pictured the granular texture as an army of fleas. For a second, she felt a surge of self-satisfaction that she would make her bed before Allison made hers, one of the tiny victories that used to fill her days.

The waiter appears with Mara's Riesling. She pulls out her phone to leave a message for Sue, the head of school.

"Hello?" the woman says coolly into her ear, and Mara startles, nearly inhaling a sip of wine.

"Oh—Sue? I didn't think you'd be in the office—"

"This is my cellphone."

"Oh, oh, sorry," Mara stumbles.

"What's up?" Sue is probably annoyed, probably at a barbecue with a beer in her hand, an eye on her children splashing in an above-ground pool. "I'm in the office today, actually," she tells Mara. "What's up?"

"I had a family emergency." Mara's mind drifts to the question of what Sue is doing in her office on Memorial Day. "My mother," Mara explains. "She, uh—she had a heart attack? She's in the hospital?" It feels fake, like she's telling a story.

"Oh, my God. I'm so sorry," Sue says. "Where is she, Boston? That's where you're from, right?"

"No—I mean, yes, but she's—my mother's in California."

"Oh. Wow."

"So I'm here. With her. In San Diego."

"Wow. Okay."

"I don't know how long this is going to take."

"You're out for the rest of the year, then."

"Well—I hope not. I mean, I think I can just get things sorted and come back in a few weeks."

"That's pretty much the rest of the year."

"I guess that's true."

"Listen, if you were a teacher, I'd say we'd have to scramble, but . . . if you have the sick days, you'll be fine. You have the sick days, right?" Sue pauses. "Of course you do. Be with your mother." Mara thanks her and ends the call in her absent way, no goodbye.

It's hard to believe Linda is even at the hospital. It seems impossible she would be nearby, in the flesh, that she's existed all the years since Mara left.

Her salad materializes, but her appetite is gone. Is Sue mad? Was Mara's story plausible?

What will her mother be like? How disabled? How haggard, how ugly? When she came out for Mara's graduation—more than ten years ago—she still looked good. She looked her age, but you could tell she'd been pretty in the eyes, the cheekbones. You could tell, too, that she thought so: the makeup, the hair, the costume jewelry, the flirting. It was in her voice.

Her voice. God.

I had three little girls once.

Where is that from? The sentence hovers in the air. Who said that? Mara puts her fork down.

I had three little girls once.

The memory tinkles in—they were outside Mara's dorm—she hears Linda's voice as clearly as if it were at her cheek. Beseeching, like you wouldn't notice the falseness, the bald ambition of it. It was nighttime, Linda was standing in a cone of yellow light from one of the streetlamps, and she was drunk, so very drunk—more than Mara had ever seen her—swaying, holding fast to Mara's arm. Her pretty mother in kitten heels, white trousers, a frilly blouse, a necklace.

"I had three little girls once," she said, "and now I got none." Her voice high and clotted. They'd had dinner in town. Mara was afraid to put her in a cab to her motel, afraid she'd puke on the way, or worse. It was the night she took her to the emergency room.

"I had three little girls," her mother told her. "The first one was my favorite."

Mara froze.

"The sea stole her away," Linda said in a childlike voice. "Just like that." She looked lost. "The second one," Linda said, "the smart one, she was too good for me, she ran away. She left me alone. With the third little girl. Who hates me."

Mara tightened her grip on her mother's arm.

"I had three little girls, and now I got none."

Mara finishes her salad. She dabs her mouth with her napkin, folds it, and heads to the ladies' room, where she runs the tap, listening to the water, watching her reflection. She doesn't look like her mother. Her big, haunted eyes are glacial ponds, not Linda's eerie blue sequin eyes. Her mouth is small—she looks like she's frowning if she isn't making an effort to smile, while her mother has the pert, pleasing mouth of a beauty queen. They are both thin, but her mother's figure is petite, an exact but miniature replica of a normal-sized person, perfectly proportional. Mara has a shorebird figure, long-limbed, knobby at the joints, her throat a stem growing from her shoulders. She is several inches taller than Linda. Or this is her memory.

She pays the bill and leaves the restaurant, and the San Diegan sun flashes back into view, filling everything, a white, bright world. She gets into the car. The GPS voice tells her where to go.

At the intersection before the hospital entrance, she knows she's turned left too quickly, she sees the Subaru headed toward her. The Subaru honks, breaks, honks again. Mara makes it through and kisses her hand to the roof.

Parking is easy enough. On her way in, she walks swiftly, her face impassive. She can seem aloof, she knows this. Cold.

Eyes forward. Don't stop.

A line. The lobby of the medical center is another atrium. She glances at her watch, scans *Times* headlines on her phone, the words on the screen just shapes floating on a white background, scrolling, scrolling. The line stutters forward. Sun beats through the glass. There are five people ahead of her.

Mara turns and walks out of the atrium, past a giant bird of paradise, out the automatic glass doors, through a fog of cigarette smoke and idling car exhaust. She fumbles for her sunglasses. She enters the parking garage and whips them off to find her rental, a shiny, anonymous car, American-made. She folds herself into its upholstered silence. She clenches and unclenches her toes.

She starts the car and flips on the radio, turning the dial to the far left, landing on a jazz station. Re-sunglassed, air-conditioned, Mara cruises out of the parking garage. The GPS woman guides her downtown, and the voice takes on a hint of domination.

She sails down Sixth Avenue, along the eucalyptus-treed expanse of Balboa Park, wishing she were driving a Mercedes, a BMW. A rich lesbian car. Ha! She could move to Los Angeles, reinvent herself as the wife of a power lesbian. She pictures herself cocooned in the hush of a penthouse. She isn't sure where she would find a power lesbian; are there bars for that? Nell could be a power lesbian if she wanted, which she definitely does not. Mara isn't completely sure what a power lesbian is. She pictures a svelte woman in a white suit with a fleet of assistants.

She follows the GPS woman's instructive purr down the sloping avenue toward the periphery of downtown, turns on a side street, and parks the car in an underground garage. An elevator—oak-paneled, jazz through the speakers—conveys Mara and her bags to the lobby of the Spreckels Hotel, a place she fantasized about when she was a kid. Built in the twenties, it was a faded but beautiful ruin by the eighties, half-full with eccentric long-term residents. It was condemned in the nineties and restored, a year ago, to its former glory. Mara looked it up that morning, read the Wikipedia entry. She hadn't imagined entering it.

She stands in line behind a man in pleated khakis, feeling tall, and allows herself the vanity of imagining how other people see her. Her understated palette, her scarf, her subtle jewelry. She doesn't look like she's from here.

At the desk, she leans in and asks for a room with one bed, preferably king-size.

"All we have right now is a suite on the twentieth floor. I have a double on the fifth floor . . ." the clerk says, checking her screen.

"The suite is fine." Mara's neck blushes. She unclasps her wallet.

"You're all set," the clerk tells her, sliding Mara's credit card and room key across the desk.

She thinks about texting Nell and drops the thought out of her mind like a bill in the mail. Another elevator, this one with an attendant who presses the buttons; too late, Mara wonders if she should tip him. She strides down the hall and presses the room card to the reader. The door is heavy, polished oak, and the doorknob catches with a satisfying click. She opens it. A terrible grin. She runs to the view.

The room has massive windows for such an old building, two of them facing southwest, the Monopoly-size downtown below, the glittering bay in the distance. The afternoon sunlight is its own chandelier, diamonds of light playing on the wallpaper. She slips her feet out of her clogs and hugs the carpet with her toes. She feels like taking her clothes off.

Mara doesn't realize she's fallen asleep until she wakes up, marooned on the massive bed, the wallpaper gilded by an orange sunset. Weak with hunger, she contemplates falling back into the confection of pillows, drifting into oblivion. She could stay here forever.

A voicemail shimmers on her phone screen. A San Diego number. She ignores it. She thumbs the app that tells you where restaurants are, and types *lesbian bar*. There it is, the one she remembers, though she has no idea why she would know it: the Pilot Light on Fourth Avenue in Hillcrest. She imagines a dark, depressing bar, empty but for grizzled, braless alcoholics hunched over their gin and tonics, music from last summer's circuit party mix blaring from the ceiling-mounted speakers. Or worse, dyke-stalgia music, Patsy Cline, Patti Smith, Ani DiFranco. There will be no power lesbians at the Pilot Light. Better to go to a gay bar. She pictures bitter old men who hate everything, including women.

But she needs to eat. She needs something.

Mara steps out of a dark, freezing sushi restaurant onto Sixth Avenue, the air balmy, submissive. It's why people move here, air the temperature of one's own skin.

The hospital is a mile from here, not even.

She passes the Palace Bar on the corner, pulsing with dance music, empty inside, a baseball game flashing across a huge flat-screen. Two sunburned men nurse drinks along a brass rail outside. It's too late for the shops to be open, too early for the bars to be full. Maybe they're never full on a weeknight, not the final night of a three-day holiday weekend. Maybe they're never full at all.

She turns up Fifth. One shop is open, a bookstore, an airy place with a ceiling fan and parquet floors and a dry, papery smell. An elegant man peers at a computer atop a glass display case.

"Hi, dear," he says pleasantly.

Mara gives him a small nod. There is a collection of first editions near the front: an Anaïs Nin from 1944, Joan Didion's first novel, Arthur Miller, George Orwell.

"Are you a collector?" the proprietor calls out.

Mara shakes her head. "Just a librarian."

"*Just?*" He laughs. "*I'm* just a bookmonger. You're a *guardian.*" She likes his smile. She pulls the Anaïs Nin and fingers its cover. "I went through hell to get that," he says. "Look inside, at the engravings. She hand-printed that, you know. Only three hundred copies in the world." He returns his eyes to the screen, leaving Mara to the book, which is beautiful, dark and weird, like a bedtime story from a strange.aunt. She read Anaïs Nin obsessively the year she lived in Paris, before she went to library school in Montreal.

It occurs to her that some of her memories are worth saving. She usually crushes them like houseflies, but remembering the open-windowed nights of her Paris summer, her brief smoking habit, her unprecedented attention to poetry and Nin's steamy diaries fills her with warm possibility.

Or maybe better to forget.

Her mother is not a nice person. The thought javelins through her mind, flying out the other side and down the street.

Without looking at the price, Mara takes the book to the man at the display case.

"Ah," he murmurs. "Wonderful." His fingers move across the keys. "$255, please."

Mara hides her surprise. She hands him her credit card.

"Question," she says. She never talks like this. "What's the best gay bar around here, do you think? I'm from out of town."

"Gay bar? Or lesbian bar?" He seems old-school, like someone who'd never dream of a bar where gay men, lesbians, and even straight people might drink at the same time. But she supposes that isn't quite what she's after.

"Either," she says. "Both."

"There's Charlie Eddy's," he says, removing his glasses. "That's an oldie but goodie. Piano bar," he clarifies. "They're nice, they'll let you in."

Mara wonders what the admission criteria could possibly be.

"There's obviously the Pilot Light, which is depressing, if you ask me. *Best* lesbian bar, there isn't much to choose from, honestly. Try Charlie Eddy's." He wraps her book in tissue paper and puts it in a bag.

"Thank you," she says. "Enjoy your night."

"Likewise." He returns the reading glasses to his nose. The door chimes on her way out.

Her phone tells her that Charlie Eddy's, which sounds awful (or wonderful, she supposes, depending on your mood), is too far to walk to, and she doesn't feel like driving. She wanders up Fifth to University, which is empty too. She surveys her options. The hospital is closer than she thought. She pictures Linda wandering out, stumbling down the street, wrapped in a blanket.

The app on her phone lists a bar she hadn't noticed before, on the top floor of a new hotel. She walks there quickly, as though someone will catch her. A young man is positioned at the hotel's entrance in a costume, like he's in a Dickens novel. He opens the door for her. Inside, the walls are wood-paneled, the ceiling crowded with birdcages and Edison bulbs. A mustached man in short pants and a vest steps out to greet her.

"Is there a . . . bar here?" Mara asks.

"Ah, yes, right this way, please," the man says. It's a hotel-wide reenactment of a fantasy of the nineteenth century—maybe this is what theater people do now instead of Renaissance Faires, she thinks. He shows her to the elevator—a rickety, ancient thing with an antique wrought-iron grille that shudders open. Inside, a vested operator pulls a big lever and lurches the car to the tenth floor.

"Ma'am," he intones, pulling the door open.

She didn't expect to find such a place in San Diego. It reminds her of the "speakeasies" in the Village that Nell dragged her to once, over a long weekend in the city with the bookstore boys, who had the run of someone's downtown pied-à-terre. The bar is dim and flickery, with a long window facing downtown, toward the water. She can see the neon letters of the Spreckels Hotel. The crowd is a mix of younger and older, hip and less-hip, gay and not-gay.

People are often surprised to discover Mara is gay, or mostly gay. She doesn't call herself gay, and the word *lesbian* sounds medical somehow when she applies it to herself. Ditto *bisexual*. She'd rather not talk about something so private.

No one knows she's here. No one.

She finds an empty stool at the bar, and a lithe woman—in a vest—leans forward to take her order.

"What's your favorite?" Mara asks coyly.

The bartender winks and begins making a cocktail. She pours drops from four or five separate little bottles, mashes something with a mortar and pestle, and lights a match under a strip of orange peel. She places a tall, luminous drink before Mara.

"This is my special. I haven't named it yet." The bartender has a lovely smile. She's young, though, too young.

"Thank you," Mara says. The bartender walks away without telling her what the drink costs; Mara can't tell if it's their policy to bill at the end, or if a cute girl just bought her a drink.

Mara has no idea whether she's attractive. Nell has told her a million times how beautiful, how elegant she is, but Nell has been in love with Mara since they were in college. It was almost too much to bear, the responsibility of her friend's unrequited longing—though *unrequited* isn't the right word. Mara's feelings for Nell had always been intense, but unpredictable and hard to access, probably owing to their intensity. It took years—*years*—for the two of them to grow into an equitable relationship. If you can call it equitable.

Would Nell forgive Mara for what she wants to do tonight?

Not that she'll find anyone to do it with.

Not that Nell would ever know.

But. Would she? Mara pushes her luck too much with Nell. She's never shaken the upper hand; it's dangerous, it isn't fair.

She takes a sip of the cocktail, which is terrible, bitter and too-sweet at once. A few barstools down, two men are arguing.

"Maybe it's because you make it really *difficult*," one of them says.

"*Me?*" Their voices drop to a tense murmur. She shifts her attention to a trio of tourists at a table behind her.

"I could live here."

"I could *so totally* live here."

"I would like—I would *live* at the beach."

Mara takes her purse and slips off the barstool. Her cocktail is melting. She wants to go to bed and book a flight home. Every minute she isn't in her beautiful hotel room feels like a wasted $20 bill.

The bartender reappears and sets a flute of sparkling wine in front of her.

"I hope you're thirsty," she says.

Mara looks at her uncomprehendingly.

"Compliments of the gentleman over there," the woman says, discreetly pointing. A man in his forties with wild silver-and-black curls smiles wanly at her. He looks like someone trying to contain his essentially feral nature. He looks like Dean Wareham from the band Luna—another of Mara's Paris-year affections.

"Thank you," she says. She eases back onto the stool and raises the glass politely in the man's direction. She takes a sip and gazes out the big window. An airplane roars past.

She pulls her phone out: just like that, she's bought a return ticket to Hartford for Wednesday morning. Maybe tomorrow she'll take a drive.

"Hi." The curly-haired man takes the seat next to her. "No one ever bought you a drink before?"

Mara assesses him.

"You're welcome." Oddly, he doesn't seem pompous.

"Thank you."

"What do you drink?"

"Mineral water. Espresso." She watches him watch her. "I like wine. Just not to the point of caring that much about it."

The man nods heavily. The animal bigness to his eyes and mouth contrast with his relatively lean body. He seems tall, though she can't tell for sure when he's sitting down; maybe it's something in the shoulders. He has friendly lines around his eyes. Fabulous hair. Hands like an ogre, which sort of breaks her heart. Every once in a while, she finds a man truly handsome; rarer than that, she finds herself attracted to one. It wasn't unpleasant the last time, a fling she had with a Frenchman in Montreal, just before she left for Massachusetts. She takes a sip.

"I'm a wine guy," he says.

"What does that mean?" Mara asks.

"I import wine."

"Oh," Mara says. "From where?"

"Australia, mostly. France. Spain. My favorite wine is from California. The other stuff's just a job. My dream is to have a vineyard." He looks like someone who derives more pleasure from dreaming than having. "What about you?"

"Why did you buy me a drink?" Mara asks.

"Why not?"

"That's not an answer."

"*I* asked *you* a question." He runs his hands through his hair. Mara pictures the rooms full of women he's slept with.

"I'm a librarian."

"You're beautiful." He looks away. "And you looked classy."

Mara allows herself a skeptical half-smile. "Are you from here?" she asks.

"I was born in Sydney, but we moved to Santa Cruz when I was a kid. My parents are American. I don't have an accent." He does, actually, have the faintest trace of an accent; Mara couldn't place it before. "Are you from here?" he asks.

She shakes her head. "Visiting."

"You look Californian."

"Thanks," Mara scoffs.

"No, you look . . . like a mermaid." He is smiling at her in the way men do when they want to sleep with you. It seems like a good idea suddenly to get lost in a stranger's idea of her, to be the classy, mysterious woman he claims to see.

"I'm Mara." She reaches out her hand. His handshake is strong, his hands are huge.

"Rex," he says.

"Is that short for something?"

"No. My parents are paleontologists."

Mara stares at him.

"I'm serious," he says.

Mara takes a sip and decides this can't be true. "What are you doing in San Diego?" she asks.

"Funeral. I'm driving back to L.A. tomorrow."

"Oh. I'm sorry."

"My cousin. We were the same age." He shakes his head. "He drove like a maniac. I always told him he'd die on a freeway, and he finally did." He takes another gulp. "What about you?"

"I had vacation time. I've never been to San Diego."

The bubbles in their glasses float jauntily to the top. "You're by yourself?"

"I usually travel alone," she says.

"Me too."

Mara pictures Rex in Europe, sleeping with women in every city. He isn't wearing a wedding ring. Probably a confirmed bachelor, like her.

Rex drains his glass, and the bartender hovers across from them. "Another of the same?" she asks. He looks at Mara. Her face doesn't answer.

"No," Rex tells the bartender. Mara sips her champagne, unhurried.

When the bartender takes her empty glass, Mara glances at her phone to check the time.

"Somewhere to be?" Rex asks.

"No," Mara says. She can't decide if she's attracted to him. Maybe it doesn't matter. "I'm staying at a great hotel," she says without thinking. "See that tall building there?" She points.

"Nice," he says lightly. He looks rich. Creamy Oxford shirt, designer jeans, good haircut. A restlessness. Mara wonders how much money he actually makes.

"Me too," he says. "I'm on the twenty-third floor."

Rex doesn't seem drunk, and his car is beautiful. Mara ignores the faint whisper of her common sense and climbs into Rex's shiny little Porsche. He slides in and turns the key, wincing.

"Are you . . . with anyone?" he says suddenly. He puts his arm on her seat as he reverses out of the parking spot, and his fingers brush her neck. Heat blooms on Mara's skin.

"I wouldn't tell you if I was," Mara says.

He deflates with what she assumes is relief. Neither of them speaks as he zooms the car downtown. In the elevator from the parking garage, he has a vague smile on his face. Either he's grateful, or he's an old pro.

"What floor are you?" he asks.

"Let's go to your room."

His room is bigger, with views along a third wall, toward Silver

Beach. He occupies it carelessly, clothes hanging off chairs, suitcase yawning across the sofa, shoes separated by a long distance from their partners.

"I'm ordering room service; are you hungry?" he asks. "Red, white, rosé, sparkling?"

She wants to tell him to order a bottle of Pellegrino, but it will kill the mood, if you'd call it a mood, this wary anticipation. "Whatever," she says. "I ate earlier." She returns to the flickering view, the mauve sky, the line separating it from the distant blackness of the ocean.

Nell is such an avowed lesbian that she's never been with a man, not once. "I'm orthodox," she likes to say. Of Mara's lovers— more than five, less than ten—Nell is the most skilled, the most attentive. The best.

Rex hangs up the room phone and joins Mara by the window.

"You didn't tell me where you were from," he says softly.

"You didn't ask."

He runs a finger along her shoulder blades. "Let me guess." He drops his hand. "You said you weren't from California." He looks her up and down, a full-body scan, and stares into her eyes. "I'm thinking . . . Blueblood. Somewhere in New England. Your family goes back to Plymouth Rock."

He is appalling.

"I'm right, aren't I? Summers in Nantucket?"

"Wellfleet," she replies. Charlie Meade's Wellfleet cottage is tiny, a dump compared to its neighbors. He bought it a few years ago with the intention of fixing it up.

"I dated a woman who had a place on the Vineyard," he says. "It's the only thing I miss about her."

Mara's parents are from southern California. Her mother's family was German, and they picked oranges and fixed cars in Tustin, an orange grove at the edge of the Santa Ana Mountains.

Her father's father had come west as a teenager with his destitute family from Oklahoma after the Dust Bowl. By the time they made it to the promised land of the Central Valley, there were no jobs left. Her grandfather improved the family's fortunes by getting a job with the post office in Indio, way out in the desert, and he worked there till he died, in his eighties. Her grandmother was a housewife.

"Are your parents still in Boston?"

"My dad is," she replies, though she hadn't said anything about Boston. "My mom died when I was a kid." She hasn't told this lie in years.

A doorbell chimes. For a second, Mara can't figure out where the sound is coming from.

"Thank you," Rex tells the porter, handing him a dollar. He brings back a bottle of champagne in an ice bucket and a plate of oysters. Nell's favorite. The last few summers, in Wellfleet, they ate them twice a day for a week. She watches Rex cover the cork with a napkin and coax it out of the bottle without a sound, the air slithering out like dry ice. He pours two glasses and joins her again at the window, his face a question.

"What do you like?" he asks. She doesn't know how to answer. But tonight she is someone else.

He holds his glass to hers. "*Salud,*" he says.

"Cheers." They clink. A plane moves across the frame of the window in silence and lands past the freeway.

"I like you," he says.

Testing her attraction to him, she reaches behind his head and dips her fingers into his hair. He sets his glass on the window ledge and leans into her neck. Men's and women's bodies are absurdly, remarkably different. Even Nell, who can stand on her hands for minutes at a time, whose muscles are hardy and firm, has feminine bones, curves, downy skin. Rex, she soon learns, has wiry black hair on his arms and chest and legs. His back is broader than she realized, his shoulders powerful, like a big cat. He slips the glass from her hand. He unravels her scarf, nudges a button open, runs a finger under the tiny chain of her necklace. He encircles her wrist and squeezes, drawing her hand behind her head, pressing himself against her. He takes her other hand and holds them together. He proceeds linearly, moving along the path of his appetite, beginning with the top of her body—his fingers dancing at her ears, his mouth snuffling her neck and collarbones—and proceeds down, like gravity.

She thinks of Nell, who is eager, not dominant. This is something else.

He's got her on the floor now, and through some combination of physics and expertise, she cannot move. At all. It disturbs her how good this feels. At the same time, it infuriates her, his control. A rich asshole turned on by what he believes is her good breeding, with his animal hands and feline face.

Her fury feels like pleasure. Ditto her shame.

Her orgasm is a shock wave. Rex is at least as good as Nell at this task, maybe better, another notch of treachery. Her hands are free now, and she reaches down to push his head away—she is too sensitive to be touched right after—but he doesn't move, his tongue presses on. It's almost painful, until it . . . another shock wave. Then another. She loses count.

She always thought women were lying when they talked about multiple orgasms.

He lifts his head, finally. His eyes are intent.

Apparently this is just the beginning. Neither of them says a word; they hurtle along the evening like a freight train, like they're outrunning death. They drain the bottle and forget the oysters. It occurs to Mara to ask Rex to wear a condom, but only after it's too late, the glitter-speck of anxiety floating up like a champagne bubble. She squeezes him hard, sinks her nails into his skin, tangles his hair in her fingers and pulls. She feels de-marrowed.

She doesn't remember falling asleep, the tumble into oblivion.

Her eyes open in the dark, and for a long, terrible moment, she can't figure out where she is. She's on a sofa, naked, a man's shirt covering her legs. Oysters are on the table, glistening in their shells; a wine bottle knocks against the bucket in a bath of ice water. A man is on his back on the floor, his forearm over his eyes, penis resting on his thigh, inert.

Mara's mouth is cactus-dry. She creeps into the bathroom and fills a glass with tap water, drinking it in a single swallow. Instantly, she remembers nobody drinks San Diego tap water, bitter as the surface of whatever pipe it came through on its journey from the Colorado River.

She steps back into the suite, thinking back to the hours— hours?—they spent tearing across the giant bed, the floor, the sofa, against the window. In a mechanical way, she remembers how it thrilled and shamed her, but she can't conjure the feeling. The room smells like sex. Maybe it's the oysters.

Rex begins to snore lightly. Mara locates her underwear, her jeans, her shirt. Her sandals, inexplicably under the bed. She pulls them on, spies her handbag on a table, lifts her scarf off the floor. She slides her phone out to check the time: three new voicemails. She darkens the screen and drops it back into her purse.

The room belongs to someone else. The man on the floor is someone else.

She closes and opens her eyes, and it's like she isn't there. She brings her hand across her face, wiggles her fingers, but the eerie feeling persists. Like she doesn't exist.

A relief or a horror? She disappears out the door, a ghost.

In the elevator, she pushes the button for the lobby, jazz still playing on the speakers, probably a loop of the same five songs. A clerk at the desk looks up when she steps out; she feels his eyes follow her across the floor.

Outside, the air is cool and moist. Three in the morning, and the city is quiet: no planes, no car traffic. She picks a direction and walks. A flutter of chirping from a hawthorn hedge, night birds. She rounds the corner and heads uptown.

The air smells different in California.

Western Massachusetts smells like coffin soil, deep reservoirs and ancient granite, pine forests and old houses. The smell of the force of the seasons, of nature putting people to shame: freezing them in the winter, seducing them in the spring, flattening them in the summer, and breaking their hearts in the fall.

The smell of California is libertine, perfumed with blooming flowers. The plants are prehistoric, Seussian in their fuzzy fringes and long tendrils and waxy stalks. The dirt, Mara would guess, is saltier, drier. She can't say she smells the ocean, but its presence is palpable, a briny density to the air at night that burns off during the day. She walks past a stand of junipers and breathes in their low, pine-gunky tartness, different from the high, airy scent of the white pines near her house.

No one knows where she is.

This part of San Diego, at the edge of downtown, is called Bankers Hill, a grid of quiet residential streets laid across numbered avenues. The streets are named after plants in alphabetical order: Ash, Beech, Cedar, Date. A huge date palm pushes itself through the old sidewalk slabs, littering the curb with hard, greasy fruit. Dark windows in every building. Windshields covered with dew. Mara walks quickly uphill with blank purpose.

She could literally go the rest of her life without talking to anyone.

In her father's house in Brookline, a three-story colonial that was too big for them, with thick walls and floors that didn't creak, she could go for hours without talking. Weekends, he'd call her to meals and, the rest of the time, he'd work in his study and she would read or do homework in one of her hiding places. She didn't have many friends. When children asked her to play or, when they were older, to hang out, go shopping, whatever—she often claimed her father needed help with chores. In fact, he paid a woman to clean the house every Friday when she was at school.

Mara knows her father is fond of her. He kept his study door open; she knew she had a standing invitation to enter at any time, to curl up in a club chair and talk, but she didn't want to abuse the privilege. What was she going to say? Their quiet arrangement seemed to suit them. When he married his interior decorator, Mara was relieved.

It could have been so much worse, her life. She could've grown up in her mother's house. She was a good student with an excellent work ethic: in college, she worked; her father paid her school fees and room and board, but that was it. The last check he wrote on her behalf was to Smith College eleven years ago.

Her comforts: books, stacks of them. Coffee, movies, knitting. Nell. Her little life. She is always smoothing the seams of her little life, repairing tears, folding and refolding it like a piece of heirloom linen. Her tragedies are minor compared to most people's. She's never complained.

Tomorrow, she'll check out of her ridiculous hotel, ideally without running into Rex. She'll drive east, out to the desert, which her family never did when she was little. There's a state park out there, a desert that looks like the Roadrunner cartoons; she looked it up on the internet. She'll take a picnic. She'll book a room at a cheaper hotel tomorrow night and fly out the next morning.

She feels for her phone to check the time.

The voicemails are sitting there at the bottom of the screen. The San Diego number. A twinge of sympathy erupts for Shannon: what if it's her? Talk about a tragic life. She presses the message and puts the phone to her ear.

Miss Meade? Mara? My name's Cindy? I'm calling from Lantern House, we're a rescue mission, down by the Coronado Bridge? Your mom checked in this morning, can you give me a call here as soon as possible?

The phone drops out of her hand and lands in a patch of damp grass. She stoops and picks it up, wipes it on her jeans. Rescue mission. Are they going to rescue her mother? Are they Catholic? Are they angry with her?

She keeps walking. The eastern sky fades, barely, toward sunrise. A mourning dove coos, plaintively. She quickens her pace.

She could lose her identity, disappear. She could work anywhere, do anything. She could grow old in a dusty town in Texas, a place she's never been, the last place anyone would look.

Up the street, an old bar, its orange sign lit from below, framed by palm trees. The Pilot Light: Cocktails Late Nite Dining. A portal opens, and two women emerge, the door banging shut behind them. Their heads are bent together, they might be laughing. The taller one slips her arm around the waist of the shorter one, and they walk up the street, trudging home. Their life: a shared apartment, a dog, the taller one sitting at a kitchen table writing a utility check. The shorter one drifting past her, touching her shoulder, pouring a cup of coffee, bringing it to her. Mara could cry.

A dark, elongated mound appears in the shadow of a storefront. The first homeless person she's seen here. A socked foot sticks out at one end and tucks itself in the arch of its twin.

She fingers the phone in her purse.

She owes her mother nothing. She shouldn't have come.

She walks faster. She's traversed the length of Bankers Hill, she's in Hillcrest, blocks away from UCSD, where her mother was, but isn't now. The same street as last night: she passes the bookstore where she bought the Anaïs Nin, a gate pulled across the storefront.

Why did she come? Why did she spend all that money? She tallies the plane ticket, the car rental, the hotel, the sushi dinner, the book. She thinks of the niceties she'll deny herself for the remainder of the year. Weekend trips, books, clothes, movies, lattes, dinners out. Nell will be annoyed.

Nell.

Mara could drop out of her own life.

She turns on University. In the dim almost-dawn, she sees movement down the avenue, a few slow figures pushing carts, people sitting on bus benches. She supposes she ought to turn around, to return to her expensive bed and sleep; she's going to be hung over. She heads south down Sixth Avenue, passes a Rite Aid, thinks of Shannon.

Alone in a string of empty parking spaces, an American-made car gathers dew. Mara doesn't know why she notices it, but it looks forlorn. She slows and walks past it, then turns around to take a second look. Her rental.

In her real life, she would never forget where she parked—she would never forget she'd rented a car in the first place. She fishes in her purse, finds the key, and unlocks the driver's side door. Inside, the car is chilly. Sheets of condensation cover the windows. Why did she tell Nell about Allison?

She isn't a good girlfriend, or a good friend. She doesn't know what Nell sees in her, she never has, except the thrill of mystery, of becoming the person with the keys to the vault.

She'll go back to Massachusetts. Nell will break up with her. Nell with her hundred friends, her crushes, her vital, vibrant life. She'll go back to Massachusetts, but she won't tell anyone about her trip.

She'll go to work, she'll recede, little by little, from her friends, she'll keep her modest pleasures, take her solitary vacations. She'll turn forty. Fifty. Sixty. She'll nurse her father through old age, death. She'll keep her job till she retires. New children every year, a different crop of tiny first graders, susceptible to Miss Meade's special, aloof charm.

She can disappear into her own life; she doesn't have to go anywhere.

She reaches into her purse, roots around with her hand, staring at the silver pixelation of the wet windshield. Where is the Anaïs Nin? She peers into her purse. It would have been too big to fit into the side pockets, but she looks anyway. Nothing but her wallet, phone, house keys, lip balm, baggage claim ticket. The book must be at the bar. Or in Rex's dissolute hotel room.

That beautiful book, that *rare* book. The nice man who sold it to her. She paid so much for it, she didn't care, she knew exactly where it would sit on her bedroom shelves, away from the sunlight, propped up so you could see its lovely cover.

Her Paris summer. Leaning over the terrace, smoking in the lamplit evenings, flirting with her eyes at the people walking down her tiny street. The music filtering in from the student apartment across the way. She'd read Nin's diaries like a teenager, like someone who'd never read about sex before, someone discovering her own existence: the entries were so delicately honest, they took such care to be true to the person Nin was becoming. Mara had never dreamt of being so frank, of taking such pleasure. She had her first female lover that summer, a woman in her thirties, grey-eyed Lise. *You are like the bird on my windowsill,* she told Mara. She adored Lise's smell: black pepper and gardenias. *That is just me,* she'd said, laughing.

Mara stares intently at the mosaic of dewdrops filtering a wan shaft of light from behind a cloud cover. She feels the path of her tears, down her nose, onto her clavicle. She sits still as a statue.

She blinks, and her eyes are a blurry swirl. She presses her knuckles into her eyelids. Her ragged breath threatens, almost, to turn into sobs, but she does not want to make a sound.

She cries and cries. Mara, crying.

She gives in to her voice, finally, a low moan that feels piped in from another part of the car. After a while, she turns it into a hum, a song she sings to herself as she comes down from the shuddering. It's a song she and Nell used to sing as they walked across campus at night.

Will she always be so sad? "I'm not *depressed*," she always says witheringly to Nell. But it isn't thoughtfulness, or reticence; it isn't some quiet mystery that seems, oddly, to draw people to her. It's sadness. Plain sadness.

She'd saved up and gone to Paris after graduation; her plane left two weeks after the horrible night at the emergency room with her mother. She went by herself and lived with some English girls in an apartment by the Jardin du Luxembourg. She took a French intensive and worked illegally at a restaurant. It was wonderful. In Paris, no one knew her, no one needed her. She made friends with a group of French graduate students, and they included her in parties and invited her out, but it didn't matter if she said no: something about being new to the city, and foreign, allowed her to live beneath a fine layer of unimportance. She could choose to be Mara, or she could fold herself into a pocket of anonymity, ignore phone calls, go for long evening walks across the city, ride the métro in silence, sit at a café and read. She wasn't lonely. She was free.

Late in the summer, she met Lise, who was finishing a summer program at the Sorbonne. Their affair lasted a month, and Lise left for Ghana on a fellowship in the fall. They talked about writing letters, but they never did.

It was the happiest year of her life.

When she came back to the States, the heaviness returned, a weight across her forehead, her shoulders, so familiar she almost didn't notice. She came home to her father's house and slept until noon for weeks. Nell called, and Mara found she couldn't explain her year away, the lightness and freedom that carried her through it. She couldn't admit the grief she felt upon returning: it seemed petulant. Her quietude in Paris fit her life there; in America, it felt pathological, ungenerous. But she sewed herself in up in it anyway. With each passing year, she grew quieter.

A stupid way to live a life.

The sunlight widens across the windshield. She can't stop crying. She sniffs, wipes the rope of snot from her nose, hunts for a tissue, discovers a napkin in the glove compartment. She blows her nose and almost laughs at the noise of it; she rests her head on the steering wheel, blinking her wet eyes, her chest stuttering.

Her hand floats back into her hollow purse.

Her mother, her wretched mother, ruining everything she touches.

Mara finds her phone, swipes it alive, presses the call log, presses the number without being able to stop herself. It occurs to her they won't answer at this hour, and she's right, it goes straight to voicemail. Lantern House: she looks it up on the map. It's in a neighborhood called Barrio Logan, near the Coronado Bridge. The place isn't far—a ten-minute drive.

She keys the ignition. Windshield wipers, defroster. She zips the windows down, and they come up clear, dripping.

She glances at her puffy face in the rearview mirror: no worse than Linda, probably. Poor, vain Linda. Mara types the address into the GPS and pulls onto the avenue.

Lantern House is an unprepossessing box of pink stucco surrounded by gravel. Bars on the windows. A row of eucalyptus towering over it from the back. Mara glances at her watch: six o'clock in the morning. The small parking lot is empty.

She could turn around but doesn't. A kind of gravity has taken over: What if she stopped fighting? What if she let herself be pulled under? Don't swim toward the shore in a rip current: swim sideways. The ocean is always stronger than you are.

She finds a parking space. A chilly breeze blows in from the water. Across the street, a handmade sign and a door: Las Posas Mexican Food Breakfast Lunch Diner. It's warm inside and smells like beans and flour; the menu is in Spanish, but she manages to order a coffee, fresh tortillas, and refried beans, grey with lard, steam rising from the Styrofoam cup. She tucks herself into a window-side booth. Across the street, Lantern House is asleep, its windows dark. The coffee is thick, almost spicy. She hasn't felt this hungry in weeks.

Little by little, the street comes to life. The dull swish of cars on the freeway; the clank of sidewalk newspaper stands; sunlight hits the pink façade across the street. Someone emerges, picking her way along a paved path. Mara drains her coffee and breathes in sharply: she's *tiny*. Her mother's self-conscious gait is easy to recognize. Linda walks as though someone were filming her every move, the strained elegance still there despite a new, obvious, physical difficulty. Her mother's steps are smaller; she holds her arms out as though for balance. She has shrunk, her skeleton compressed, her hair flat against her head. She wears a pink sweater, white slacks, slippers. Her old ballerina posture nearly gone, but not quite. Mara can't make out her expression.

She is so small, this mother. Mara could scoop her up and do whatever she wanted.

She collects the table's detritus, dumps it in the trash, and ventures outside. Linda heads down the block, and Mara follows her, watching her from behind. The folds of her mother's pants give away how emaciated she has become: her mother loved being thin, but this is grotesque. Mara thinks of her stepmother's old cat in the years before he died, the way his bones felt when you picked him up.

Linda walks into a convenience store on the corner. Mara hangs back, following her at a distance, and enters the store without being noticed. Linda is at the counter pointing out the cigarettes she wants—Virginia Slims, of course. Her mother's voice is warbled and uneven, like there are stones underneath it, but her tone is unmistakable.

Where is Mara's anger? She feels only pity for this branch of a woman, in her cheap slacks and pink cardigan, with her old-lady voice, *her slippers.*

Her mother wanted so much. She wanted to be beautiful, to be famous, to be a singer, an actress, a dancer. She wanted to be the wife of a big-shot lawyer. She wanted. Mara remembers all the photographs her mother had of herself, the way she'd pause in front of the mirror in the foyer, her bracelets tinkling. She'd been so pretty, the prettiest mother in the neighborhood. When they were really little, before their parents' relationship soured, Mara and Allison were enamored with Linda in the way little girls worship beautiful young women. Sparkle-eyed, perfectly dressed, laughing all the time. Mara hides in an aisle of chips and watches her. Was the emergency room visit ten years ago? She doesn't remember leaving, putting Linda into an airport shuttle, saying goodbye: only her beating panic in the waiting room at Cooley Dickinson, Linda doubled over next to her.

She can't find her anger. Like the fury of her interlude with Rex the wine importer, she can't conjure it. She steps out of the shadow of the aisle and stands behind her mother in line.

"Thank you, dear," she hears her mother say to the clerk as she takes her change. Linda takes her time placing the change in her wallet, tucking the pack of cigarettes into her purse. She turns around, barely glances at Mara, and walks out.

"Next?" the clerk murmurs. Mara steps out of line and watches her mother cross the store's threshold and disappear. She steps out and looks up the street. There is her mother, hitching daintily up the sidewalk, savoring her cigarette, smoothing her hair.

"Mom!" Mara hollers.

Linda keeps walking.

"Mom! Hey!" Mara is frantic. She runs to catch up and taps Linda on the shoulder. Startled, her mother turns around. She managed to look young for so long, but nature has its revenge: up close, face to face, Linda looks ancient. Like she's lost her teeth, her cheeks sunken. Her eyes, though, bright as ever, an eerie color Mara has never seen on another person.

"Mom."

Linda is confused.

"It's me."

Linda's eyes widen. Her face lights up the way Mara's first graders do when she brings them a treat. She tosses her cigarette in the gutter and throws her arms around her daughter, her arms like Lilliputian ropes tightening across Mara's shoulders. After a strange beat, Mara puts her arms around her mother and holds her there.

"You came! You came to get me!" Linda cries. "You came!"

Chapter Eight

The dreams are insane. Carnivals, terrors, urgent tasks that never finish, giant outdoor raves, and everything else in the entire world, swirling through Shannon's head.

Sleep, wake, smoke, repeat.

On what might be the third day (?), she wakes up at an hour with no shape, just grey light. Noises in the apartment. Why? Who? A wedge of foam between each thought.

A surprised voice. A scratchy voice. Women. What women? Are they coming to seize the apartment? Has she been here for months, blazed on her bed eating Chex Mix, long enough to get herself evicted? She sits up, stares through the window at the oleander for answers, the power lines stretched behind it, the stucco cube across the street, the colorless sky. The voices go on, but she can't make out the words.

Hunger pushes her out of bed. Unless she's eaten it all, there's a cupboard stocked with shiny bags and boxes of chips, crackers, cookies, puffs, kernels, corners, combos, all the best nouns, their bright, familiar logos like billboards on the road of her new life, post-Texas, post-Brandy, post-Linda. She should have kept a journal. There were big thoughts—she can't remember them now.

She cracks her door and peers through it, but it's just the voices, no people. Maybe she's dreaming them.

Ah! She remembers a big thought: Shame cripples you. Stand tall and be proud of your beauty, even if you're ugly. Was that it? She straightens, squeezes her thighs, throws her shoulders back, and marches into the bathroom. The mirror greets her with a horror: side ponytail, a halo of bedhead fuzz, eyeliner (why?), a wrinkled t-shirt she doesn't recognize, *boxer shorts.* Whose boxer shorts?

No shame!

She'll face the evictors. Maybe the police have come to confiscate her looted weed; too bad there's none left. They'll repossess her junk food. She threw the credit card in a parking-lot trashcan when it stopped working, but she could still be arrested.

Better, maybe, to go back to bed.

A presence in her bedroom. Unclear how much time has passed: a minute, an hour, a month. Everything is a little sharper, louder, like she took off her headphones. She blinks a crusty eye open.

A tall, beautiful woman is staring at her. A linen dress the color of mud. A necklace at her collarbone, a bracelet. One of those women with long, bony limbs, who will grow old skinny, who has never been fat. Grey-brown hair that falls to her shoulders, the same family of color as the mud-colored dress, shades you see in a marsh or a beach. Grey-green-blue eyes that make Shannon think, if you were going to find a pool in a forest that would tell you the future, this is the color. This woman knows her. Shannon opens her other eye and half-sits up.

The woman sighs.

Shannon sits all the way up, crosses her legs. Everything she'd imagined or remembered about Mara is right: she's perfect. She's an adult in a way Shannon will never, ever be an adult. If Mara makes a rare bad decision, she won't apologize for it, she has a reason, and if that reason is wrong, she'll have you believe it's right. It's a scary authority her half-sister has—like she doesn't have to work to be in charge, she just *is*. She's a teacher or something. That makes sense.

Mara looks at Shannon's bed, her floor, her piles. She turns around and stares past the oleander. She's looking for somewhere to sit. She folds her arms around her middle, lowers herself to the edge of Shannon's mattress, and it bends toward her weight.

"I'm not in jail," Shannon says, surprised at her voice.

"Mmm," Mara replies.

The pieces find each other and form the corner of a jigsaw puzzle. If Mara is here, her mother is here. The owner of the other voice, Linda, alive, possibly with a bedpan, a walker, an IV, a paralyzed face, drool. Shannon is not in Tennessee. She's never going to be friends with Brandy again. Her boss probably won't give her another chance; she'll have to get a job at CVS. How will she work if her mother is drooling over a bedpan? There's no more weed left.

"Do you need a minute?" Mara asks.

"Huh?"

"Take a shower . . . ?" Mara looks around, her eyes stabbing the room's little disasters.

Shannon remembers her hunger. The snacks are in the kitchen, which is one hundred dragon-filled miles from her bedroom. She reclines and pulls her sheet up over her head, wiggling down.

With a gentle but decisive hand, Mara pulls the sheet back.

"Please get up. Take a shower, get dressed, eat lunch with us."

You can't say no. Shannon would love to find the one person in the world who could say no to this woman.

"Mom doesn't eat," Shannon says.

"Sure she does," Mara says, and rises from the bed, tipping Shannon back toward herself. "She's a lot better than I thought she'd be." Mara seems neither pleased nor surprised as she lets herself out and closes the door behind her. A moment later, she opens it again. Shannon has not moved an inch or breathed a breath.

"It's time," Mara says.

The bathroom looks different: Shannon imagines Mara having to pee here, wash her hands, her pool-eyes landing on the soap hairs, the layers of sink scum, the toothpaste-spattered mirror, the dark corners of the tiled floor, the mildewed shower curtain. The beach towels filled with images of manic, ecstatic cartoon characters, the pinkish toilet bowl, the wrinkled stack of Pennysavers on the hamper. She takes the longest shower in the world and puts her wet hair into a bun, as though this will do something. Back in the bedroom, she fishes out an ancient blouse, an ancient pair of shorts, clean, but dense with the smell of years in a drawer. It occurs to her to iron them—her mother had an iron, once—and she laughs to herself. No shame: no shame.

For days (or who knows), the apartment was an oasis of solitude, Linda-free, little comfort stations everywhere: mid-couch was for Chex Mix and fresh bowls, the armchair for cans of beer and Cheetos, the kitchen chair for Combos and orange juice. Now, in the stark light of Mara, it looks like what she imagines a frat house would look like, or a halfway house that has been taken over by its residents, or the apartment of someone whose life is so depraved they've ended up on reality television. You have to assume it smells extremely skunky, but Shannon doesn't have a great sense of smell.

Linda is back in her spot, reclined like a sultan on the couch, ready for her closeup in a muumuu. The untrained eye thinks, *Elizabeth Taylor,* but Shannon knows it's the only position that doesn't make Linda want to puke. She has a cigarette in one hand, her arm extended like she's mid-story at a big dinner party, after the dinner, when everyone is gathered with their cocktails in the sunken living room. Her mouth is open like she's talking, but she's silent, watching the smoke float up. She doesn't look paralyzed. She looks, basically, the way she always looks—terrible, but very much alive.

Mara is busy in the kitchen. Her pace, her vibe, her *velocity*. She's standing on a chair, reaching far back into a high cupboard, pulling things out and examining them, calling out for a verdict from Linda, who says nothing, and tossing them into the garbage in a flawless arc.

"Was the Tang purchased in this century?" she calls out. Linda looks in Mara's direction. The Tang sails into the trash, landing on an old box of Froot Loops. Shannon switched to Fruity Pebbles years ago. She shifts her weight and tries to fade back into the shadow of the hallway. The movement catches her mother's eye.

"You!" she cries. "Mara, she's here! I found her!"

Mara tosses something heavy into the trash.

"Where were you?" Linda asks, lively, curious. She takes a drag like an old pro, blows the smoke toward the ceiling with the elegance she learned when she was a movie-obsessed teenager. "I was in the hospital! Surgery, *me,* can you imagine? They said I was a miracle."

Shannon stares at her.

"Get me a cup of tea, would you, darling?" Linda asks, holding up her mug and shaking it like a spare-changer on Obsidian.

"You're out of tea, Mom," Mara calls out. "What do you like, Lipton? I'm making a list."

"Shannon knows how I like it." Linda winks, shakes the mug. Shannon's feet refuse to move.

"Mom, you're out," Mara repeats. A box lands in the trashcan, perfectly upright.

"Please?" Linda's voice loses its honey. "Shannon."

"How do you know she hasn't poured it out already?"

"Shush," Linda instructs. "I watched her. *Bring me a cup of tea. Please.*"

"Get your own tea," Shannon says, surprising herself. Linda glares at her and slowly swings her legs down off the couch. What was left of her agility is gone now. She sets her cigarette in the ashtray and steadies herself. With effort, she rises to a standing position, wobbling for a moment, and finds something like balance. She lurches across the living room and stumbles into her bedroom. Shannon watches her, agape, and can't bring herself to offer an arm or hand for support. The bedroom door clicks. She always helped Linda before, retching inwardly at her mother's bag-of-bones quality.

"She makes tea in her bedroom?" Mara asks, standing at the entry of the kitchen, a can of Folgers in her hand. Shannon is frozen. "Help me tie this?" Mara asks, setting the can on the counter. She pulls the trash bag up, the plastic stretching from the weight of its load. "Just grab the . . ." Shannon watches her. Mara yanks the bag, and it rips in half. Shannon looks at her in surprise, fear. "Shit," Mara murmurs.

"What's wrong with her?" Shannon asks quietly.

Mara straightens, cocks her head slightly. "Heart attack. Decent-sized."

"What else?"

"A stroke."

Shannon nods.

"Late-stage alcoholism, obviously," Mara continues, going into the living room, the trash bag's contents slowly expanding on the floor by themselves. "Dementia. Peripheral neuropathy. Wernicke-Korsakoff's syndrome. An ulcer." She stubs Linda's cigarette in the ashtray. "Emphysema. Cirrhosis of the liver. Probably bipolar disorder, but they didn't keep her long enough to diagnose it for sure; they just hinted. Narcissistic personality disorder, if you ask me."

"The doctor with the brown hair said she could make a full recovery. If she quit everything."

"That was the heart surgeon. Nobody else said that."

"So . . . what?"

Mara folds her arms. "Rehab?"

"They don't take you if you don't want to go," Shannon tells her, unsure if this is true.

"Plus, there are waiting lists," Mara agrees, "and it's expensive, and it would need to be longer than thirty days . . ." She stares at the nubby ceiling. "Honestly? I feel like it's more of a hospice kind of thing at this point."

Shannon has heard the word, but she doesn't know what it means.

"But she's also, like, bionic woman," Mara says, returning to the kitchen. "It doesn't seem like she's dying." She says the word out loud, without whispering.

Shannon always thought her mother would outlive her. They both make terrifically bad choices, but Linda floats above the fray, immune to the indignities, physical and otherwise, of being a drunk, yammering on about the same things, her youth, her acting/singing/dancing career, how to stay beautiful. Like Mara, her mother is in charge.

"She's gonna live forever," Shannon says.

Mara seats herself in a kitchen chair and removes a pile of old mail from the other one, offering it to Shannon. Shannon approaches carefully. She sits, folding her hands in her lap.

"We have to make a plan," Mara says. It's so perfect she's a teacher. She should be someone's mother, too, someone's wife—a whole collection of people to be in charge of.

"Why aren't you, like, the principal?"

"What?" Mara says, thrown off.

"You're a teacher, right?"

"I'm a librarian."

"I'm saying. You should be the principal."

Mara eyes her, like maybe Shannon has bigger problems than she thought. Then she softens, the way you do when you're talking to a special-needs person.

"We need to make a plan," she says again, slowly.

"Okay." Shannon had a plan, and look where that ended up.

Mara crosses her legs. She's thought about this. "First, we talk to her about rehab. At least give her a chance to say yes."

"She's not gonna—"

Mara cuts her off. "Sometimes, when you have a near-death experience, you see things differently. And a stroke literally changes your brain—an addict can have a different attitude toward recovery after a brain injury."

"What rehab?" Shannon asks, rolling *brain injury* over in her head. "We're on Medi-Cal." Shannon feels a shred of pride at knowing this, an actual relevant thing.

"The ones that take Medicaid have long, long waiting lists. There's one in Claremont that doesn't take Medicaid, and it's really expensive, but it's good." Mara winces. "I could talk to my dad."

Shannon is out of her chair, drawn to the cupboard, hoping to God Mara hasn't thrown her Combos out. She opens it and finds a lone, gleaming bag of SunChips on the bottom shelf. She grabs it, rips it open, and brings it to the table, setting it between them. She gestures to it and dips a hand in.

"Let's say she refuses," Mara says, ignoring the SunChips. "Which she probably will."

Shannon nods, her mouth full.

"Either way, she needs help. Lantern House said she'd qualify for a part-time home health aide through Medicaid for eight weeks; they gave me the paperwork for it. Which might be enough, unless she gets worse. But if she gets worse, and the doctor says yes, she's worse, she could qualify for more. Like hospice." Mara lights up at this word.

"What's hospice?" Shannon asks through a cheek packed with chips.

"It's, um. Like when a doctor's official assessment is that you're dying, and rather than treat you and make you well again, their main objective is to make you as comfortable as possible until you actually die. It can be at a hospice facility, or a hospice nurse can see you in your own home."

Shannon swallows and leans back in her chair. "It's a *death* nurse?" she whispers.

Mara reaches over, paws through the bag for a SunChip, and, after some time, selects one, examining it. "It's not like the nurse kills you. You're already dying."

"Did the doctor say she was dying?"

"Which one?"

"I don't know! The *one*."

"She doesn't qualify for hospice. Yet."

Shannon gets up and takes in the living room. Mara must have thrown open the curtains when she came in: the overcast morning has turned into a sunny blue sky. The sunlight, brightly even, illustrates the smallness of the room, crowded with furniture from the seventies, tables and chairs meant for a house, not an apartment. Smudges on the TV screen and coffee table, layers of dust, the splotchy color of the couch, the stained carpet. She whirls around.

"Is this the same furniture? From when you . . . ?"

Mara nods.

"Does it feel like your old house?"

Mara nods again, rests her chin in her hand. Shannon finds her spot on the couch, on the center cushion, and plays the last few days (weeks?) over in her head. She can taste the Chex Mix, the way the salt mingled with the funky, grassy taste of Brandy's weed, the finest weed she ever smoked in her life.

"You want this to be over," she tells Mara. Her half-sister's face, uncomposed for once. Shannon rests her feet on the coffee table. "Get Mom squared away so you can go home."

"Define squared away."

"Locked up in a home."

"She doesn't need to be institutionalized."

"No, but like—you want to *fix* it, and fixing it means she isn't your problem anymore."

"Or yours."

"Your rich dad would pay for Mom to be locked up somewhere?"

"She doesn't need to be *locked up*. She's not a psych patient. And my father isn't rich."

"No?"

"Define rich," Mara says.

"So he is."

Mara sighs.

"I heard your dad paid our rent."

"That's ridiculous. Why would he do that?"

"Search me."

"Who told you that?"

Shannon pulls a pillow to herself and lies on her side. "I don't know. Doesn't matter." Her eyes droop.

"Wouldn't you know if he paid the rent? Who does the bills?"

"She won't let me touch rent," Shannon murmurs. "She just asks for cash, and I give it to her, and we still live here, so."

"You handle the other bills?"

"Sort of."

Mara finally puts the SunChip in her mouth and crunches. She gets up from the kitchen chair and walks into the living room, where she clears a pile off the easy chair. She pulls her legs underneath herself as she sits. She seems like someone who has a lot of abdominal strength.

"I should stay long enough to see about the medical stuff. Do you want me to do that?"

Shannon doesn't answer.

"I didn't totally understand the home health aide thing, to be honest," she says. "Medicaid is this labyrinth of rules and claims and paperwork and terrible websites. But if I deal with it, you can go to work, whatever you normally do."

Shannon smiles at the thought of what she "normally does."

"You're gonna stay *here?*" she asks.

"You don't think I should stay here?"

"No, just. You *want* to stay here?"

"Hotels in Silver Beach aren't cheap."

"Where are you gonna sleep?"

"The sofa. I'm not picky." This is probably a lie, but whatever.

"I quit my job," Shannon tells her.

"Well, now you can find another job. I don't mind dealing with Mom." Mara gets a funny look on her face. "For some reason."

"How do you know I want another job?" Shannon drops her arm over her eyes.

"Shannon." Mara sounds the way she must sound to children all day. "Are you going to sleep? Or are we having a conversation?" She waits. "If you don't want my help, I can be back in Massachusetts by Wednesday."

Shannon removes her arm from her face and takes her time sitting up. She slides her feet off the coffee table. "I was gonna get a job in Tennessee," she tells Mara. "I was gonna be an electrician."

"In Tennessee?"

Shannon shakes her head. "Never mind."

"Is that something you want to do?"

"I don't know."

"Maybe I can help."

"How?" Shannon asks.

"I'm a librarian. I find things."

"Do you pay for them, too?"

Mara looks at her a long time. Shannon is so much more pathetic than Mara must have imagined.

"Where did you go?" Mara asks. "Why did you tell me you were in jail?"

Shannon flops down again on the armrest, and her arm falls back over her eyes. "Why did you come?" she asks the ceiling.

A car alarm goes off down the block, burps to silence, and starts wailing again. If Mara is trying to answer the question, Shannon can't tell. Her own breathing grows heavy waiting.

When she wakes, she can't remember what the VCR clock, which is comically off but the only timekeeping device in the house, said before. The shadows have slipped across the television screen: afternoon. Silence from her mother's room. She can feel Mara's absence; a survey of the apartment doesn't turn up a purse or a cellphone.

The radio comes on in Linda's room, her mother's favorite station, oldies from the forties, the AM hiss running beneath the songs.

If Shannon had any guts at all—any sense—one teeny ounce of self-preservation—she would walk out, get in her car, drive to the bus station, and get out of town. She could do whatever. Wash dishes. Dishwashers in every town in America manage to go home and feed their families—or at least themselves. (Right?) Shannon could do it.

She finishes the SunChips.

"I need to talk to her caseworker," Mara's voice says out of nowhere, her half-sister materializing through the front door, grocery bags in each hand, phone pressed between her cheek and ear. "I mean, the lights are still on." Mara gestures incomprehensibly to Shannon. "Dad, hold on a sec?" She sets a bag on a patch of countertop. "Help me with this?" she says to Shannon.

"It's already here," Shannon says.

"In the *car*."

"Oh," Shannon says, and puts on her flip-flops. Downstairs in the street, the trunk of Mara's gleaming rental is open, welcoming any local weirdo to take what he wants, not that a weirdo wants all that broccoli, all those leaves, bags of rice and nuts from the bulk section, Luna bars. Not a single shiny box or bag from the snack aisle, not even cereal. She struggles up the stairs with several paper bags and wonders how long Mara's staying.

"Did you close the trunk?" Mara asks. Shannon lets out a sigh. "I'll get it," Mara says, swishing past her, babbling on her iPhone to Charlie Meade himself, something about a low-interest loan. In the kitchen, Shannon opens the fridge and stares inside: empty except for a two-gallon container of distilled water. By the time she fills the shelves with Mara's vegetables and fruits and soy milk, it looks like someone else's fridge. She is seized suddenly with how much she loved Brandy's fridge, the kind with the freezer on the bottom, better lit somehow, and there'd be all these containers of roasted potatoes and chicken salad and quiches and things, little mini-yogurts lined up, six different kinds of juice, cold cuts and presliced cheese, a million sauces. She crams the rest of Mara's stuff into a single cupboard, mentally designating it Mara's, because she is not going to eat any of it. Maybe Mara will get them takeout Chinese for dinner.

Mara is just outside the front door, talking softly. Shannon wonders if she realizes Linda's window faces the balcony.

"Mara!" Shannon calls. Mara sticks her head in, her face unreadable. "Can I talk to him? Your dad?"

"Why?" Mara asks. Not hostile, just confused.

"I haven't seen him in twenty years. Let me say hi," Shannon says. She remembers his height, and that he was kind to her, though she can't remember the specifics. Mara murmurs something into the phone and hands it to her. "Hello?" Shannon says, suddenly nervous. "It's Shannon. Yeah. Hi." She fingers the hair in her stupid bun, which is falling out. "How are you?" she asks. Charlie Meade's voice sounds older but familiar. "Um, I wanted to ask you something," she says, holding her breath. She eyes Mara, who is staring at her. "Do you pay our rent? Me and Mom?"

"Shannon!" Mara yelps, and lunges for the phone. Shannon steps back, keeping it to her ear, but she can't hear his answer. "I'm sorry, I didn't hear you," she says. Mara snatches the phone.

"Dad, I'm sorry," she says.

Linda appears, lightly gripping the side of a bookshelf.

"Hello, dears," she says brightly. She's a half-pint of tea into her afternoon. "Yes, darling," she tells Shannon.

"What?"

"He pays the rent. Charlie's always paid the rent. What did you think, we had some kind of public *voucher?*" Her face wrinkles in distaste.

Mara's mouth is open.

"Ask him," Linda says. "It was my recompense. I lost my little girl, and he *took* my *other* little girl, and it was just me and the baby out here, and we had to move into this ghastly apartment, and it was the least he could do. He had the money." She turns to Shannon. "My ex-husband has done well for himself." This is how she says it, every time, but she never said a word before about the rent, not in Shannon's whole life. Her monologue continues; Shannon knows it by heart. "He's a good lawyer. It's lucrative, being a good lawyer. That's why I hung around the law school, you know. I was smart."

Her mother was *actually* smart, too. She was valedictorian at her high school, and she was offered a scholarship to Berkeley, but she chose Fullerton instead, because she didn't want to be with all the hippies. She graduated early and skipped commencement to get married. She earned an English degree. Shannon saw it once, it was real, Linda wasn't making it up.

Linda's muumuu slips down her shoulder, exposing the tip of the bandage on her chest.

Mara's phone is back at her ear. "Is that true?" Mara whispers into it, like they aren't going to hear. Her face clouds with disbelief. "But *why?*" she asks her father.

A chill lands on Shannon. It hits her exactly how broke they are: how broke she'll be by the time Linda finally shuffles out of this life, how Mara is, now, effectively trying to cut off the lone benefit she received for being the one left behind, while Mara grew up in a huge fancy house and went to good schools and a preppy girls' college and lived in Paris and probably speaks *French,* and one day, she'll inherit all her dad's money, one day, she'll die rich and alone, which is better than alone and broke.

Mara is a cunt, basically. Maybe she can't help it, but there it is. Cunts are worse than losers, because they know they have power, and they use it against you on purpose.

She'll wash dishes somewhere. She never wants to see either of them again.

She turns and heads quietly into her bedroom. In two minutes, she has a sweatshirt on, a duffel over her shoulder, car keys in her hand. Linda and Mara and Charlie Meade are still stuttering their half-sentences, sorting out something that doesn't need sorting, a trio of clowns. She's out the door, about to turn the corner, when Mara pokes her head out.

"Where are you going?"

"Out," Shannon says, and hustles down the stairs. But her ugly brown Toyota isn't in the carport. She hyperventilates for a second before remembering she parked it at Denny's the day she drove home from the hospital. She sets out on foot, praying it hasn't been towed.

Chapter Nine

She's the string between their tin cans. Her father in one ear, his lawyer voice, the Vulcan logic of it. Her mother, holding onto that bookshelf for dear life, chattering and chirping about how this was their *arrangement,* as though Mara's father were arguing with Linda, but he isn't. Neither is Mara, not really, but neither of them is listening to her.

The apartment was a murky hollow when they came in this morning, the underwater light through the dark-blue curtains exactly as she remembered. Even through the haze of pot smoke, she could smell the skin cells and funk buried in the upholstery, the same furniture she left behind in 1984, piled higher now with stacks of unopened mail and catalogs and Pennysavers and cellophane wrappers and random objects like a fire-wire cord, in a house without a single computer. She opened the curtains and the window and turned on the fan, but it didn't help. She is seven years old again, a feeling she can't shake.

The books on the shelf are the same, arranged in what looks like the same order, as though the shelf and the books had been transported from the old bungalow to the apartment without the slightest disturbance, and no one had touched them since. An odd, dust-covered collection: Ellis Peters mysteries, biographies of old movie stars, paperback copies of English classics, the color and shape of their spines preserved in her memory. She doesn't think she's ever seen her mother with a book. Is her mother a reader? *Was* she a reader, once?

Mara has the vague sense that Shannon is a comic-book reader, but she can't remember if it was a teenage thing or something more recent. Their conversations over the years have been brief, horribly awkward, and after the first five minutes pointless, because, once the critical information was conveyed, neither sister wanted—knew how—to have a conversation with the other. Shannon seethed with a defensive resentment that ran under everything she said.

Mara has had a nice life: this is her crime.

It didn't feel like a nice life. It didn't feel nice that Linda was still her mother, even 3,000 miles away. It didn't feel nice to know it should have been her who drowned in the ocean, but instead it was her magical older sister, and because she survived, it was her fault, and no one in her family ever got over it.

But here she is on Diamond Street in her mother's apartment, and it's clear Mara is guilty of having a nice life. Shannon is a twenty-seven-year-old feral child, operating on base instincts, no skill at life, unable to stand up to anyone, not even a ridiculous drunk person. Shannon is perhaps in more grave danger of imminent tragedy than Linda is.

And where, by the way, did she get the money to buy *so much* pot? Mara is no expert, but it smells like what you would buy, say, in an expensive dispensary in L.A. Shannon has quit her little minimum-wage job, and Mara guesses she's never applied for benefits herself, so the two of them subsist, have subsisted for *years,* on what? Some kind of welfare, her father's rent payments, and Shannon's paltry paychecks? Even with her father's help, how in the world is that possible? Gas in California is over $3 a gallon. Groceries in Silver Beach are no cheaper here than in western Massachusetts, not that Shannon and Linda seem to *buy* groceries—the refrigerator, the cupboards were basically bare when she arrived, except for long-expired non-food, like Kool-Aid packets and an ancient bottle of ketchup.

Her father's rent money infantilizes Shannon. Shannon has never had the opportunity to be an autonomous, grown-up person with actual responsibility. She's barely responsible for Linda, her duties limited to filling their mother's coffee mug with cold vodka and bringing home cartons of cigarettes from Rite Aid.

Cigarettes: $7 a pack!

Mara's heart nearly broke when Shannon said she wanted to be an electrician.

She is here to save Shannon, not Linda.

Mara watches her mother and hands her the phone. "Here," she tells her, "you talk to him." Linda is confused; she's never had her own cellphone. She takes the thing and gingerly places it near her ear. Mara remembers suddenly how her mother used to crack her and Allison up when they were little by grabbing a banana and holding it to her ear, saying, "Hello? Hello? *You* called *me!*"

"Charlie," her mother purrs. "*Como sah vah,* my dear?"

Mara leaves the room and heads down the hall, peeking first into her mother's bedroom. Oddly, it's neater than the rest of the apartment—no random detritus, just a bed, made by someone without strength or coordination, a nightstand with a purse and a coffee mug on it, a dresser with a giant mirror, a tray of perfume bottles and costume jewelry. An old lady's room. She must keep the vodka hidden.

"Oh, Shannon—*you* know." Linda speaks loudly. "Do you know she *barely* finished high school, by the skin of her teeth? Never went to college like we did." Linda must say this all the time.

Mara tiptoes down the hall to Shannon's room and eases the door open, feeling like a thief but unable to stop herself. If the rest of the apartment smells like pot, this room smells like the inside of a bong. The mess is funkier, more intimate, piles of clothes, crumpled tissues. The only anomaly is a pristine crate next to Shannon's worn dresser, crammed with comic books in their plastic sleeves. Mara crouches next to it and pulls one out: she doesn't recognize it, a Marvel superhero thing. She thought maybe Shannon might be into the subversive, independent titles, like Lynda Barry or Drawn and Quarterly, which tend to appeal more to women. Maybe Shannon's never seen alternative comics. How does she buy them, how does she buy anything?

Mara begins to curate a reading list for Shannon. She wonders about her reading level. It's hard to tell how intelligent she is, how much of what seems like dullness is just willful, stubborn anger. What would Shannon sound like if she felt free to be herself? Mara peers at a bookshelf under the window: dime-store copies of hippie/stoner paperbacks. It's possible Shannon has never read them, that she bought them because they seemed cool: *Zen and the Art of Motorcycle Maintenance, The Doors of Perception, The Lord of the Rings, Stranger in a Strange Land, On the Road.* It's possible she has read them.

Mara's father means well, paying Linda's rent. There is mercy in the gesture.

It's possible, once they deal with Linda's immediate medical needs, that Mara could convince her father to actually help Shannon. They could go in together. Shannon could go to rehab in Massachusetts. Mara could move Shannon into a studio near her own place and help her register for classes at one of the community colleges. In a year or two, her sister could have momentum, sobriety, skills, a recovery community. She'd be one of those friendly, grateful people who gather at the coffee shop on Main Street on Saturday mornings for the twelve-step meetings downstairs. She'd be on her way to a degree, a certification, a job. She'd pay her own rent.

Mara pictures it, almost brings herself to tears.

It would never work.

Or maybe it would.

"Charlie, it was an honest-to-God heart attack, the real thing," Linda is saying. "I *know*. You're absolutely right. And a minor *stroke,* whatever that means. Oh, me? A bit of surgery. But I'm fine. Fit as a fiddle." There is a pause in her mother's static. "Oh, sure, sure. But I'm telling you, I'm fine. Fit as a fiddle."

Linda repeats herself, Mara notices. Frankly, her mother only has only ever had two or three things she wants to talk about; Mara has heard her stories a thousand times, even without living with her for the past twenty-six years. But she's starting to sound loony. Mara wonders how long it will be until she has full-blown dementia.

"*All* right, Charlie. I will. *Thank* you, as ever. I will. You too. Bye, now." A brief silence. "Mara! How do you turn this thing off?"

Mara appears and slips the phone from her mother's frail hand. "You don't have to, he hung up," she says softly.

"It's all settled," Linda tells Mara. "You can stop worrying about us."

Mara decides she'll call her father later. She goes to the window and shrinks her irises in the bright haze of the afternoon. Shannon is right: their mother will never touch rehab. She is a happy drunk.

"You know what Lantern House was, right?" she asks Linda.

"A mental institution?" Linda snaps. "A homeless shelter? A pen for derelicts and undesirables? All of the above?"

"It was a rehab facility," Mara says, not sure this is actually true.

"I don't need rehab, darling. And that girl told me expressly that it *wasn't* a rehab."

"Why did the hospital send you there?"

"Because *you* two never came to pick me up!"

"If you didn't have a drinking problem, they wouldn't have sent you there. The doctors made an assessment."

"An *assessment*. That I'm a drunk?"

Mara turns to look at her mother, who clings proudly to the bookshelf.

"Is that what you're saying, Mara?"

Mara sighs.

"Because you know what, *yes*, I'm a girl who likes her cocktails, but I'm *fine*. Obviously." She unclaws her hand from the bookshelf and steadies herself. Mara watches, fearful. Linda walks in her strange new gait, knees high, flapping the air, until she reaches the sofa, which she grabs at once. She guides herself to the other end, collapses into it, and arranges herself in her reclined-movie-star pose.

"Can I make you something?" Mara asks, giving up. "I got groceries."

"No," Linda replies. She brings a coffee mug to her lips and drinks her elixir, her face beatific. Mara watches her discreetly from the kitchen pass-through, knowing her mother loves being watched. Linda sets the mug down with the careful flourish of someone at tea with the queen. She pulls a hard pack of Virginia Slims from between the sofa cushions, tips one out, places it lightly on her lips, and produces a pack of matches from the same place. Never a lighter—too masculine. She waves her match and tosses it into the massive orange ashtray Mara remembers from childhood and inhales, deeply satisfied, a look of performed satiation on her face. Instantly, she begins coughing. Mara doesn't know how she missed it before, the awful mucusy depth of it—a chronic cough if there ever was one. As Linda recovers, her cigarette hand shaking, Mara hears her ragged breath—she must have been hiding it before, though Mara can't imagine how. She sounds like a much older woman, like Mara's old neighbor, Miss Honey, a pack-a-day smoker till the day she died at ninety-three, breathing like an idling truck engine. Linda focuses intently on the space in front of her nose, recovering her composure.

"Mom?"

"I'm fine," Linda rasps.

"I'm making sandwiches. I'm going to make you a little one; you don't have to eat it, but if you want, it's there. Okay?"

Linda doesn't answer and stares at the air. Mara fills a glass with water and brings it to the living room, clearing a place on the coffee table.

Linda coughs, shallower. "I'm fine," she gurgles, miserable, not wanting to be seen, for once. Mara leaves her alone and returns to the kitchen. She turns the radio on, shifting the volume way down, dialing the station to NPR. She sneaks another glance at her mother, who is concentrating, her face clouded with fury.

Mara tries to make the most normal American sandwiches in the world, nothing Northamptonish: sliced bread, mayonnaise, mustard, lettuce, tomato, sliced cheese, turkey. Will her mother and sister eat Dijon? She'll only use a little. First, she cleans the counter, the sink, and the stray dishes, dries them and puts them away, though it isn't clear where they're supposed to go. She pulls out her ingredients and discovers she forgot to buy mayonnaise. Mayonnaise is essential.

"Mom?" she calls. Linda doesn't answer. Mara ventures into the living room. "Mom?"

"Mmm," Linda murmurs. She is far away now, the ash growing long on her cigarette.

"You know the minimart up here?" Mara says, pointing. "At the gas station on Obsidian?"

Linda looks at her blankly.

"Do they have groceries? Little stuff? Mustard and mayo, Chef Boyardee?"

It's as though Mara is speaking Chinese. Linda finally takes a drag from the cigarette, and the ash falls to the carpet.

"I'm just going to be a minute. I have to pick something up— you're okay here? I'll be right back."

Linda narrows her eyes. Is she angry again? Angry at Mara?

"Do you mind?" Mara's voice softens, and she gently takes her mother's cigarette from her hand. Linda seems not to notice. Watching her, Mara stubs it in the ashtray. "Water?" she says, holding the glass up. Linda shakes her head slightly, a little shiver. "I'll be right back. I promise. Okay?" Linda's eyes are open, but Mara can't tell what she's looking at.

She'll be five minutes, max. Shannon leaves Linda here all the time; she'll probably fall asleep.

Everything in San Diego is cleaner and shinier than on the east coast, even crummy gas-station minimarts. It isn't so densely populated out here, maybe, or it's because people don't tramp through every winter with salt and mud on their boots, or it's because everything seems newer by about fifty years. Mara grabs a mini-jar of mayonnaise off a shelf, pays the clerk, and is back in her rental, pulling up at the curb on Diamond Street, in exactly six minutes.

She trots up the stairs, opens the door, and breathes a little sigh of relief: Linda has not moved. She's resting, her eyes closed, her breathing labored but even, a smoker's sleep.

Mara sets to work in the kitchen. How long till Shannon gets over her huff and comes back? She has to be hungry; the afternoon is sliding toward evening. It's not like she has the money to eat out. Mara places a sandwich on the coffee table for Linda, her mother's snoring steady and shallow. She finishes her own sandwich at the kitchen table in the companionable hum of *All Things Considered*.

She cleans her dishes and pulls her wheeled suitcase into the kitchen. She takes out her laptop and opens it, connecting to the Internet through her phone's hot spot.

She will make sense of Medicaid. Medi-Cal, whatever. She is a reader; she is a trained librarian; she has an elite degree; she does Nell's complicated taxes, wading carefully, patiently, through tax code to ensure the correct deductions and payments on Nell's varied freelance gigs. When Shannon comes back, Mara will have answers about what they're going to do next.

She cancels her Wednesday flight to Hartford.

All Things Considered becomes *Marketplace, BBC World Service.* Hours pass, hunger doesn't occur to her, nor time, nothing but the complicated—but knowable!—intricacies of Medicaid. She makes her way down endless message boards of informational gold. On *Fresh Air,* someone is interviewed, then someone else, and Mara tunes them out, zooming along on the oddly sexy rhythms of Terry Gross's voice. As Linda dozes on the sofa, Mara goes to her mother's room and opens drawers in search of their benefits paperwork, finding instead an infinite supply of tiny bottles of vodka. She searches the closet and finds a file box way in the back. She pries it open, and of course it's a mess: useless copies of forms from the late eighties; important documents nowhere to be found, nothing with the caseworker's name. She could just ask her mother.

She glances at her watch and is shocked that it's well after eight o'clock. The sky is still pale; she imagined it was five at most. She can't very well go *looking* for Shannon. The first thing Mara will do when this is all sorted is get Shannon some kind of cheap little cellphone; she'll pay for it, and the plan, herself.

She puts her mother's closet back together, resisting the temptation to organize the vodka by size and type. She lugs the file box to the kitchen table. Her laptop makes the sad, low warning of a low battery, and she fishes the power cord out of her suitcase, running it around and behind the kitchen's fire hazards to plug it in. She stands up and stretches.

"Hey, Mom?" she calls out, soft at first. She walks into the living room.

Linda doesn't look right. "Not right" in reference to Linda, who generally looks like hell, is a weird thing to define. Mara can't put her finger on it, but her mother looks . . . inert. She goes back to the kitchen and turns the radio all the way down, listening for the rattle of Linda's breathing.

The apartment is quiet. In the distance, an airplane. Mara approaches Linda, kneels down, pushes the coffee table back. She gingerly tries to find Linda's neck pulse with her finger. She places her hand beneath her mother's nose. She lays her ear on Linda's chest. Somehow, she isn't convinced her mother has stopped breathing; she feels like she's playing pretend EMT.

"Mom," she says loudly into Linda's face. She shakes her mother's shoulders. If she isn't dead, she's certainly unconscious. Did she have another heart attack, another stroke? Did everything simply stop? Did she struggle? If she did—if she made a sound—Mara didn't hear it. But she wasn't listening.

Mara takes Linda's hand, searches for a pulse in her wrist. She has trouble finding even her own pulse this way. Linda's hand is cool, floppy, giving her the creeps. She notices a thin trickle of dried blood from a scab on the inside of her elbow—her mother's skin is delicate, papery like an old lady's. Mara sets her mother's arm down at her side.

Mara should feel: what? Panic? Urgency? Grief? She has one mother, and her mother's life might be ending—might have ended—just now, here, in this room. Relief? Mara feels none of these things, in fact feels nothing at all. Maybe she will, later.

Maybe Linda isn't dead. She's never been dead before, despite seeming so close to it.

Relief would make sense, wouldn't it, if her mother were dead? Mara is allowed some relief? This is what people feel when a relative dies after a long decline, and Linda's decline has lasted at least since Allison drowned in 1984.

It isn't relief. It isn't anything.

For a second, she longs for Linda to wake up suddenly, brazen and satisfied, gesturing with a levitating cigarette, letting loose with one of her loopy but deeply held opinions on something that mattered very much when she was in her twenties and the world was younger. You had to admire her vivaciousness, her defiance. Mara secretly enjoyed how *right* her mother believed she was. Or, she didn't, not until now—now it's a story. Maybe.

A feeling enters the room. Mara doesn't believe in this sort of thing, but it's so distinct, so strange and palpable. Not a chill; not quite a presence; a heavy *something* saying *something*.

Mara is sure then that Linda is gone. It stops feeling fake. She can't bring herself to go through the routine of calling an ambulance; she'd rather let her mother, and the feeling, take their moment. She would rather not interrupt her mother's death.

Should she call an ambulance? Would calling an ambulance be the difference between Linda living a while and dying tonight?

Mara decides she will take her chance. She'll live with not knowing.

Nell told her that when her father died—he was at home after a miserable fight with stomach cancer—her family opened all the windows in the house so his soul could make its exit. Mara opens the front door and stands on the balcony, leaning her elbows on the railing. The air is still warm, the sky fading to the peculiar blue of late-spring twilight.

Chapter Ten

Linda opens her eyes, and the afternoon comes into focus. Her middle daughter isn't in the kitchen. Maybe she's gone, finally. Maybe she's ransacking Shannon's room, throwing Shannon's ghastly things into giant garbage bags. Shannon is off somewhere, she's sure of it. Mara is tiring, is what she is.

Linda is so *tired*. It's the worst time of day, afternoon, soap-opera time: when you might as well call it quits. The optimism of the morning, the beauty and possibility, when it still tastes good, slides like leftovers into the trash.

What can you do, when your children disappoint you? She learned a long time ago to get used to the letdown. She thought her daughters might be dancers, like her—singers, actresses— wives, certainly—pretty and bright and fun. Mara's going to be a spinster if she isn't careful. She isn't bad-looking, but no man is going to find that sour disposition attractive. Shannon hasn't brought a boyfriend home, not once.

What about her, what about Linda? A spinster, technically! But who'd fall for her now? She hasn't willingly looked in a mirror in years. She hangs her clothes neatly, presses her slacks, chooses jewelry every morning, and combs her hair, but she can't admire herself the way she used to.

This house, these hands, these daughters, this pain in her stomach. Rising from the sofa isn't as easy as it once was.

She hates the afternoon.

It's not a dream that overtakes her then; it's like watching a film of her life, her brain a perfect projection of Tustin, California, in the fifties. Her parents' boxy little house, the carpeted stairs, the lawn, the tree, the swing. The mountains rising out of the orange groves to the east, reflecting the sunset. Her great-aunt Ada's garden, its little gate. Aunt Ada, the only one in her family who loved her or even liked her.

Aunt Ada was her mother's aunt. She had a big Bakelite radio on her kitchen table, and they'd listen to Artie Shaw while she smoked cigarettes and baked and thumbed through magazines. Cookies would be warming in the oven as Linda sucked on peppermint candies. Aunt Ada was tall and thin—like Mara, actually—and she had a patrician face like Katharine Hepburn, and she favored long white slacks and straight-shouldered blouses that looked fabulous on her. She was in her seventies by the time Linda was born; she had been in Europe as an army nurse in the Great War and never married. She died in '62, when Linda was twelve. It was awful.

One afternoon, Linda walked to her aunt's house to escape her mother's wrath. Linda's mother was a fiend about dishes and dusting and ironing and mending and helping in the kitchen after Linda's homework was finished, and meanwhile her horrid brother Tommy could play baseball with his friends as long as he liked, waltz in for dinner with muddy dungarees and filthy hands, and nobody said a word. Her mother could have tracked Linda down if she'd wanted to, but she was afraid of Aunt Ada.

Linda slipped in through her aunt's screen door, careful not to let it bang behind her. There were no cookies that day, and the house smelled simply like itself: tobacco, Emeraude perfume, peppermint, book dust. Aunt Ada was getting older. A reflective quiet, a kind of gloom, would settle over her some days, and she'd stare into the distance as she smoked, silent for minutes at a time. Linda found Aunt Ada in her rattan rocker in the living room, music levitating from the kitchen as the winter sun sank gently to the bottom of the sky.

"Hi, Lindy," she said softly, like she didn't want to disturb some great, quiet creature nearby. She gestured for Linda to sit in her lap, something Linda could still do at nine—but only just—because she was such a small child. Linda climbed into her aunt's lap and leaned forward to resume the chair's gentle rocking. What happened next might not have happened right then, but it did happen, and this is how she always remembered it.

"You're starting to look like your mother," Aunt Ada said. Linda wrinkled her nose. "Not Gail," Aunt Ada said. "Audrey. Her little sister."

Maybe Aunt Ada was going senile. Her mother, Gail, had an older sister, Betty, and that was it. She'd never heard of an Audrey in the family in her life.

"Your grandparents had three girls," Aunt Ada went on. "Betty, Gail, and Audrey. Audrey was the baby, nine years younger than Gail."

The shadows grew another centimeter. An uncanny feeling shivered along Linda's arms.

"She was wonderful," Aunt Ada said. "Bright, clever—and *what* a talker. They'd never admit it, but she was their favorite. She was *my* favorite. We'd have coffee after dinner, and Audrey would get up and perform for us, little dances, little plays she made up on the spot. When Gail and Betty would argue, which was always, she'd get between them and make them laugh until they forgave each other."

Aunt Ada's living room had a big picture window, and you could see three palm trees in the neighbors' yard across the street, higher than the house. As the sun fell, the trees became black silhouettes, outlined in sad, gold light.

"Betty graduated," Aunt Ada was saying, "and Gail graduated, and she married Henry, and they had your brother Tommy. And Gail wanted a girl so badly. But anyone could see there weren't going to be any more children between them."

Linda didn't know what Aunt Ada meant, but she stayed quiet.

"And when Audrey was sixteen, she became pregnant."

"How come nobody ever—"

"Hush," Aunt Ada admonished. "I'm not supposed to tell you this. Your parents would be very upset. Your grandparents would be *very* upset."

Linda held herself tightly as her aunt rocked the chair.

"Audrey became pregnant. She was too young, and she didn't tell anyone. No one knew there was a boyfriend. But she was clever: she told us she was rehearsing a play at school, and to prepare for the part, she had to wear the costumes at home. We didn't *see* the pregnancy because she hid it in these medieval dresses."

"Didn't her sisters share the room?" Linda asked.

"They'd moved out. She had the room to herself. She didn't seem different at all, I thought. She laughed like she always did; she performed scenes from the play for us. None of us knew what was happening when she had a seizure and they rushed her to the hospital."

"What's a seizure?"

"She had eclampsia." There was a catch in Aunt Ada's voice.

"What's that?"

"It's when a pregnant woman develops high blood pressure," Aunt Ada explained. "If it goes untreated, it can get *very* bad. Which it did. At the hospital, she had a stroke. They did a C-section. You were more than a month premature. And she died," Aunt Ada said.

The sun peeked from behind the palm tree. Applause filtered through the radio.

"She could've told me, but she didn't. Your grandparents didn't call me until after she was gone. I was right here."

Linda felt an odd pleasure in the bath of her aunt's grief. As though everything was more real. Why did bad things feel like that?

"Gail wanted a little girl, and she got her. They adopted you at the hospital; they filled out the paperwork on the spot. Your grandparents told everyone Audrey had died in a car crash."

Linda could imagine her grandparents doing this, not wanting the shame of it. They were proud and unhappy.

"Mama never got big," Linda pointed out.

"Your mother was enough of a homebody that I don't think anyone doubted her story, not to her face. I never heard gossip about it. They don't have a lot of friends."

"I don't believe you," Linda said, testing her.

"It was like she never existed. They didn't have a funeral. They took her picture down and hid the old albums away, and your grandmother, she was absolutely clear: we weren't to mention Audrey again. It was a pact of silence she laid down. Everyone bent to her will, like they always do. But I thought you had a right to know."

Linda blinks the room into focus again. She never got anyone in the family to confirm the story. She dug around in her grandparents' closet when they were at church—a federal offense if she'd been caught—and found nothing. She dropped hints and scrutinized their expressions. Maybe Aunt Ada was crazy. But the story made sense.

She liked her tragic secret.

If she'd stayed in touch with her family, she might have gotten the real story. Her grandparents died in the eighties, after Shannon was born—her brother sent the obituaries. Her parents, who couldn't stand each other, died almost simultaneously, when Shannon was in high school. Her brother sent the obituaries in an envelope again, no letter. Somehow, it was forwarded from the old address she'd had with Charlie.

Aunt Ada was the only one who understood. Linda never had anyone who loved her, who *got* her, the same way, again. Allison seemed like a soul mate when she was born, and then she was gone, too.

From the moment Linda came into the world, she was baptized in loss.

She leans forward, shifting her center of gravity, and lets her legs slide off the sofa. Her throat still hurts from the tube they tried to suffocate her with. She grips the cushion with two hands and takes a raspy breath. She heaves herself up: the room swims. Her arms cast about for ballast. Like standing on top of a light pole.

Back on the sofa. Failed again.

She tried to stop drinking. She knows they aren't cups of tea. She isn't stupid.

When Stan lived with her, they drank too much, more than she ever had before. She gained weight with all the beer, the wine coolers, the tequila shots. Stan loved getting to that water-eyed, maudlin state where you declared your love and loyalty, no matter who had punched his fist in a wall the night before. He'd get weepy and lift her up from the kitchen chair and tell her she was too good for him. Which was true. She hadn't meant to get pregnant. She almost—*almost*—got rid of it, but she kept putting it off. Then she started showing, and it was too late. Stan, of course, was thrilled.

She cut back on her drinking through each of her pregnancies; it wasn't hard. She hardly drank at all when she was breastfeeding, but she weaned each baby after six weeks because she wanted her body back.

She really, truly quit when Shannon was eight months old, the girls seven and eight. She didn't go to meetings or anything; she just quit. She put Stan's beers in the alley with the trash and poured all the liquor and a dozen little bottles of Bartles & Jaymes down the sink. Stan was furious. It was the first time he left for more than twenty-four hours. She got so sick she thought it was the flu, and she stuck the girls with a neighbor while she waited out the fever, the nausea, the shakes. She didn't call in at Safeway, and they let her go.

It's a stupid story. When Stan returned, it had been three weeks, Linda was sober and working on her boss to give her back her job, and the girls were fine. Everything was fine. She was playing cards with the neighbors when he came through the door, puffy-faced and repentant. It was a crime against nature that he was so good-looking.

She was glad when he finally left for real. She was about to quit drinking again, and stay quit, because she was the only mother those little girls had, when Allison got lost in the current. And then it was too much.

She never let go of the pleasure of a cocktail, the icy warmth, the tart edge, the feeling of doing something grownup and illicit. Her family were teetotalers except for Aunt Ada, who liked Scotch in the evenings and swore Linda to secrecy about it.

Someday her daughters will soften and become better people with their own lives and houses. Shannon will move out. It sounds nice, living alone. No one interfering with her routines. No one burning enough incense for a Turkish bazaar.

She picks at the scab on her arm from the IV, and blood threads down her elbow onto the sofa. She stares at it before trying to blot it with a tissue.

The fan's feathery croak as it turns back and forth. An airplane. A nail gun from a construction site across the alley. The fuzz of freeway and ocean, the sound of the white sky itself. Harder to comfort herself since she got home. Everything feels deflated, the afternoon of it all. She settles back against the sofa cushions and closes her eyes.

She startles from sleep in a sweaty fury, gulping air. The sofa is a sarcophagus. She rises and stumbles to the TV for balance, walks high-kneed to the kitchen, hands splayed, listening for signs of anyone else in the house, but she can't tell. Mara is sneaky, secretive—she always was—she could be in one of the bedrooms, rearranging things. Linda is too tired to care.

In the freezer, a fresh little bottle. Apparently Mara couldn't bring herself to trash it on her rampage through the kitchen. Linda doesn't want a mug, every surface outside the freezer is too warm. The bottle itself is cool, alive, the vodka viscous as it comes out. It vibrates in her mouth and stings her nostrils, soothes her throat, burns her chest. She drinks it like water, more than usual, claiming herself. It's always in her ear, feathering her cheek: yes, she says, *yes,* the love returning.

Oh, to be a classy drinker again! Martinis, heels, a man in a jacket paying the tab. This was before she turned twenty-one. She'd sneak off to Los Angeles by bus in her best outfit: she was going to be discovered. Her favorite bar was at the Chateau Marmont. They mistook her for Ann-Margret. Twice.

She never went anywhere with the men who bought her drinks, not even up to their rooms. They didn't usually have rooms: they were trolling for girls like her while their wives cooked dinner at home.

They said they were casting directors, managers, producers. Of course they weren't. One man's business address was a cheap bungalow in Century City; she got a friend to drive her, just to see. Another's phone was answered by his teenage daughter.

No one wanted to hear her sing.

She screws the cap back on and places the bottle gently in the freezer behind a bag of ice. She smooths her blouse, her slacks, her hair, and returns perilously to the sofa. She is too tired to light a cigarette. Sleep falls on her like a wave.

Chapter Eleven

Shannon has a fantasy of herself. In high school, her fantasy self did homework; she sat in front and raised her hand; teachers liked her. Fantasy Shannon didn't smoke weed and only partied on weekends, a little, like *one* drink. Fantasy Shannon lived in a house with her father, a mild-mannered guy with a decent job, a plumber or electrician or something. Fantasy Shannon wasn't rich, but her life was solid. She graduated on time.

Fantasy Shannon's life was a movie that kept going in Shannon's head. Fantasy Shannon went to Mesa the fall after graduating from high school. She earned her associate's in two years. Fantasy Shannon transferred to San Diego State, which she commuted to in her silver Honda Accord, which she washed and vacuumed every week and paid off in monthly installments. Fantasy Shannon worked her way through college, but the actual job was fuzzy in Shannon's mind. Fantasy Shannon got a four-year degree in four years. She started her career, also fuzzy, but she works in an office in a tall building downtown.

Fantasy Shannon's apartment is small but nice. She doesn't have roommates; she has a cat. Houseplants near the windows. A clean coffee table. Framed posters on the walls. Fantasy Shannon is always making dinner as the setting sun bathes the apartment in yellow light—she's still in her work clothes, a blouse and a skirt, shoes off, making a stir-fry in a wok, her shoulder cupping the phone as she talks to a friend, who's coming over later and bringing a bottle of wine. Fantasy Shannon likes wine, not too much, not to get drunk. Fantasy Shannon looks like the real Shannon, but she's thinner. She wears makeup, just enough to look polished. Her hair is up in a French twist. She gets a regular mani-pedi. She makes dinner at her father's house every Sunday. She isn't depressed or listless or pissy or suicidal and doesn't hang out with losers. She goes to Rite Aid to pick up a prescription, and in the parking lot she sees actual losers, people like Shannon, and thinks, Ugh. Tough life. Glad that's not me.

The traffic pulls to a stop on Obsidian, and Shannon crosses. She wonders if it's time for Fantasy Shannon to find love. Shannon's only experiences with love—of course it wasn't *love*—were dumb, embarrassing, a waste of time every time. Lame, gross guys. Cute guys who turned out to be lame and gross. Cute, cool guys who went for Brandy instead (always). She basically doesn't believe in love.

Fantasy Shannon would believe in love.

Fantasy Shannon would date a nice guy from work, or someone she met through friends, cute but not drop-dead, a guy who would make a nice husband. They'd date; he'd propose; they'd get married, maybe by the time she turned thirty. She'd make her father so happy.

There is her car—yes? Yes—at the edge of the Denny's parking lot. She unlocks the driver's side door and climbs in. The upholstery is warm, the air dense and hot. She turns the ignition and rolls down the windows, watching the needles on the dashboard. An eighth of a tank left, enough to get her to the bus depot downtown, probably. She turns off the engine.

A familiar figure in big sunglasses crosses the lot from Marina Boulevard in the distance. She's by herself, leggy and confident, a purse Shannon doesn't recognize slung over her shoulder. She looks super-young from this far away, but Shannon is sure it's her.

Brandy has been Shannon's only real friend since eleventh grade, but let's be honest: she never trusted Brandy. Their closeness, their loyalty, it didn't make sense. Brandy was resources, a listening ear, constant companionship—in high school, she tried to get Shannon to study with her and finish homework—and Shannon was nothing. Brandy thought Shannon was funny, and Shannon didn't see why. Then Shannon fucked their friendship forever.

The girl in the distance stops at a car that isn't Brandy's red Del Sol. She takes a phone out of her purse and starts talking into it like a walkie-talkie, which Brandy never does. She pushes the sunglasses up on her head. It isn't Brandy. The girl is a teenager. The girl and Brandy could be sisters, cousins. Maybe they are.

Shannon counts the change in the tray between the front seats: a little over $3, mostly nickels and dimes. She unfolds a wadded ATM receipt, the one from the morning she drove home from the hospital. $151.23. Enough for a bus ticket?

What is she doing?

Her mother's friend emerges from Denny's right then, with a crowd spilling out behind him. In the daytime, he is a tall, rangy white man, grey hair cut so short it glitters on his head. Huge sunglasses take up most of his face, and he throws his straight shoulders back with a weary confidence. He always wears the same outfit: pastel button-up shirt, open at the chest with the collar turned up, tucked into white jeans. A sleek little purse with long straps down to his hip. He is extra tall in high-heeled sneakers.

Her mother started taking her to the drag show at Golden's, the piano bar on Obsidian, Friday nights when she was in elementary school. She'd drink Shirley Temples and mouth the words to the songs, the patter between numbers, the jokes they repeated every week. Linda's friend performed as Desert Rage, the look inspired by actresses from old black-and-white movies. Desert Rage was always in a terrible mood and made mean, wickedly funny jokes; she wasn't much of a dancer, but her stage presence dramatically outshone the others. She was Shannon's favorite performer at Golden's, not that anyone asked.

He introduced himself to Shannon as Des, but everyone, including Shannon, calls him Garbo. In and out of drag, he has something of Greta Garbo's melancholy, a regal disappointment with everything that has ever been or ever will be. A despairing, chin-in-hand beauty. When Shannon asked, her mother explained who Greta Garbo was, pointing to her picture in a giant book of silver-screen actresses she kept in her room. She always tried to get Shannon to watch old movies with her when they came on TV, but Shannon didn't have the patience.

Garbo is the higher-functioning version of Linda: an alcoholic who still works, pays his rent, stays groomed, holds normal conversations. He told Shannon once that he could get her into the restaurant business, which he'd worked in for decades, serving, bartending, cater-waiting, if she was interested. "It's better than whatever the hell they're paying you to work here," he sniffed one afternoon at Rite Aid as she rang him up. Brandy had told her the same thing. But she figured waiting tables was out of her league: you had to be fast and cheerful and hardworking. And cute.

Shannon gets out of her car and waves Garbo down. He doesn't notice at first, but someone nudges him and points discreetly toward Shannon. He lowers his sunglasses and saunters toward her. Like Linda, he bases his existence on the premise that he is correct and the rest of the world has a problem. While Linda's premise is mistaken, Garbo's might not be. Shannon has always marveled at the way he seems like displaced royalty.

"Hey, you," he says, leaning down to peck Shannon on the cheek. She has known him since childhood, and still she burns with the thrill of encountering a celebrity. His breath is alcoholic.

"Where the hell is Lindy?" he purrs, swaying a moment, gathering himself. "Where's your mama at, boo?"

"She was in the hospital." Shannon swallows.

"The *hospital*?" Garbo rears back. "Fuck." He pushes his sunglasses back onto the top of his head, and Shannon can see how his face has gotten older in the last few years, after seeming ageless for so long. His big dark eyes, naked without eyebrows, full of worry. "What happened?"

"Heart attack."

He gasps, drawing his hand to his heart. "Is she okay?"

"Yeah," Shannon says vaguely. "She'll be okay. She's home." Shannon coughs. "My sister's there."

"Your—I thought your sister . . ." He flicks his head in the direction of the ocean.

"My other sister. From Massachusetts."

"Ohhh, right," he says, nodding, his expression hard to read. "I forgot about that one." He cocks his head. "Darling, I'll be honest with you," he says. "I never thought *I'd* live this long." As far as Shannon is concerned, Garbo is immortal, but she does the math: he must have lost dozens of friends in the eighties. Who knew what horrors he'd seen?

"I know what you mean," Shannon finds herself saying.

"You do?" Garbo says doubtfully.

How does anyone learn to be a woman? It's strange how Shannon didn't hold on to the beauty-pageant know-how of her elementary years. Her mother had dressed her up, styled her hair, dabbed lip gloss and blush onto her second-grade face. When Linda stopped bothering, Shannon opted for shorts and t-shirts and sloppy ponytails. Brandy tried to teach her about makeup— Shannon has a drawer full of cast-off makeup, plus whatever Brandy felt like "borrowing" from Rite Aid and forgetting in Shannon's car—but it looks freakish when she puts it on.

"How old are you, anyway?" Garbo asks.

"How old are you?" Shannon replies.

"I'm *sorry*?" he hoots. "I asked you first, little girl."

"Twenty-seven."

"Jesus Christ. You got your whole life ahead of you, pumpkin."

"What if it's not the life I wanted?"

"Like how?" He places a hand on his hip.

This is not what Shannon means, exactly. "What if it mostly sucks?" she asks quietly.

Garbo assesses her.

"I mean, like—" Shannon sighs. "I just know what you mean," she says. "I almost died when I was eighteen," she says, unable to stop herself. She's never told anyone about it, not ever.

"How?" he asks, softening. Shannon's face reddens. Literally her mother's only friend. She is an idiot. He stares at her, waiting for the story.

"It's—it wasn't a big deal," Shannon says, backpedaling. "I was sniffing shoe polish. Out there on the pier." She gestures with her eyes. "I ended up in the emergency room. They said I almost died." She shrugs, like maybe he'd been exaggerating, the ER doctor, so serious with his lab coat.

Garbo takes a long time to speak, gazing at Shannon until she has to look away. "Shoe polish?" he finally says. "Like, shoe polish?"

Shannon stares at the sky.

"Girl, stick to booze. Huffing is for white trash," he says. "No offense." He stares at her, reading her fortune. "It isn't that bad," he tells her. Shannon returns his gaze. "I'm still here," Garbo says, smoothing his invisible eyebrows. "Lindy's still here. Look at us!" he cries with a kind of despondent joy. "How bad can it be?"

"I'm leaving town," Shannon says, testing the idea.

"What about your mother?"

"My sister's there," Shannon says. "She's, like, super-responsible."

"Where to?" Garbo asks, folding his arms, and Shannon imagines him ringing her mother on the phone, tattling. "You should go to New York," he tells her. Maybe he won't say anything. Maybe he understands what it means to be trapped in the house with Linda.

"Have you ever been to Tennessee?" Shannon asks.

"*Yes.* Ew." Garbo makes a face. "What's wrong with New York? Or at least San Francisco. Jesus."

"Too expensive."

"Not if you *work*! Learn how to tend bar, you'll be fine."

Shannon imagines herself as a bartender, wasted at the end of every shift.

"Make it work. Anybody can make it work, if you have the heart," Garbo says.

"Do you know that old transit depot downtown?" Shannon asks. "The pretty one? It's, like, Spanish-looking?" It dawns on Shannon she doesn't know exactly where it is or how to get there.

"You're going *now*?" Garbo asks.

"No," Shannon lies. "Just thinking it over."

"You're young," he tells her. "You're cute. You got your whole life. Go to New York."

Shannon plays it over and over in her head: *You're cute.*

"Do I have the heart?" she asks.

"Who are you talking to? Bitch, *yes*." He fans himself, looking around the parking lot. A tight circle of his friends are laughing and gesturing, but they're too far away for her to hear what they're saying. Garbo unsnaps his purse and fishes out a shiny little flask. "Here," he says, offering it to Shannon. "Take my blessing."

Shannon puts it to her lips, wincing. It's vodka, a sacrament she imagines coming from both Garbo and her mother, the best parts of them anointing her, sending her on her quest. She tips it and swallows. She wipes her mouth and stares at the sun for a second, silvering her vision.

"Your mama's gonna be okay?" Garbo asks, taking a quick sip before tucking the flask back into her purse.

"Yeah," Shannon says casually. "She's good."

"Tell her to get her skinny ass back out here, then." He winks and pecks her on the same cheek. He squeezes her shoulder for a second, looking past her. "Ciao, babe. Don't leave without saying goodbye."

She climbs into her car and starts the engine. She rolls down the windows and turns on the radio. Her second most absolute all-time favorite song, from her all-time favorite album in the entire world is playing, which never happens, and she turns it way up, backing out of the parking lot. *Bre-eathe . . . breathe in the a-air . . . Don't be afraid to care . . .*

She sails through a flume of green lights down Obsidian. She literally can't remember the last time that happened.

What if, like her mother's friend, she just *decided* her life was worth living, and that she was good at it? Just decided not to be ashamed? She shakes her head, pulls onto the Five. She yanks her hair out of the bun and lets it blow behind her in the warm wind. The song goes all the way to the end, just like on the album, and begins to fade into the next one, a pulsing instrumental with spooky vocals, the sound of her own momentum, the concrete tearing past the car. Maybe they're playing the whole thing. They are: the next song from the album comes on—on the radio!— and this, *this,* is her absolute, hands-down, all-time, number-one favorite song *ever.* When she first got the car, she was nineteen, and she used to keep the tape of the album—dubbed from a friend—in the tape deck and save it for after work. She'd go out to the parking lot, sit in the driver's seat, roll up all the windows, and get stoned, always starting with this song. Pure release, liberation. *Ticking away . . . the moments that make up a dull day . . .* She's never felt so loved by God, which she doesn't really believe in, except she sort of does. She doesn't want to believe God (or whatever) despises her, which is her fear. But maybe she is lovable and not despicable. Maybe.

She pulls off the freeway and has no idea where to go. She's running on intuition and faith. Downtown is a maze of one-way streets, but she doesn't care. She'll find the depot, with its beautiful, high ceilings, birds perched in the rafters. How does she even know this place, what it looks like, the birds in the rafters? She never hangs out downtown, never went there as a kid. She has distinct memories of it but can't place them in their time or context.

She does find it, eventually, after the radio has played the remainder of her favorite song and moved on to other songs that mean nothing to Shannon (they weren't playing the entire album). She turns the radio off and pulls into the parking lot in silence.

Inside, the place is just like she remembered. Spanish tile floor, great big windows at both ends flooded with light. Long wooden benches, quiet echoes. Train signals clanging on the tracks.

The ticket booth is at the far end; the line is short. She has her debit card in her sweaty hand, the balance floating in her mind. She tells the clerk she wants a bus ticket.

"Just train tickets, ma'am," the clerk says. He has a little Amtrak hat, like a bellhop.

"Huh?"

"Just train tickets. Amtrak and Coaster. No buses."

"This is a bus depot."

"It's a train station, ma'am. The bus station is about ten minutes from here."

Shannon is dumbfounded. How could the music have played on her radio and guided her *here*? What about Garbo's blessing?

"Are they still open?" she squeaks.

"They're open till midnight." The man is patient. "You want to take Broadway all the way to 14th and make a right; take 14th all the way to Imperial, make another right; make a quick left onto National Avenue, and you can't miss it. Big parking lot. Greyhound sign."

Shannon stares. She doesn't want to be mad at him.

"Next!" he calls out over her shoulder. A woman with two small children comes up behind Shannon, and they crowd the window. Shannon skulks off and sinks into a bench with her duffel. This is the station for trains, for the kind of people who take trains.

Poor people take buses.

She thinks of the apartment, of Mara and their mother, Charlie Meade's voice on the little iPhone. Two big doors are open to the tracks, where the sun is still setting: a beautiful day, like all the other beautiful days. She wants to stay in this room, pretend she belongs, as if sitting here will transport her to Tennessee. And she wants to be somewhere else, a place she doesn't recognize, a place so different they have accents and strange trees and weird light and different food.

Brandy said, "Why Tennessee?" and Shannon didn't have an answer. She liked the sound of it.

She raises herself up and hoists her duffel over her shoulder, wishing for something to give it weight. She gets back in the car. The man's directions are easy to follow, and there it is. A grey box in the middle of a parking lot, idling buses at one end, rumbling engines, diesel fumes. Shannon parks, locks her car, jiggles the keys in her hand. If she's leaving for good, she'll never see this car again. Maybe she should leave the keys in the ignition for some-one who needs it. She imagines a meth head on a bender trashing the interior and stuffs the keys in her pocket.

Inside, the freezing air is stale and close. It reminds her of her elementary school cafeteria. The line isn't long, but the people in it look like they've been there for days; the clerk window is empty, and people sigh over giant suitcases, check their phones, give agitated looks to the floor, the wall, and the clock, which hangs high and huge like a sun.

Shannon hypnotizes herself, watching the clock. Literally forty-five minutes later, she makes it to the clerk behind the glass.

"Ticket to Nashville," she says. "One way." She's practiced in her head. The clerk's hands fly across a keyboard. The woman leans her mouth toward a little microphone.

"$255. Cash or credit?"

"Two hundred and fifty-five *dollars?*" Shannon stutters.

"$255," the clerk repeats without emotion, her eyes on the screen. "Leaves tonight at 10:30."

Shannon's face reddens. "Um," she says, stalling, thinking. "What about Texas?"

"Where in Texas, ma'am?"

"Wherever. The cheapest one."

More key strokes. The woman has dark brown skin and a crisp, straightened bob with a pink streak near the front, a diamond ring on her finger. She could be Shannon's age. She leans toward the microphone again.

"Dallas is $171." She looks at Shannon, who would like to die.

"What about Albuquerque?" Shannon stammers. The clerk sighs. Taps the keyboard.

"$124.50."

Not enough left over. "Arizona?" she asks.

"Where in Arizona." The clerk's impatience is in her voice but not her face.

"Phoenix?" More keystrokes. The clerk looks up, twists behind her, and calls out to someone. She laughs at the person's response and returns to the screen.

"Phoenix, $89 one way," she tells Shannon with finality. "Six-thirty tomorrow morning. If you want to leave tonight, it's $103.50."

The benches in the waiting area are made of widely spaced metal bars. She's not going back to the apartment, only to leave again in the morning. She'd never get up that early.

Phoenix is too close: she can't just get on a bus to Phoenix.

Life without Brandy is different.

"Thank you," Shannon says and turns around. She walks to a wall and stands against it, duffel in hand.

So that's it. She's not getting on a bus. She was supposed to get on a bus.

She pushes the glass door open and makes her way across the parking lot to the car she almost left to tweakers. The sun still lights the western sky. She starts the car, turns the radio on, and it's a song Shannon hates. She turns it off. Her keychain swings back and forth.

She pilots the car out of the parking lot, drives north, back through downtown, onto Highway 101. She'll run out of gas before making it even thirty miles past Silver Beach. But if she had gas: what about L.A.? What's north of that, before San Francisco? *After* San Francisco? Maybe she needs to head north, not east. She'll get her stupid job back, start saving up.

Saving up. Ha.

She pulls into a Jack in the Box. If she was with Brandy, they'd smoke in the parking lot, Shannon overdoing it, Brandy holding back, laughing at her.

Inside, the Jack in the Box is cold. There's one guy at the tables, eating a meal so big it's like his own buffet, everything set out across two trays. Shannon stares up at the menu. A teenager behind the register watches her nails. Shannon steps forward.

"Can I get a Chick-n-Tater Melt Munchie Meal?" She's heard of this, heard it's good.

"The Munchie Meal menu is only after 9 P.M.," the teenager tells her. Literally the late-night stoner menu. Shannon sighs. She orders a chicken ranch club, curly fries, onion rings, and a large Dr. Pepper. She might even get dessert, now that she isn't buying a bus ticket.

She fills her soda and makes her way to the tables. The man is eating slowly, concentrating, like it's a ritual. He's white, skinny and goateed and dark-haired, not as young as she is, not old. His t-shirt has the name of a metal band she's heard of, but sometimes people just wear random t-shirts; it doesn't mean they like the band or went to the show or whatever. She trains her eyes on her soda.

They call her order number over the loudspeaker, disturbing the relative quiet. She's always liked the labeled cardboard containers at fast-food restaurants, the little fry bags. She loves the sensation of a warm, foil-wrapped sandwich. She decides she'll eat slowly. Why is she always rushing things? What's the hurry?

The amount of food the guy has on his two trays is shocking. He's been eating since she walked in, but there are still—she counts them—three unopened sandwiches, a large curly fries, two tacos, and a teriyaki bowl steaming in its Styrofoam tub. The guy is totally skinny. Maybe this is his one meal a week, like he's on some kind of program.

She's staring again. He catches her eye, and she looks down. Squeezes a ketchup packet onto her tray for the onion rings. Takes a leisurely, self-conscious sip of soda.

"How's it going?" the guy says when he finishes chewing. He's casual; it's not a creepy greeting. Shannon looks at him. He has weird eyes, but not too weird.

"You know," she says vaguely. "Long day."

"Tell me about it," the guy says to his burger, taking another bite. She *would* tell him about it. If that's what he meant.

"What's your field?" he asks. She stares at him blankly. Baseball fields, football fields. Magnetic fields. "Long day at work?" he clarifies.

"Oh," Shannon says. "Not really." She drags an onion ring through a lake of ketchup. "My mom was in the hospital. So I had to deal with that."

The guy nods, chewing. He swallows thoughtfully. "She okay?"

"Yeah," Shannon says. "No."

"Yeah no?"

"Yeah. No." Shannon would like to be in a bar right now, in the dim shadows as the brightness faded outside. Maybe that's her next stop.

The onion rings at Jack in the Box are superior to the ones at Burger King, definitely better than the ones at Wendy's, but not *quite* as good as the ones at Carl's Jr. For some reason, curly fries are the same everywhere. Shannon hates when people—girls, usually—say, "Oh, I *never* eat fast food. I haven't had fast food since I was a kid." Like it's not food, like you're eating literal garbage. Her sandwich is delicious. Warm mayonnaise drips onto her tray, and she sponges a curly fry into it.

She can't help staring at the guy's trays. "That's a lot of . . ." Shannon finally says, trailing off. He's onto the tacos, but he still has three sandwiches, plus the teriyaki bowl. He nods, cheeks full.

"It's called the Warrior Diet," he says after swallowing. "You fast most of the day, exercise till you're really tired, then eat like crazy before bed."

"Oh," Shannon says, mystified.

"Helps you build bulk. I just started."

"I've never exercised in my life," Shannon tells him, shaking the ice cubes in her soda.

He eyes her. "You're actually in pretty decent shape, then, considering. Do you eat well?"

"No."

"You probably have great metabolism."

Shannon smiles, flattered.

"If you started working out and eating more intentionally . . ." He slides the remainder of a taco into his mouth, finishing the sentence with his eyebrows.

"What do you mean?" *Eating more intentionally* sounds like eating on purpose, which everyone does.

"Like being picky about protein, carbs . . . when, how much . . ." He laughs. "You're not supposed to eat at Jack in the Box. I'm just here 'cause I was starving and I don't get paid until Friday. Usually I eat all organic."

Shannon looks out the window, hiding her disappointment. "What's your job?" she asks.

"IT."

Shannon has no idea what this means.

"How about you?" he asks.

"TI."

"What's that?"

"Just kidding. I wait tables," she lies. "In La Jolla."

"So you're on your feet a lot. That's exercise," he says approvingly.

"I'm thinking about getting out," she says, echoing Brandy's old coworkers. "It's, like, stressful *and* boring?"

The guy nods. He pries the lid off the teriyaki bowl.

"I might go back to school," she tells him.

"Right on," he says between mouthfuls. "Go into IT. Training doesn't take long, and the money's good." He grins at her. "We need more women in IT. For sure."

Italian Toppings? Incident Tips? Iron Tunnels?

Maybe it means International Transportation. The guy could be a trucker. Shannon imagines herself at a truck stop, men banging on the door of her tractor trailer to sexually assault her. Relieving herself in a Pepsi can.

She finishes her sandwich and tries not to watch him eat all that food. She slurps the last of her soda through the straw, making the sound Brandy hated. As she gets up to order dessert, she hopes the guy is watching her and that he isn't. She returns to her table with a slice of pie in a plastic shell, a cup of coffee, and a fistful of creamers. She catches the guy's eye, and her face reddens.

"How long did the training take?" she asks, shy.

"For what?"

"IT."

"Oh. Two years. I did a lot of my stuff online. I had to take out loans, though."

She nods like she understands.

"Do you like computers?" he asks.

"Sure." The last time Shannon used a computer was in the high school computer lab nine years ago.

"Good. Just do a search. There's a million programs. They're all basically the same, if you ask me."

She'll ask Mara what IT is. Is she going back to Silver Beach? What else would she do? Crash with this guy? Find a shelter? Sleep in the park? She knows people besides Brandy, but no one she'd ask to stay on their couch; they're just people she sees around. Some of them are people she'd like to be friends with, but how do you do that, when you aren't *already* friends? Some of them are people she doesn't even like: she has the same relationship with all of them. Her coworkers at Rite Aid probably think she's nuts the way she told the manager off.

She has $150 to her name, minus whatever dinner cost. She is almost out of gas. She is so stupid.

The guy finishes the teriyaki bowl. He stares at the remaining two sandwiches on his tray. "Guess I overestimated, huh?" He smiles at her and takes the trays to the trash, and Shannon is mournful for a second. When he returns, he hikes a backpack over his shoulder and approaches her table. He holds up a hand for a high-five. "Good luck with everything, all right?"

She high-fives him, and it fills her with courage. He digs around in his backpack and comes up with a dog-eared business card.

"My email's on there," he says. "If you want to network or whatever."

She takes the card and examines it. *Mark Browne, IT Systems Manager, Afillis Industry Solutions.* Truckers don't have business cards. Do they?

"Thanks," she tells him, not wanting him to leave.

"Take it easy," he says, walking backward. "Nice talking to you." He waves. All Shannon can do is half-smile. She watches him leave, his figure darkened through the tinted glass. He climbs into a little hatchback sedan with no muffler and buzzes out of the parking lot. She didn't tell him her name.

She eats her pie slice slowly, counting the chews, ten each, and whitens her coffee with creamer. The little clock over the CPR sign says 8:30, but it doesn't feel late enough.

Would Fantasy Shannon read in the evenings, or watch TV? Or talk on the phone? What would she read? What would she watch? Who would she talk to?

She has a stomachache. She clears her table, dumps her half-full coffee in the trash, grabs her duffel. She drags herself into the parking lot, her body heavy. She thinks of the man she saw in a tabloid who weighed a thousand pounds. In the car, she turns the radio on and switches it off without even waiting to hear the song.

Maybe she'll get lucky and run out of gas on the way home. Have another adventure.

She takes the long way home, past Brandy's house, the windows yellow against the blue twilight, Brandy's father's Audi in the driveway. No sign of the Del Sol.

The gas gauge is down to nothing, but her car drives on, making an extra loop around the bay. The sunlight is a thin pink line over the ocean.

She pulls into the carport and turns off the ignition, the car dripping and ticking as it cools. If she had a hose, she could end things right here and never have to go back in the apartment again. She doesn't even know what kind of hose people use. Garden hoses? How does it stay on the exhaust pipe? A smelly way to go. She's such a pussy. The only way she'd commit suicide was if it didn't hurt at all and was really easy.

At the door to the apartment, she hovers her key over the lock, listening. She leans her forehead on the door. Suddenly, it opens, and Shannon stumbles forward.

"You scared the shit out of me," Mara breathes. She doesn't sound like herself. All the lights are on. The apartment is—somehow—more disheveled than usual. An inside-out pair of blue rubber gloves is on the coffee table, a strip of medical tape is stuck to the TV screen, and little antiseptic towelette packs are on the couch. Mara seems to be hyperventilating. The sofa is empty.

"These EMS guys are just *assholes*," Mara seethes, as though they're in the middle of a conversation.

Shannon goes to her mother's bedroom, Mara trailing her.

"They treat it like it's a *crime scene.* They call the police! Don't get me started on the police. It's, like, such an *inconvenience* for them."

Linda's room is empty, the bed tautly made. She turns to Mara. "Where's Mom?"

Mara closes her eyes and breathes.

"She had another heart attack?" Shannon asks. Her duffel is still on her shoulder. "She passed out?"

Mara looks for words but can't find them. She goes into the living room and collapses onto the couch.

"Where is she?" Shannon asks.

"Gone," Mara says very, very quietly.

"Gone to the hospital? In an ambulance?"

"Gone like . . ." She throws up her hands again, shakes her head. "I'm sorry," she tells her lap.

"Gone *where?* What are you sorry about?"

"They pronounced her. Here." Her voice is small. "Sort of. They can't do it officially, a doctor has to do it. We have to meet them at UCSD and pick up the body."

The body.

But Linda doesn't die. She floats over death, keeps floating, like someone in the ocean.

"She'll come back," Shannon hears herself say. Mara looks at her, horrified.

"She had another heart attack." Now Mara's voice is clear. "She might have had more strokes. She looked like she was asleep, for a while. I was right there, researching Medicaid. They had, like, five different ways of being sure she was dead. They put her on the stretcher, and she looked—" Mara's voice shrinks to a whisper. "Stiff." She lifts her eyes to Shannon. "I'm sorry."

"Why are you sorry?"

Mara looks away. Shannon sets her duffel on the floor and folds her arms tightly over her chest. Mara is still pretty, even with her shoulders hunched, her eyes spooked. That necklace at her throat. Composed. Grown up. Competent. Rather than solving their problem by getting Linda into rehab, she solved it by getting rid of Linda.

"Where do I go?" Shannon says softly.

"What do you mean?"

"Where am I supposed to go?"

"We have to go to UCSD." Mara doesn't get it.

"I'm hungry," Shannon says for no reason. She could crawl out of her skin.

"I made a sandwich for you," Mara says, a catch in her voice. "It's in the fridge, in plastic wrap."

Shannon wonders what sort of shelter she could stay in. If she didn't have to pay rent, she could—maybe—save money faster, once she got a job. Shelter: what does that even mean? Like a cot in a gymnasium, people wheezing all around you? Or like, they give you a room? How long do they let you stay?

What could she fit into her duffel bag?

She imagines the old framed pictures of Linda, dusty and yellow with time, stacked in a garbage bag. All the living-room piles, the kitchen piles, her mother's clothes, the makeup and perfume and cheap jewelry, in garbage bags, nothing in the apartment but the scuffs on the walls and a bottle of vodka hidden in the freezer.

She'll never afford a bag of weed again.

"Come on." Mara is at the door.

Chapter Twelve

Mara concentrates on the road, on the tail lights of the Civic ahead, creeping along Obsidian in mysterious evening traffic.

She never knew her mother, is the thing. Why was Linda the way she was? Why was she fixated on this, oblivious to that? Why did she inhabit her own Linda-sized universe? What was her family like? Why didn't she talk to her family? Mara will never know, not ever.

She always thought, when someone doesn't know their father, it's not such a big deal. Fathers walk away from fatherhood all the time: look at Shannon's father. But when your mother does that—when she seems like she shouldn't have had children at all—it's crippling, somehow. Is that fair? Is Mara crippled?

Maybe it isn't Linda, and never was. Maybe Mara needs to deal with her shit and keep it moving, as Nell would say.

Nell. She should text her now, probably.

Your sister died, your mother was crazy, and what? Join the club. You turned out fine. Keep it moving. Take care of whatever needs it. Bring Shannon back with you to Massachusetts. The light changes, and she merges onto the Five.

At the front desk at UCSD, Shannon hangs behind Mara like a child. Mara is surprised to hear the word *autopsy,* but she supposes they always do one, just to make sure.

"*I* can tell you what she died from," Mara mutters to the woman at the desk, regretting it. The woman tells them to wait in the lobby; they'll call her when the body is ready. There will be paperwork. She hands Mara a flyer with a list of mortuaries on it.

"They're required by law to quote you a price over the phone," she says. "Don't be afraid to ask." The flyer is pink. Mara finds a seat as far from the ceiling-mounted televisions as possible, which isn't much. They're playing the same news program, and one has a millisecond delay. Shannon trails behind and sinks into the seat next to her.

"There were no end-of-life directives," she tells Shannon. "She didn't have a DNR. So they want to make sure I didn't kill her." Shannon gives her a look that, for the life of her, Mara cannot read. They sit in silence. Mara resists the urge to look at her phone because Shannon has nothing to read, or do, unless she wants to paw through a germy, outdated copy of *Us Weekly,* which apparently she does not.

"Did she ever talk to you about—like, her life? Her childhood?" Mara finally asks. "Did she get along with her parents?"

Shannon stares at the floor.

Mara answers her own question: "Obviously not."

"You know the stories," Shannon says. "She was the best in her ballet class, blah blah blah." It was a litany, Mara knew it too, a transparently curated series of anecdotes supporting the idea Linda had of herself as a special, tragic figure whose potential no one understood. The stories never featured anyone else.

"Do you know her parents' names?" Mara asks.

"Her brother's name was Tommy."

"What was her maiden name?"

"Tiegert? Taggart? Something with a T."

165

"We could probably find her birth certificate."

"Why?"

"I'm curious."

"You weren't before."

Fatigue hits Mara then, a heavy cape of exhaustion. She hasn't properly slept since she left Massachusetts. The massive bed in the Spreckels Hotel cruelly looms in her mind. It'll be a lifetime before she spends that much money again without thinking. Not even then.

"I know this is a weird question," Mara says, scanning the flyer in an attempt to keep her eyes open. "But are we thinking burial or cremation?"

After a moment, Shannon twitches and tries to put her hair back into the bun she'd had earlier. The physics of the task elude her.

"Turn around," Mara says gently, and she is surprised when Shannon complies. She smooths Shannon's long yellow hair and pulls it into the hair tie, wraps it expertly around itself, and secures it tightly with the scrunchie in Shannon's hand, tripling it around the bun so it will stay. A trio of fourth-grade girls seeks this service from Mara on an almost daily basis after the lunch recess. Shannon gingerly touches her head.

"Thanks," she mumbles, and drops back into her slouch.

"Do you have a preference?" Mara asks.

"For what?"

"Cremation—"

"Can we talk about it later?"

"I have to call one of these places," Mara says, "and tell them what we want to do."

"Which one do you think?"

"Cremation?"

Shannon's face is bitter. "*Ew.*"

166

"You think it's *less* gross to embalm a dead body and put makeup on it?"

"Don't you think Mom would want to look nice?"

"I don't know what Mom wanted," Mara sighs.

"She'd want to look *nice*. Her friends would want her to look nice."

"What friends?"

"She has friends!"

"I'm asking who they are, not whether she had them." Mara can't picture her mother having real friends, unless they were exactly like her.

"She has friends," Shannon repeats.

"We can have a memorial service without laying her out in a coffin in a funeral home," Mara points out. "Her friends can come. We'll serve food. We can do whatever we want."

"We can afford to do more than just burn her up," Shannon says. "You can. Your father can."

"I'm not suggesting cremation because it's *cheap*. Jesus," Mara says. "Do you know how many chemicals they use to preserve the body to make the person look like they're alive, but they still look dead? And the chemicals in those coffins, sealed in lacquer? It never biodegrades. It just sits there in the ground, leaching all that stuff into the soil, the water table." She is not entirely sure about the details here. "And a burial plot, we'd have to buy a plot in a cemetery."

"You're so *cheap*," Shannon says. "*Stingy*. Both of you."

"My dad paid his ex-wife's rent for twenty-six years because he's *cheap*?"

"No, he felt guilty. And now he can stop."

"I don't know what he wants to do."

"What would you do? Would *you* pay my rent?"

Not for a two-bedroom, Mara thinks.

"I'm so fucked," Shannon says to herself.

"You're fine through the month. Through at least the end of next month," Mara says. "I promise."

"And then what?"

"We'll figure it out."

"'We'? You probably already booked your ticket back to Massachusetts."

"I didn't, actually." Mara breathes, using the technique she learned years ago to control her anger with children. "There's a lot of stuff to deal with, and I'm going to deal with it. I told my boss I was taking the rest of the term off. I don't have to go back until the end of August."

Shannon is suspicious. "What stuff?"

"Every agency that sent her a check, anyone who billed her regularly for anything, Medicaid, Social Security—they all need to know she's deceased. We have to deal with her estate."

"What *estate?*"

"Everything a person owns is their estate. Even if it's a hundred tiny bottles of vodka and a closet full of muumuus." Mara turns the flyer over. "Maybe we'll find something interesting in her room. Maybe she wrote letters."

"Her body's not even cold, and you're talking about digging through her stuff."

"She's not going to get less dead," Mara says. Their mother's body probably is cold, especially if it's in a morgue. She realizes too late how angry Shannon is. Maybe it isn't anger, but helplessness, which is its own sort of rage.

"She's just a problem for you to solve," Shannon cries, unaware or uninterested in the intrigued looks from other people in the room. "And now it's *done.* Now you can go home, back to where you came from."

"You know what?" Mara says without raising her voice. "You don't have any idea how I feel about Mom. You weren't there, and you're not me." Her face is hot. "If you don't want my help, say so. I'm not trying to prove something."

Shannon stands up, looking for an escape route.

"Where are you going?"

"Who cares? You don't need me." Shannon stalks out, chin tucked into her chest. Mara follows.

"Hey. *Hey.*"

Shannon's pace slows, but she doesn't turn around. Mara catches up to her, touches her shoulder. Shannon jerks her body around. *"What?"* The woman at the front desk watches them. A man pushing a cart of flowers pauses, eyes them from the elevator.

"You can't just disappear every time you get mad," Mara says, her voice low.

"I'm not *disappearing.* It's a free country."

"We have a decision to make."

"Make it yourself."

"I don't want to. It's important." Mara can't read Shannon's face, but her eyes are shiny. "You want a burial, we'll do a burial. You're right, my dad can help cover it. Maybe he'll take care of all of it."

"It doesn't matter. Seriously. Do what you want." Shannon turns around and marches through the automatic glass doors.

"Oh, for fuck's sake." Mara glances at the woman at the desk, and the woman looks away. She jogs through the doors and catches up with Shannon, planting herself in her path.

"Excuse me," Shannon says.

"Stop it."

"Excuse me." Shannon tries to walk past Mara, but Mara stays in her way, inching sideways like a crab.

"Where are you going?" Mara asks.

"None of your business."

"Nothing around here is open late. Except bars."

"*None of your business.*" Shannon's hostility is transparent, pitiable, like a kid starting to rebel against her parents.

"If you go to a bar, how are you getting home?"

"I'm not going to a *bar*."

Mara sighs. "Wherever you're going. How are you getting home? Are you coming home?"

"What are you, my chaperone?"

"What are *you,* coming and going mysteriously while *critical events* are unfolding in your *family?* Who does that?"

Shannon stares at the ground.

"I said I'd take care of things, but I need your input, your help," Mara says.

"To do what?"

Mara gathers her hair on top of her head. "We can start with what to do about our mother's body in this hospital."

Shannon takes a deep breath, looks Mara in the eye, and waits. Mara feels her pulse slow to its normal rate. After a long moment, Shannon speaks. "I don't like you," she says.

This is not what Mara expected to hear.

"I don't know you," Shannon says. "We're not family. Mom's gone. I don't need to throw her a funeral, I don't care. Her friends don't care. You're gonna go back east, your dad's gonna live his life and keep his money, and I'll figure it out. I don't want an audience."

It's the longest, most articulate, most coherent statement Shannon has made to Mara, possibly ever.

"Bullshit," Mara says.

Shannon rolls her eyes. "Fuck off," she mutters, and steps around Mara to continue toward the street.

"No way," Mara says, following her. She puts her hand on Shannon's elbow.

"Do not! Touch me!" Shannon yells, shaking her off.

"I'm not *asking* that much! We *are* family, that's *our* mother, and *we* need to deal with it! You and me! She isn't some kind of Jane Doe. Let's be dignified here."

Shannon rolls her eyes again. She might be trying not to cry, Mara can't tell. "I'm going to a bar," Shannon announces. Mara watches her stuff her hands in her pockets and trudge to the street. She doesn't look back.

"Fuck you, too," Mara whispers to herself.

Her mother is dead. Like, actually dead. Mara wishes it would sink in, she keeps repeating the sentence to herself. Should she be sad? *Is* she sad? The image of herself sobbing messily in the rental— what was that?

She wasn't crying for Linda then, anyway.

Are these people waiting for dead relatives, too, or is it a catchall waiting room, everyone with his own particular medical misery? A plump middle-aged white woman in a frilly blouse dozes with a magazine overturned in her lap, her hands folded over it. A Black teenage boy in Elvis Costello glasses, wide awake, stares at his jiggling legs, eyebrow raised. An old light-skinned couple, tiny in their chairs, teary and sniffling, hold hands and murmur in Spanish.

Her phone rings. *Dad,* the screen on her phone says, shimmering as she thumbs it.

"Hey, Dad," she says softly.

"I was thinking," her father says. He never begins with hello. "Your mother didn't sound too good. Did they evaluate her for dementia? I don't remember if you mentioned . . ."

This is the part where, if Mara were a normal person with feelings, she'd begin to cry. She wouldn't say, *She's dead;* she'd say, *She's gone.* Or just burble *Dad,* and her voice would catch.

"Mar?"

"Yup." She feels the ice melting in his highball, the stacks of paper on his desk neatened after an evening of work. She can see him penciling an answer in the crossword, torn from the *Globe* and folded back to the size of a napkin. "How did you meet Mom?" she hears herself ask. Her father chuckles.

"I kept running into her on campus, she was everywhere. Turns out she wasn't even a law student."

"She said you met at a party."

"Maybe. It took me a while to understand she liked me. I'd never—" He pauses. "I didn't know anything about women."

She wonders how long it took before he realized his mistake.

"She was different then," her father adds.

"How so?"

"I thought she was brilliant." He sighs.

"Was she?"

"She's *very* smart. But alcohol changes you."

Mara can't imagine describing her mother as *very smart*. And with Linda, it wasn't just the booze—it was everything. To say she was a drunk didn't begin to describe her. "She drank when you met?" Mara asks.

"Not like she did later. It was social."

"What about her family?"

"I met them once. I don't remember if they were drinkers."

"What were they like?"

"Strange." He pauses for a second. "I don't know—*I* was strange. I was awkward, I wasn't used to being tall yet, I'd grown up in the sticks with old parents, I didn't have any money. They didn't, either." Mara's father doesn't string clauses together like this until he's had his evening Scotch; perhaps, tonight, he's having seconds. "Linda's family . . . I would say they were gloomy. She didn't get along with them. I never figured it out."

172

"What were their names?" Mara digs in her purse for a pen.

"Oh, goodness." He is probably scratching the side of his face, pulling on his ear. "It was almost forty years ago."

"What was her maiden name?"

"Taggart. Her brother was Tommy." He pauses, thinking. "If I remember the others, I'll tell you."

"What kind of house did they live in?"

"This was her grandparents' house. They were incredibly old, in their nineties, if I recall, and they still lived there on their own. Her parents didn't like each other. They were a tense family. And they all lived on the same block."

"In Tustin?"

"Yes."

"Did they come to the wedding?"

"We didn't have a wedding."

Mara finds this astounding. But there are no wedding pictures on Linda's wall of photographs of herself. "Why not?" Mara asks.

"I don't know. I said we didn't need anything fancy, but she insisted, no wedding. Of course, I was happy to elope. She probably didn't want to involve her family."

Mara keeps hoping she'll dissolve into tears, but it doesn't happen. "She died," Mara tells him quickly. "I'm at the hospital."

"What?" her father sputters. She can hear the ice cube in his mouth.

"She was lying on the sofa, and I checked on her, and she was— that was it. Probably another heart attack. They're finishing the autopsy."

"Oh, my goodness," he says quietly. "Mar, I'm sorry."

"It's okay," she tells him, but it feels like a bizarre thing to say. She supposes it's true.

"I can come out there and help. I'll be there in two days. Let me have a look at the calendar . . ."

"I got it, Dad. It's not that much. If I have a question, I'll call you. My boss let me take the rest of the year off, so."

"Do you need money?"

"No." Maybe.

"I'll help with the—burial, or whatever you decide."

"Okay. Thanks." Her phone peeps: the battery is dying. "Um, what's happening with the, uh . . . Mom's rent?"

"I suppose I'm off the hook now," he says ruefully.

"Shannon still lives there."

"Oh," he says, startled. "Really? You know, Linda said something about . . . I must have chalked it up to dementia, that she was living in the past. How old is Shannon? What does she do?"

"She's twenty-seven. Oh, Dad." Now, strangely, Mara feels she could cry. She won't, but she could. "She worked at Rite Aid for ten years and quit; she had some kind of yelling match with her boss. She's broke. She's a pothead. She has no skills. She's depressed." Mara sees her father tipping the glass in his palm, watching the whisky slide over the ice shards. "I want to help her," she says.

"Well," her father says. He hasn't thought about Shannon, not in years. Mara's phone peeps again. It's shutting down.

"Dad—" The screen goes black. Her charger is on the kitchen table in the apartment.

Someone wakes Mara by squeezing her shoulder.

"Ms. Meade?" a man says. Mara blinks in confusion. "Ms. Meade, they're ready for you. Have you called a mortuary?" Mara stares at the man. She scans the room. A wall clock suggests it's 2:30 in the morning, but this seems impossible.

"Are they open?" she mumbles, searching for the pink flyer. The man plucks it from the floor and hands it to her.

"They answer the phones twenty-four seven." He lowers his voice. "Would you like to see your mother?"

"Um," she stammers. "Is my sister here?"

"What does your sister look like?"

Mara scans the room again.

"Maybe she stepped out," he suggests. "We'll keep your mother here for seventy-two hours. When you make arrangements, they'll come and pick her up. Okay?" He hands her a folder full of forms. "You don't have to sign these yet, but the funeral home is going to want them." He steps back and folds his hands. "I'm sorry for your loss." He's like someone from *Saturday Night Live*. Mara opens the folder and hopes he goes away.

At this hour, the forms are incomprehensible. She might not be awake enough to drive. With a sad thrill, she spies a row of coffee urns along one wall, Styrofoam cups in tall stacks on a table under a coffee-stained tablecloth. She wades across the room and serves herself. The coffee burns her mouth but startles her awake, sort of.

On her way back to her seat, she sees Shannon, her sister's walk unmistakable, arms folded across her chest. She beelines for the chair she'd occupied hours before, as though she'd never left. She doesn't look around, just sinks into the chair and waits to be found. How does she know Mara is still here? Mara hangs back and watches her, gingerly sips the scalding liquid in her cup.

Shannon places her chin in her hand. She stares at her knee, her foot, the floor—anything that doesn't require lifting her eyes. Her self-pity is profound. She doesn't seem drunk, but Mara can't tell from here. It probably takes a lot for her sister to get drunk.

Imagine being raised by Linda, only Linda, who was drawn to beauty like a moth to a bare bulb. She probably decided early on that Shannon wasn't what she'd hoped for. It didn't occur to her that Shannon's character, her self-esteem, her autonomy in the world, were Linda's responsibility, that you have to teach those things to your child.

Allison was what she'd hoped for. You only hit the jackpot once.

At Amherst Friends, troublesome kids are malleable, redeemable—whether they're five or twelve, you give them structure and boundaries and teach them to get with the program of coexisting with everyone else. No one lets a tantrum-prone fourth grader go on being a miserable lout—they help him become a citizen of the community. If they don't, the child's wealthy, assertive parents will intervene or transfer him somewhere else, taking his tuition with him.

Those precious, expensive children.

Can you teach a woman who is almost thirty to get with the program of living in society? Did anyone ever see Shannon as precious? Their mother must have, on some level, at some point. She wasn't a psychopath.

If Shannon keeps drifting, she'll end up homeless, deranged, worse. She's young enough to still seem like a kid, more innocent than willful, but the window is closing. Soon, she'll seem like a lost cause.

She hates Mara, though. Wouldn't you?

Mara blows on her coffee. She sits in one of the chairs, obscuring herself behind a potted plant. She can see Shannon through a break in the foliage.

Mara, so arrogant.

Shannon settles back into her seat, stretches her legs out in front of her, and closes her eyes.

They'll bury Linda. Why not? Mara wants to see these supposed friends. Shannon's right, Linda would want a beautiful corpse, not that you should get what you want when you're dead, but maybe it's the nice thing to do. Her father is having a moment: she'll persuade him to pay for it, she'll talk him into helping her transform Shannon's life. She finishes her coffee and tosses the cup into a trashcan. Closer up, she sees that her sister hasn't dropped off, her face is too tense.

"Hey," she says, sitting down next to her. Shannon says nothing, doesn't open her eyes. "You're right," Mara says. "We'll do a burial, we'll have a service."

"Whatever," Shannon says.

"I'm going to call them," Mara says, scanning the sheet. She selects a number at the center of the page and walks to the front desk to use the phone.

When sleep finally finds Mara, she doesn't care that she's on the lumpy sofa where her mother breathed her last breath, that she's wrapped in an old set of sheets redolent of the mildewy linen closet, her nose inches from Linda's ashtray. She sleeps and sleeps. When she finally wakes the next morning and her phone says it's after ten, she is appalled. She flings the dark curtains back to let in the grey, oceany light.

She can't find anything to make coffee with, not that it matters, because she forgot yesterday to get beans. She changes in the bathroom and knocks softly on Shannon's door.

"Shannon?" No answer. "I'm going to get coffee, do you want anything?" Silence. Maybe Shannon is one of those people who sleeps until the afternoon.

At Java Jazmin's, a thatch-roofed hut with a drive-through window off Obsidian, Mara finds a little table inside and sips her Americano, which is bitter and hot. On her phone, she searches local apartment rentals—studios, roommates. There is one studio apartment in Silver Beach under $1,000: $988, to be exact. Mara expands the geography of her search. Near San Diego State, roommates advertise living rooms as bedrooms for $400 or offer to split their own bedrooms for $375. Rooms near Tijuana go for $250. There are pricey weekly rentals by the beach, and an SRO called the Friendship Hotel in Hillcrest. She does the math on Shannon's (former) job at Rite Aid. If, because of longevity, her sister made more than minimum wage—let's be generous and say she earned $14 an hour—and she worked forty hours a week, which is unlikely—she'd make around $2,200 a month, before taxes. It might be enough for a share, somewhere. She can't imagine who would choose Shannon for a roommate, but there are probably sloppy, pot-smoking guys who would be happy to take Shannon's money every month, as long as she paid on time. Then there's the phone bill, gas, food, clothes, car repairs—and for Shannon, pot. She'd need a better job, and a budget.

It won't work.

But Mara already knew that.

The apartment is too dense, too depressive, to make breakfast in. Mara knocks on Shannon's door again and is startled when Shannon opens it, dressed, hair combed and pulled into a pony-tail.

"Denny's?" Shannon asks, reading Mara's mind.

The waitress gives them a window booth. Mara cups her hands around her coffee, chilly in the cavernous, air-conditioned restaurant. Shannon empties two creamers into her coffee, stirring it with her finger.

"Mom used to come here. With her friends."

"Tell me about them."

"They're, um." Shannon fiddles with her stack of ripped-open sugars. "Drag queens?"

"Mom was friends with drag queens?"

Shannon shrugs.

"Where did she find drag queens in Silver Beach?" How lovely, how perfect, Linda with the drag queens, Linda who was such a drag queen.

"There's a drag show at this bar on Obsidian. She used to take me to it."

"Really," Mara marvels.

"We should tell him."

"Him?"

"It's really just one who's her main friend. Garbo. We need to tell Garbo." Shannon's eyes are shiny for a second.

"We should." Mara is dying to meet them now. She wonders if Shannon knows Mara is basically gay. Probably not. Sitting across a table at Denny's from one another is less excruciating than their phone calls. There's a window to look out of, something to drink, little objects to occupy the hands. They can be silent.

"Usually the food comes faster," Shannon says, gazing at the napkin dispenser.

"I don't mind," Mara says.

She doesn't want it to be true that Shannon doesn't like her. She doesn't blame her. Still. What would it be like to have a sister again?

"Do you want to know something crazy?" Mara asks. Shannon glances at her, returns to her study of the napkin dispenser. Does it take work to cleanse the emotion from your face? Or is this how Shannon interacts with the world generally? It's not like anyone taught her how to be gracious.

"What?" Shannon finally asks.

"My girlfriend didn't know about Allison. I've known this woman since college. She swears I never mentioned it."

Mara watches the gears shifting in Shannon's consciousness, the rearranging of the narrative. Their food comes. The waitress sets each plate down, then switches them.

"Can I get you anything else?"

"No, thank you," Mara says.

"You've had a girlfriend since college?" Shannon finally says.

"We got together a year and a half ago. We were good friends before that." She hates the phrase "best friends." She doesn't have best friends.

Shannon forks a bite of omelet. She holds her utensils effortlessly in the European style, fork in the left hand, knife in the right. Linda taught her something.

"She's mad at me," Mara says.

"Why?"

"Because I don't share myself with her," Mara says, surprising herself.

Shannon sets her knife and fork down. "Why not?"

"Because I'm depressed and want to be a hermit for the rest of my life." Mara smiles strangely, her cheeks warm. She takes a sip of coffee. "But maybe I just need to get it together. Whatever that means."

Sunlight penetrates the marine layer, and it plunges diagonally through the big windows along the booths, bathing her sister in gold. She ate here with her parents and Allison, Mara suddenly remembers. The girls on one side, mother and father on the other. She and Allison would get up and inspect the pie case, and the waitress would yell at them for pressing their noses against it. She dips a forkful of hash browns into ketchup.

Across from her, Shannon is fascinated by her omelet. Minutes pass. This is why you don't say what you mean.

"How did you become a librarian?" Shannon asks.

"I went to school for it," Mara answers.

"But how did you decide that's what you wanted to do? Did you always want to do that?"

Mara gathers a bite of potatoes and runny egg, considers it. "I majored in art history," she says.

"Are you an artist?"

"No."

Nell is perpetually astonished at how slowly Mara finishes food. She eats plenty, she just takes three times longer than anyone else at the table. She sits back in the booth, thinking.

"I liked sitting in the dark looking at slides of old paintings." She lifts her fork, sets it down again. "I had to spend a lot of time in the library. I always loved libraries." It seems obvious, but she never connected it before. "Now I get to work in one."

"So, what, you sit behind one of those counters, and check people's books out? The kids, you check their books out?"

"The person who does that at a branch library is usually an hourly employee. They don't need a degree in library science."

"Library *science?*"

Mara nods. "It's complex. You're organizing information, and there's *infinite* information. And in the last ten, twenty years, with the Internet . . . library science is kind of exciting. It keeps changing, I have to keep up with it."

"So you don't check the books out."

"Actually, I do, because I work at a school. My job is a lot like teaching—I have the different grades for an hour at a time, and I'm reading to them, and we talk about books, and they get to check out something new every week. But I also, like, manage the collection. And organize events. And a bunch of other stuff." She's been advocating for years for Friends to hire another librarian, to no avail. Sue just keeps adding to Mara's job instead.

The waitress refills their coffee. Shannon's empty plate is whisked away.

"Picking a career has a lot to do with how you want to spend your days," Mara says. "I have freedom at my job—the main people I have to deal with every day are children, which I like. I'm sort of insulated from having to deal with the rest of the staff. I get to hole up in the library, which is its own little building." Mara takes a bite of cooled egg. She's talking too much. "What sort of place do you see yourself working in?"

Shannon gives no indication of having heard the question. She sips her coffee and stares out the window in the direction of the old transit depot, a disgusting hull of a building covered in bird poop.

"I want to work in an office," she finally says.

Who actually wants to work in an office? Haven't *Dilbert* and *Office Space* and *The Office* captured everyone's feelings about working in offices, which are generally suicidal?

"I want to wear a skirt and a blouse and work in an office with my own desk," Shannon says.

"Doing what?"

"I don't know."

"What are you . . . interested in?"

Shannon sets her coffee down and rearranges the stack of spent sugar packets. "I don't know."

"Do you like working with other people?"

"If they're not, like, assholes."

Mara nods. There will be assholes. "Do you want the sort of job that requires a degree?"

"What's IT?" Shannon asks.

"Information technology. Computer systems. Tech support. It's a growing field," Mara says approvingly. "It pays well." And it's probably full of potheads, she thinks. "Are you good with computers?" Where on earth would her sister have gotten good with computers? Talking to Shannon is like talking to someone out of a time machine.

"Sure," Shannon says vaguely.

"The trick with IT," Mara says, "is finding a program that's affordable and actually leads to a job. There are lot of scam schools with slick advertising, and they're really expensive but not very good. Basically, if you see it advertised everywhere, stay away from it."

Shannon looks glum. "What should I do?"

"Do you want a career in IT?"

Shannon shrugs.

"Start with community college. Take the required courses. See what you like. After a year, you can decide whether you want to go the IT route, or something else. You'll meet people in a bunch of different fields, see what's out there." Mara's heart fills.

Shannon's eyes are far away. She disappears from the conversation.

"Why not?" Mara says.

"I can't do all that," Shannon says. "I'll be back," she says, getting up out of the booth.

"'You can't do all that' why?" Mara asks.

Shannon hovers, half-standing up. "I'm broke," she tells the table, "and I suck at school." She turns and makes her way to the bathroom, quick little steps.

Chapter Thirteen

"Are you really depressed?" Shannon asks when she comes back. Mara drags a piece of toast through a congealed egg puddle. She taps pepper onto it and takes a year to chew and swallow. Then she takes a slow sip of coffee.

"Yes," she finally says. "I guess."

"Like. How do you know?"

"I've never seen anyone for it. I probably should."

"But why would you say you were, if you weren't sure?"

"I'm pretty sure."

Shannon could stay in the booth forever. Order all her meals here, the waitresses replaced one by one as they grow older and die. Maybe heaven is a Denny's.

Should she apply to wash dishes here? Would that ruin the pleasure? Could she eat for free?

"You should come back to Massachusetts with me," Mara says.

"What?"

Shannon's sister takes a deep breath, then another. She pushes her plate away and folds her hands, reading invisible notes, a silent conversation with herself. Lifts her eyes.

"The community college near me has rolling admissions. You can start in the fall. My father and I can pay whatever financial aid doesn't cover. You can get a job in town. I'll help you look, I'll be your reference." She pauses. "Stay with me until you find a place."

The room becomes airlessly silent, like the inside of a corked bottle. The waitresses, the people coming in through the vestibule, the dish tub slamming on the counter, soundless as clouds. The bottom falls out of Shannon's stomach, drops to the center of the earth and out the other side, picking up speed as it falls.

"What if my car dies?"

"We'll find you a car."

"I'm a shitty student. I almost failed out of high school."

"High school is really different from college. College is less annoying."

"What if I fail?"

"Why would you fail?"

"Because I'm stupid?"

"Do you *want* to go?" Mara asks.

"Where?"

"To college."

"Maybe?"

"Look. I don't know who's going to pay you more than minimum wage without some kind of degree, even a two-year degree. If you want to answer phones as a receptionist in an office, you need *something*."

"I know."

"And you're not *stupid*."

Shannon wants to hear this over and over and over.

"Are you afraid?" Mara asks.

Shannon makes a nest out of her forearms and sets her head down. Mara taps her.

"I don't want your money," Shannon mumbles.

"I can't understand you."

Shannon lifts her head and stares at Mara's elegant, stony hands. "I can't keep taking your dad's money."

"Shannon." Mara is in teacher-mode now. She could help Shannon with her college homework, sit next to her at the kitchen table after dinner. "You're family," she says. "It's your money, too."

This is a revelation.

"What if I fuck it up," she whispers.

"Don't fuck it up."

"Don't fuck it up. Got it." Shannon puts her head back down.

"Would you go to rehab?" Mara asks. Shannon rears back.

"Why do I need to go to *rehab?*"

"You smoke *a lot* of pot," Mara says.

"So?"

"Well. If you're broke, I don't see how you're going to keep paying for it. I don't know how you paid for it before."

"I had a friend . . ." Shannon trails off.

"If you stay with me, you can't smoke. I'm sorry. You can drink—within reason—but you can't smoke."

"Lots of people smoke weed. Doctors and lawyers smoke weed."

"I'm just saying. This is a weed-free offer."

"I don't need to go to rehab."

"Okay."

"Would your dad pay for rehab?"

"Maybe."

Shannon rips a packet of sugar open and pours it into her half-empty coffee mug. She plucks another one and repeats. The sugar rises above the coffee in a dissolving mound.

"You don't have to give me an answer right away. You can think about it," Mara says.

• • •

On their way out, the pie case is fogged. Shannon used to stand and stare at it when she was little. They must have come here when she was a kid, but the memory isn't connected to anything.

Did Linda cook when Shannon was growing up? They ate somehow.

She wants to take Mara around Silver Beach, like show-and-tell, but keeps the thought to herself.

"I'm gonna take a walk," she says when they reach Mara's rental.

"How long do you think you'll be?"

"An hour. Give or take."

Mara, sunglassed, shrugs and climbs into the car. Shannon steps back and watches her drive off, the car followed by its own shadow. The morning grey is gone. She is a helpless specimen under the high sun, no sunglasses, no hat, no sunscreen. She often makes this mistake and has the peeling, pink shoulders to prove it.

Linda's liquor store is down the street from Denny's, a building from the sixties, the gravel-topped roof low on one end and high in front with huge windows. An island in its own parking lot, two palm trees arching over the entrance. It used to be Linda's first stop on her daily rounds, but lately she sent Shannon, with strict instructions.

The door beeps as Shannon steps through. The man behind the counter is the same; he could be Dan from the sign on the roof, but probably not, because the store seems older than time, definitely older than him. He's tall, blue-eyed, with long legs and arms; he looks like he still surfs in the mornings, his hair a beachy mess, grey-brown with silver streaks. He studies Shannon over his chained reading glasses.

"Hey, sweetie."

Shannon lifts her chin in greeting, stuffs her hands in her pockets. She turns down the rum aisle and knows he is pulling Linda's 200 ml. Fleischmann's from the wall, setting it on top of a little paper sack. The store smells like cardboard and tobacco.

She passes a huge display for T.G.I. Friday's Mud Slides. When they got along, Shannon would bring home a jug of it, and she and Linda would spike it with vodka and watch *Wheel of Fortune*.

Expensive bottles on top, cheap stuff on the bottom with the dust. Rum, then cognac, then whiskey, bourbon, Scotch. Icy six-packs hum in the refrigerated cases along the wall. She and Brandy used to take hours, days, setting up an evening's partying—the right substances and paraphernalia, the right people, the right setting. Being friends with Brandy was like having a rich boyfriend: she could turn to you and say, "Why not?"

If Brandy walked in right now, Shannon could say, "Thank you. You were good to me." Or, "I can't believe we lasted that long." Or, "My mother's dead, and I don't know how I feel."

At the counter, she pays for her mother's vodka with a $5 bill. The man slides the bottle toward her, the paper sack, the change. She hesitates; he breathes in her pause. She turns and lets her feet carry her out the door, the door dinging on the way out.

Shannon despises Silver Beach afternoons. Everyone else at the boardwalk seems fine with them: the tall herd of sunburned Germans brushing sand from their feet, deciding where to have dinner; the rollerblading man in short shorts and headphones, hips shimmying; the lifeguards scanning the water in wraparound shades, stoic and superior.

She asks a vendor for a cup of ice. He squints at her in the shade of his umbrella, leans down, and scoops a waxy red cup through his cooler. In the restroom, Shannon locks herself in a damp, sandy stall. Next door, a woman pleads with her daughter to pee, and the little girl starts to sing. Shannon unscrews the cap on her mother's vodka and pours it over the ice. She delicately sets the bottle behind the toilet and flushes. The first sip is already icy.

Outside in the knifing glare, she shakes the ice and scans the boardwalk for her mother's friend. He'll be disappointed she didn't make it to New York. But not surprised.

The boardwalk regulars grow older in the sun, year after year. Their worry lines deepen; their eyes develop a metallic sheen. The gloomy, tuneless girl with her guitar—she might be Shannon's age, or older, singing into her open instrument case. The man with the long beard and a parrot on his elbow—Brandy and Shannon called him Father Time—walking up and down the boardwalk's length, talking to himself. The rollerblading guy, who seems happy, but he's always here, as though some god has sentenced him to this task for eternity.

Shannon finishes the vodka quicker than she means to. It barely touches her.

Garbo isn't anywhere along the boardwalk. He isn't at Denny's. Golden's isn't open yet, and she's never seen him hanging out in front when he isn't working. She doesn't know where his apartment is, just that it's in Silver Beach.

She walks as far as the jetty beach, pays respects to her dead sister, sucks on her ice, and watches the waves, which don't stop.

Chapter Fourteen

The first week, Mara did the living room. The piles, which probably took years to form their topography, eroded as she filled garbage bags with paper for the recyclers, trash for the dump, and donations for Goodwill. Shannon didn't say what her plan was, but she made it clear she did not intend to keep living in the apartment and stayed in her room while Mara worked. Layers of dust filmed Mara's hands and arms and hair, and a gummy, ashy substance clung to her fingernails.

No smells or sounds came from Shannon's room.

They ate simple meals together in not-unpleasant silence: sandwiches, fruit, glasses of water. Mara couldn't read Shannon's quiet. She figured Shannon had consented to Mara's plan to move back to Massachusetts with her, because where else would she go? But Shannon hadn't said yes. Yet.

She texted Nell about her mother and her plan to stay in California at least through June, and Nell knew her well enough not to say, or ask, much. To wait.

The second week, Mara did their mother's bedroom. She asked Shannon what, if anything, she wanted to keep, and Shannon had no answer.

Mara made the room disappear, down to the furniture, which she hired a local crew to cart away. She poured the vodka down the kitchen drain, and when she put the bottles together in one bag, they made a clamor vastly out of proportion to their size. The only thing she set aside were the photographs, which went up to the eighties and stopped. She took them out of their frames, bundled them with rubber bands, and mailed them to a company that scanned old pictures and returned them to you in a USB drive. In the empty room, she made a pallet for herself with clean blankets.

In the afternoons, when she returned from wherever she had taken the latest round of garbage bags, she noticed how Shannon remained in her bedroom. Mara couldn't find evidence her sister had gone anywhere. Sometimes, she stood and listened; once, she pressed her ear to the door. Nothing but the subtle movements of a person inhabiting a room.

From sundown until late at night, Mara cleaned: kitchen, bathroom, walls, floors, windows. The insides of cupboards and drawers; edges, baseboards, corners, crevices. She went through packages of sponges, reams of paper towels. She bought a vacuum cleaner. Shannon had mentioned that the old woman next door was functionally deaf and the guy downstairs played video games all night, so she couldn't imagine she was disturbing anyone. Shannon's light was on even as Mara fell into a dead sleep.

The third week, she started the admin. She passed whole days on the phone at her laptop, typing notes into a detailed Word document. By now she was used to Shannon's three daily appearances at meal times. Her sister answered basic questions with basic answers but otherwise said nothing, or next to nothing. She didn't seem particularly drunk or high, but she didn't seem *not* those things, either.

By late June, the apartment was sunny, bare, and smelled like chemical citrus. Marks on the walls indicated where furniture or frames had been. The landlord would have to paint and replace the carpet.

The rent was paid through July. Mara had plans to call the land-lord and give notice for Shannon, but she was putting it off. Maybe Shannon just needed time.

Linda's ashes waited for them at the funeral home. After com-ing back from a long walk that first day, before initiating her bedroomed silence, Shannon had insisted cremation was fine, they didn't need a funeral. They hadn't talked about it since. They hadn't talked about anything.

The last Thursday in June was overcast and almost cool. The clicks of the oscillating fan in the living room echoed across the empty walls of the apartment, and Mara figured Shannon was asleep. She had eight or nine things to tick off her main list. She wondered if she should make more of an effort to communicate with Shannon, to see if something was up, but Shannon seemed self-contained. It was a relief.

Mara's mind wandered from her Word document. Something occurred to her. It made her sit up, finger her necklace.

It couldn't be. It was impossible, nearly impossible, had cer-tainly never in her life been possible.

She must have lost track of the days. She checked her phone.

No. Yes.

She yanked her ear, and her pulse raced.

She counted. She was five days late.

She was never late, had never been late in her menstruating life. She opened her calendar, scrolled back to the previous month, did the math, and felt herself dissolve into the kitchen chair.

It was the stress. She was approaching her mid-thirties; her cycle was changing. It was a record-keeping error. (No.)

She told herself she'd pick up a test at the drug store. Of course it would be negative. She was upset over nothing, five days was nothing. She went back to typing.

At ten o'clock, Shannon's door opened, and she came into the kitchen. She set a spiral notebook on the table next to Mara's laptop like an offering. Mara looked up and searched her sister's face.

"Hi," Shannon said. Her eyes were intent, alive with something Mara had never seen. Mara touched the corner of the notebook's cover, silently asking permission; Shannon granted it. She stood and watched Mara open it to the first page, where a title was written:

Finnicle Bade
An Adventure Comic
By: Shannon Falcon

The lettering was painstakingly small and square. What a name, Finnicle Bade: Tolkien-ish, but modern. What was an adventure comic, aside from the obvious, and what was Shannon doing drawing one? Were there other works that billed themselves as adventure comics? Weren't all, or most, comics adventures of some kind? Was this one of many comics in Shannon's body of work and, if so, where was the body of work? Mara was awash in a reader's anticipation. She turned the page.

The paper felt like vellum, thickened with hard lines in pencil and pen. A neat nine-panel grid filled the first page, each pane containing a densely shaded, complicated image and a box filled with the same tiny, squared text. Mara peered at the drawings. Finnicle Bade was an androgynous, pixie-haired superhero: harmless cubicle dweller by day, airborne warrior princess by night. Certain details were rendered beautifully: the movement in the protagonist's cape as she soared over sleepy neighborhoods; the texture, shape, and shadow of royal palms, just like the ones in Silver Beach. Other details were clumsy: hands, fingers, certain facial expressions, a skewed perspective in the office scenes—but maybe it worked, maybe it was intentional. It reminded Mara a little of Lynda Barry in its crowded, exuberant chaos, and—rather uncannily—of the voluminous drawings of a former student. Evan, the student, was on the autism spectrum, and between third and sixth grade, before he moved to another state, he produced *metric tons* of comics and murals, accompanied by careful, elaborate indices of names, places, and plot lines that explained what you were looking at. They were somehow both unpolished and precise, the style never changing in the years she knew him. She had a series of them framed in the library with archival matting.

The story of Finnicle Bade was straightforward: the protagonist was a young woman with a boring, predictable life—a more stable life than the author's—who became powerful, sexy, and heroic at night. The problems she solved were vague, but the people's gratitude was not. Finnicle Bade acted alone; she wasn't part of a crew of superheroes. Mara wanted to know the character's back story, the inciting incident that led to the double life and the superpowers, but it wasn't clear in the first ten pages. She flipped further in the notebook and gasped. Shannon had filled the entire thing. Mara ran her fingertips over the pages, feeling the strain of her sister's effort.

"This is incredible," she murmured, looking up. Shannon's face was ablaze, open. For the first time in Mara's memory, her sister was completely *there*, in the room. Mara returned to the notebook's beginning. She noticed new things, funny little details in the corners and margins, like a half-naked surfer, a centimeter high, changing out of his wetsuit.

"I draw sometimes," Shannon said from the back of her throat.

"This is incredible," Mara said again.

"You like it?"

Mara nodded.

The notebook's force pulled her back, and she read the entire thing without pause. It took over an hour, which surprised her—she hadn't noticed the minutes go by and was startled to see that Shannon was no longer standing there. When she finished, she sat back. The story itself was interesting enough but unremarkable; it rambled, dissolved in confusing tangents, and recycled the same redemptive plot thread. Her sister didn't have a great command of punctuation. But there was something about it—the stiff, textured pages, the quantity of detail in each pane, the indomitable spirit of the protagonist—that rattled with energy. Here was an artifact, a statement of aliveness. Shannon was in there, she lived, she was full of something.

Mara got up and went to her sister's room. The door was closed, but a note was taped to it: *IM ON THE BOARDWALK BY THE JETTY BEACH.*

The inside of the Albertson's on Obsidian was bright as a tanning bed, thirty times the size of the little health food store Mara went to faithfully in Northampton. She meant this to be a quick stop, but she had to navigate acres of produce, bread and bread products, snacks, pet food, a maze of frozen food cases, before locating the pharmacy in the back.

The pregnancy tests were behind the counter. She felt a teenager's shame as she requested one. The cashier, efficient, expressionless, handed her a bag and a receipt. In the car, Mara opened the package and read the directions. *Use the first urine of the day for most accurate results,* it read. She'd have to wait until morning. She dropped the test into the glove compartment.

She knew what to do. Of course it would be negative, but if it wasn't—if it wasn't—she'd go to Planned Parenthood. Obviously. She had friends who'd made the same choice, more than you would think. It was not the end of the world. Anyway, no one would know.

She didn't feel anything. She felt like herself.

She certainly didn't want to add to the number of children Rex had littered the world with.

When she got out of the car on Marina Boulevard, Mara felt strong, capable. She was in touch, for once, with the extraordinary fortune of her life. Hers was not a precarious or rocky or deprived life; she had many things and people to be grateful for. She was a pro-choice woman in a pro-choice country, and she could do what she wanted with the probably-nothing in her body. She was in love with a woman who was intelligent, funny, and brave. It was a difficult love that unfolded slowly, but it was love, she knew this. She had a job she looked forward to most days; it paid well enough. She had the resources to be generous to her sister, who needed her. This was her next step, her next chapter. She usually hated that phrase: *the next chapter of my life.* But she didn't hate it then, she even said it to herself, almost out loud.

She came to the beach entrance with the sea-lion fountain, a steep spiral of stairs that took you to the boardwalk and wound down the cliff to the sand. Strange how you reverted to your old trails when you returned to a place. She wondered if it would be painful—if she might be overcome somehow—but instead she felt warmth in her chest, an old love. A spring that had not dried up. She had had an older sister once, and she loved her. She was loved by her.

At the bottom, she took off her sandals and tied the hem of her dress at her knees. The sand was warm and dry. Her footsteps broke the crust from an earlier high tide; sharp bits of dried sea-weed pricked her toes. If you looked down the beach, you could see the moist haze that hung below the cliffs and, in the distance, the jetty.

Rip currents are common near jetties; she had looked it up. Parents brought their children to the jetty beach because there was a warm inlet along the rocky wall that drew water in and out of a small lagoon. It was perfect to play in, to build structures and dig moats around.

In the off season, there are far fewer lifeguards on duty, less than half the number employed in the summer. This stretch of beach, for example, is patrolled by a skeleton crew between October and March; response times are slower then. She'd looked this up too.

It was Allison who convinced their mother it was Saturday, that they didn't have school. Their mother was having a bad day: Shannon was feverish, vomiting. Linda took the baby to the doctor and told them not to go far. Why didn't she just take all three of them? Mara was eight, Allison nearly nine. Mara remembered suddenly: Allison had insisted. She didn't want to go along to the doctor; she wanted to play with Mara. They were old enough to go outside alone, to go to the store, to watch themselves after school if their mother wasn't home. Even if they hadn't been old enough, or if this hadn't been so common in that era, in that neighborhood, Allison was very persuasive: she could convince their mother, and most adults, of anything. You didn't feel manipulated; she glowed with authority. She made people feel like they were in on her conspiracy.

An unseasonably foggy Tuesday in October 1984. They walked to the boardwalk; they descended the sea-lion stairway to the beach. They hiked the sand that hugged the cliffs. The marine layer was dense enough that they couldn't see the jetty until they were right there. The windows of the lifeguard tower were shuttered. The air was warm-cool.

Mara plopped down and began building a sand castle, one that would upstage the castle Allison had made late in the summer. She'd just learned how to make "witch castles," squeezing wet sand through her fingers to make surreal, drippy towers.

197

Allison went into the water.

They could swim. They'd taken lessons, they were both a level ahead of their age group at the Y.

A rip current can take you so quickly you don't notice; suddenly, you're further out than you want to be, and you imagine the solution is simply to swim back. The solution—another thing Mara had looked up—is to swim parallel to the shore to get out of the current's path. Your instinct is to swim back to shore in a straight line, the way you came, but the current is too strong. You exhaust yourself.

Sometime later—long enough to finish her castle—Mara looked up. She saw a pink dot near the end of the jetty.

Everything is crystal-clear up to this point, and then it gets patchy. An older woman, an ambulance, men running into the water with rescue tubes and a stretcher, their tanned, hairy legs, her mother trudging across the sand with the baby on her hip, Allison buried under an oxygen mask and a blanket, the empty beach after everyone had gone. Then it was just the three of them.

When you're the one who survives, it's your fault the other one didn't. That is the logic of things like this. It was so clear, so apparent and distinct, that Mara took it as truth and has carried it with her ever since: it was her fault. If it wasn't *quite technically* her fault that Allison drowned—she could see this might be true, even if she couldn't feel it—it was her fault for not drowning instead. If one of them had to drown, obviously it should have been Mara. It was a misalignment of universal forces, a mistake.

Perhaps this wasn't the only way to read what had happened.

Mara would never have gone in the water past where her feet could touch the ground, without a lifeguard there; Allison would absolutely have done such a thing, and did, all the time. It wouldn't have occurred to Mara to talk Allison out of it; Allison was wiser in all things.

But deference wasn't Mara's mistake. Her mistake was not dying. Somehow, Mara not dying meant Allison had to die.

The rest of Mara's beliefs about the way the world worked were fact-based, rational, sensical. She wasn't superstitious. She didn't believe in fate or karma or reincarnation. She lived in one of the most New Agey precincts outside the state of California, where people made a living doing "energy work" and selling herbal tinctures, but she, Mara, did not go in for any of that.

So why did she think she killed her sister?

If there hadn't been a rip current—if Allison had stayed on shore, or in the shallows, where the waves broke—if they'd gone instead to the park, to the playground, or to school, where they belonged—if Shannon hadn't been sick—if their mother had been less harried, less desperate, less everything she was—if Allison had been a less manipulative child.

Mara stopped where the cliff tapered and dug her toes in the sand. The beach was full of tourists and families with young children. Two lifeguards in red swimsuits were on the deck of the lifeguard tower, their feet on the railing. Next to them, a bronzed young man in red trunks and mirrored wraparound sunglasses hunched over a foam rescue tube. He sat up and blew the whistle, gesturing at someone in the water to get herself back between the flags.

Mara could see the boardwalk from here. Shannon was leaning against the railing, shielding her face from the sun. Just like she'd said.

If Shannon saw her, she didn't indicate it. Abruptly, Shannon turned her head; someone had called her name. Mara watched her turn toward the voice and assume a posture of shame as a young woman approached her. The young woman was beautiful in a *Seventeen* sort of way, Audrey Hepburn in a Noxzema ad. She looked like she'd have similarly lithe, beautiful friends; Mara felt the prickly potential for cruelty from her. The young woman and Shannon were talking. They stayed a peculiar distance apart; they didn't seem quite like friends. The young woman became more expressive: surprised, aghast. Sympathetic. Remote, then pained. Shannon remained in her hunched pose, head down, her back to Mara.

To Mara's surprise, they hugged, briefly. The young woman said something more and walked away, down the boardwalk. She put in a pair of earbuds, pulled out her phone, and disappeared into the crowd. Shannon watched after her; then she turned and resumed her post, hand to forehead, shielding her eyes from the sun.

Did Shannon think Mara had killed their sister?

In twenty-six years, Mara had never put words to these thoughts. The feelings surrounding that day, those months, everything before her first plane ride to Logan and the life that followed, had been dark, dense, unreadable. The terror that woke her up most nights in her elementary years. A wordless force that couldn't be reckoned with.

Maybe it was a cluster of bad decisions and coincidences, none of them Mara's fault.

Shannon saw her and waved. Mara waved.

They didn't say much as they walked back to Mara's car. Mara didn't ask about the young woman, or the adventure comic. It was a companionable silence they shared. It reminded Mara, almost, of the afternoons that passed between her and her father.

The next morning, a Friday, Mara woke up before dawn, her bladder full, her nerves pointy. She turned the light on in the bathroom and reread the directions. There were five tests in the box, and she opened one, set it on the edge of the sink, and read the directions a third time, her pulse battering her chest and forehead. She reached down and placed the stick in her urine stream as directed and set it again on the edge of the sink. The digital display had a crude hour glass that turned itself over and over as she waited. She watched it for a half-minute. Blinked.

Pregnant.

The word floated into the room, spinning like a mobile. It was just a word, nothing to do with her, Mara, this body, this life, this hour. It meant nothing. It meant everything. A bubbly dread deep in her stomach, a stark regret like thorns across her lower back.

She didn't do foolish things. She had done the most foolish possible thing.

Pregnant, a hideous word. She looked again at the display, which said something else: *2–3 weeks.* The test came with a "weeks predictor," which told you how far the pregnancy had progressed. She imagined a poppy seed growing into a monstrous beanstalk that burst through the top of her head. Her whole life would crack.

Abortions hurt for a day or two. You bled some; this is what her friends said. None of them regretted it. "The biggest relief of my life," one of them told her. "I wanted to dance in the streets."

She took some toilet paper and wiped the test clean. She pulled her sweatpants up and stood. She closed the lid, flushed, and sat back down. She stared at the display, the word, the numbers.

Someone knocked lightly. "Mara?" Shannon said.

"Yeah! Just a minute!" Mara leapt to open the door.

"Sorry," Shannon said. They stared at each other. "Can I—?"

"Yeah, no, of course," Mara babbled, and went to the kitchen, the only room that still contained chairs. It was dead quiet outside, the purple dark blurred by the streetlamp. "Do you have a coffee-maker?" Mara heard herself call, knowing full well they didn't. It was too early to go get coffee.

"What?" Shannon yelled from the bathroom.

"Do you have a coffeemaker?"

"Hold on." The toilet flushed. Shannon came into the kitchen with a strange look on her face. "There's like a filter thing up here,"

Shannon said, brushing past, jumping up to reach a cabinet over the stove. She pinched a plastic cone and a box of paper filters and presented them to Mara. Mara had seen them as she cleaned, but it hadn't registered as being coffee-related for some reason, after years of Moka pot espresso. All those trips to Java Jazmin's had been a waste of money.

Mara nodded. "Thanks."

Shannon seated herself and put her chin in her hand. Mara set the water to boil in a saucepan.

There'd be a Planned Parenthood nearby, probably right in Silver Beach. It wasn't like they were in Alabama. It wasn't like she couldn't afford the procedure. It would probably be some nondescript building, an office among offices. Mara watched the water, willing it to simmer.

"Um. What's that thing in the bathroom?" Shannon asked.

"Huh?" Mara said vaguely. She'd never watched the water on a stove so hard in her life.

"I thought . . ." Shannon trailed off.

"Sorry," Mara said, deeply, horribly regretting leaving it behind. "I'll throw it out."

"But—are you, like—"

The water came to a boil. "Where's your grinder?" she asked Shannon suddenly, opening cupboards, knowing it was futile.

"We don't have one."

Mara's shoulders sagged. Why didn't she grind the beans at the store? She turned the burner off and watched the bubbles die.

She turned to Shannon. "My offer still stands. Come to Massachusetts."

Shannon stared at Mara. "I don't get it."

"What do you mean?"

"Are you—"

"It's fine," Mara told her. "I'm going to take care of it."

"You're pregnant?" Shannon whispered. "With a baby?"

"It's not a *baby*."

"But I thought—don't you have a—"

"It's none of your business," Mara said, regretting her tone, regretting the words. It was not how she wanted to talk to her sister. "I did something stupid. I'm going to take care of it."

Shannon couldn't stop staring at Mara, who wondered how bad the coffee in the burnt carafe at the gas station minimart could be at this hour. She hunted for her shoes. Surely, you might find yourself in a store in your pajamas late at night in Silver Beach, and no one would call you crazy.

"What are you doing?" Shannon asked.

"Getting coffee. Come with me."

Shannon found her flip-flops and followed. It still surprised Mara how damp and chilly it could be at night in California, even in June, especially in June. The earliest birds were awake, but otherwise it was so quiet you could hear the ocean.

"Who was that girl you were talking to yesterday?" she asked Shannon.

"What girl?"

"Up on the boardwalk. When I was on the beach."

Shannon swallowed the quiet between them and stuck her hands in her pockets. "Just some girl," she finally said. "We used to be friends."

"Is that why you don't want to come back east? You don't want to leave your friends?"

"I don't really have friends. That was my friend, but I fucked it up."

What a strange pair they must have been.

"I didn't say I didn't want to come," Shannon said softly.

"Do you?" Mara tried not to let her eagerness show. Shannon was like a moody, standoffish cat; you didn't want to spook her.

Responding to questions with silence was apparently a family trait: Mara was starting to understand what Nell went through. Shannon let the question hang until it faded. At the gas station, speakers mounted high in the rafters played a song from the eighties that Mara could have gone the rest of her life without hearing again. Inside, the minimart smelled like stale coffee and churros. A nonplussed night-shifter in a red uniform eyed them from her stool.

If she was pregnant, should she switch to decaf?

She wasn't pregnant. She wasn't *staying* pregnant.

A friend told her 20 percent of pregnancies ended in miscarriage, and this was probably a low estimate, because so many women miscarried before realizing they were pregnant in the first place. Mara would just finish off the remaining percentage points. Who needed another human? She'd never questioned her beliefs about abortion access; she never, ever pictured herself raising a child. Pregnancy itself repulsed her, a feeling she kept private, especially as more of her friends started having children. If she and Nell wanted kids—which they didn't, Mara was fairly sure— Nell would be the gestator. Not Mara.

She filled a tall foam cup with three-hundred-degree coffee, black. She looked over her shoulder. "Are you having?" she asked Shannon. Her sister held up a stick of beef jerky, eyes hopeful.

Mara paid for the coffee and the jerky and a canister of Tic Tacs, and they walked into the chilly predawn as they sky began to fade. Mara burnt her tongue and went over her list in her head. Plane ticket. Tickets? There was still so much to do.

"You don't want kids?" Shannon asked, swallowing.

Mara's answer was swift. "No."

"Are you sure?"

"Why wouldn't I be sure?"

"What about your girlfriend?"

Mara didn't answer.

"What's her name?" Shannon asked. They rounded the corner of Diamond Street and slowed.

"Nell," Mara said.

"Nell doesn't want kids?"

"She might." She had to admit this was true, and the truth of it intensified the taste of the minimart coffee. "Nell could totally have kids."

"Are you guys, like . . . like *life partners,* or . . ."

"She'd probably marry me." As Mara said this, she was suddenly unsure whether it was true. Kids, yes. Mara? For life? "She is going to be so *fucking* angry with me," Mara said. "I am such an idiot."

"Guys sleep around and it never matters. Even when something happens, they can just walk away. It's not fair."

"I could have told him to use a *condom*. It's not like I don't know how this works." Mara shivered. "Ugh. It's so gross."

"It happens," Shannon said simply. She seemed unfazed, uninterested, even, in the scandal of Mara's random affair with a man.

"Not to me."

"What if Nell wants to raise a kid with you?"

It was a good question. A question she'd never ask, because Nell would never know, because Mara would take care of this immediately. When did Planned Parenthood open, nine? She would be herself again when it was over.

"I could help out. I could babysit."

Mara stopped, closed her eyes, and rested a hand atop her head. She wanted to bundle Shannon up and carry her to Massachusetts, guard her for the rest of her life, watch her grow, flourish. She felt it in her arms first, then across her chest and up to her forehead.

"Are you okay?" Shannon asked.

"Would you come back east if I had a baby?"

Shannon's face emitted a slow grin. "Yeah. Maybe."

Mara squeezed her eyes shut before opening them again. "That doesn't mean I'm having a baby."

Shannon let out a horse's sigh. "What the fuck else am I going to do?"

"Really? You'll come?" Mara turned to Shannon and squeezed her shoulder. They never touched, it was so strange—her sister's shoulder surged with a crackling current.

"Yeah."

"Yeah?" Mara said.

"Yeah." Shannon shrugged. Mara couldn't contain the joy in her veins. Her face went red. "What are you gonna do?" Shannon asked.

"I don't know," Mara lied.

She made her appointment, but rather than take the earliest available, she made it for the end of the following week. She finished the Word document, the phone calls; she drove with Shannon to all the agencies and municipal offices that required her notarized signature. They picked up their mother's ashes in a neatly labeled box at the mortuary. They decided they'd take them back east, for now, because they couldn't decide what to do with them.

"You said Mom had a friend. The drag queen," Mara said.

"Yeah." Shannon dropped quarters into a parking meter. "I went to look for him, but I couldn't find him. It was weird, he's always around."

"We should tell him before we go," Mara said.

They had tickets to leave on the fourth of July, a Sunday. Mara's appointment was scheduled for the weekend before. She would ask Shannon to pick her up.

Three days before the appointment, Mara called Nell. Shannon was down the boardwalk hunting for Linda's friend; Mara leaned on the railing and watched the waves tin-foil in the sun. Mara envied the seagulls, who hovered in the air, the angle and position of their bodies equal to the force of the air current, a perfect balance, until it wasn't, and they'd swoop down, then float back up.

"You," Nell breathed into her ear. She was good at the phone; she sounded the same as she did in person, as though you'd come a long way to tell her something she wanted so much to hear. "Hi," Nell said.

"Hi." Mara was not, had never been, good at the phone.

"Where are you?"

"The ocean."

"It's—what color is it?" Nell was remarkable, the way she could meet you in a moment, even when she should have been angry with you, probably *was* angry. She could be there, and be angry later. It was a generosity that would serve her if she ever raised children, a generosity Mara was only ever able to muster around children, and never enough.

"Same as the sun. A white mirror."

"Amazing," Nell said. "You know I've never been to the west coast? Dumb, right?"

"Really?"

"My family didn't go on vacations." Nell was the youngest of five. She had a full scholarship at Smith.

"Me neither," Mara said. For her, it wasn't the money; her father simply didn't want to go anywhere, and Mara never asked. The few times they came to California to visit his parents—and Linda and Shannon—were brief. Her father hated flying, hated spending money on the car, on restaurant food.

"Mar," Nell said. "I'm sorry about your mom."

This was why Mara hated the phone: it took your silence and made it cold. Mara said nothing. Nell was patient as the moment stretched itself further and further. The skittering flashes on the water drifted toward the horizon.

"How are you?" Nell finally asked.

"I don't know," Mara said.

"Relieved?"

"I thought I would be. I can't describe it. It feels like nothing, but it takes up a lot of room."

"I remember that. For about six months after Dad died."

"Then what?"

"It changed. It still changes, just more slowly."

If Nell were next to her, she could tell her everything, but without words.

"What are you going to do?" Nell asked. Everyone wanted to know. If she moved to a place with no people, she'd never be asked this question again. "Are you back at Friends in the fall?"

"Shannon might come. She is coming. She has a ticket."

"Oh, my God. Really?" Nell sounded excited. "Like to visit?"

"Like to live. She's going to stay with me. I want her to register at Whately."

"Okay. Wow."

"You think it's a bad idea?"

"You tell me."

"If I leave, and she stays here . . ." Mara pictured Shannon with a shopping cart and matted hair, settling to sleep on a park bench.

"How old is she again?"

"Twenty-seven. But she has the life skills of a middle schooler."

"And you've invited this person to live with you."

"I need to," Mara said. Her arsenal of caution and doubt had been inhaled by the nothing-feeling. "I need to," she said again. Shannon didn't feel like a burden the way her mother had.

"I think that's lovely," Nell said. "I want to meet her."

Mara smiled at the sky.

"I have to do something else," she said, scanning the horizon for the words. Nell waited. Mara closed her eyes.

"What?" Nell asked.

Mara's thumb hovered over the red circle that would end her call. Her throat sealed itself.

"What's up?"

"I did something stupid," Mara whispered.

Nell waited.

"I'm sorry."

"For what?"

"I'm going to take care of it." If she hadn't said anything, she could have dealt with it and never told Nell. Why on earth did she say anything?

"What are you talking about?"

"The first night I was here, I couldn't pick up my mother. I just—I couldn't. I sort of left myself. It was the weirdest night of my life."

"Okay."

"I met this guy at a bar."

"Oh, God," Nell said suddenly. "I don't want to know. Let's pretend it never happened, can we do that? Literally, delete, erase. Don't tell me."

Mara knew better. She'd ruined everything.

She'd move, she'd never have to see Nell again. She'd let Shannon take over her lease, give her a lump sum of cash and tell her not to fuck it up, and she'd move to a small town where she didn't know anyone. She'd become the librarian everyone loved but no one knew, and someday she'd die there, having winnowed down the space she took up in the world to the smallest possible dimensions.

"I have an appointment at Planned Parenthood," Mara said quietly.

"Wait, what?"

"It's early, it's not even a—it'll be done by Saturday afternoon. We don't have to talk about it. He was—it was the stupidest thing, I didn't—it was like I'd left my body. It was very strange. I don't even know his last name."

"You're *pregnant?*"

"Not really."

"You're *pregnant,*" Nell marveled. "That guy fertilized the egg strolling out of your ovary at that precise moment, and if you don't go to Planned Parenthood, you're going to have a *baby.*" She almost didn't sound angry.

"I'm not going to have a baby."

"You don't want a baby?"

"No!"

"Why not?"

"No. No, no, no, no."

"What if you couldn't get an abortion? What would you do?"

"I am not going to have a baby."

"I always thought I'd be the one who got pregnant," Nell said quietly. "But you would be great." Nell breathed on the other end of the line, her words elusive, for once. Mara made herself blind staring at the sun. Nell spoke again. "If I think of him as a donor, I don't really hate him."

"A donor?"

"What if we had a kid? Would that be so terrible?"

"A child should have two parents who are committed to each other, who have children on purpose."

Nell snorted. "Name one person you know that that's true of."

"You."

"My parents had a *terrible* marriage, and they did not have five kids on purpose." Nell paused. "*We're* committed to each other."

"I am the worst girlfriend. How can you say that?"

"I know you. I like you the way you are."

When Mara crawled out of her dark head and connected with other human beings, she realized how much she liked Nell.

"Where am I going to stash a kid?" she asked. "Where in my life . . . ?"

"What are you talking about? You have great hours, an okay salary, health insurance, enough cash piled up in your Scrooge McDuck savings account to put a down payment on a house . . ." Nell took a breath. "And me."

"And you," Mara heard herself say. She sensed Nell was wise enough not to mention marriage. "I'm sorry," Mara said again.

"I know you are." Nell waited a second before adding, "So am I."

"Why?"

"I hooked up with that woman from Mass MoCA last summer, when we had that big fight. It was stupid, she was married." The woman from Mass MoCA had an otherworldly charisma and looked like Tilda Swinton.

"You hooked up with her?" Mara asked.

Nell sighed.

"What was it like?"

"It was whatever. I felt cheap. It wasn't, like, *good.*"

Mara put the woman out of her mind, half-horrified, half-pleased, a little jealous. "If we want kids, maybe you should have them. I don't want to be pregnant."

"Do you really want to get an abortion?"

"You sound like Focus on the Family."

"Seriously, though. You're already partway there."

"I could miscarry. I'm literally two weeks pregnant."

"Have a baby with me."

It was the pivot of the rest of her life. The gold spots on the water changed position; the sky softened its blazing white, pinkening; all the gulls dipped at once. It felt reckless, like it would be the worst mistake of her life, but it wasn't.

Shannon was coming up on the boardwalk. Mara's phone was back in her pocket, and she was elated and terrified, like a kite. Her sister was accompanied by a tall, stately white man with a deep tan and movie-star sunglasses that flattered his regal face: Garbo. Linda must have envied his beauty and thrilled to his attention.

Mara waited as they approached, a rare grin lingering in her mouth. She stuck out her hand, and he took Mara's fingers and lifted them.

"*Enchanté*," he murmured.

"*Enchanté*," Mara replied. "*Comment vous appelez-vous?*"

"Huh?"

Shannon laughed.

"I'm Mara," she clarified.

"Des," he replied, withdrawing his hand and removing his sunglasses. "A.k.a. Desert Rage, every Friday night at Golden's, nine o'clock sharp." He winked without smiling. "You can call me Garbo."

"It's lovely to meet you," Mara said. "Finally."

"Likewise," he said. "You don't look like Lindy," he mused. "Neither of you do."

"She always told me I looked like this aunt she had," Mara said.

"Aunt Ada," he told her, studying her face. "That's who you look like. I think she was a dyke."

"Well," Mara said.

It had never occurred to her that her mother had friends: Linda who was so alone in her grandeur, so lost and deluded. But here was her friend. He was real.

"I'm sorry," she told him.

"Me too," he said.

She wanted to ask him so many questions. He seemed congenial but prickly, good at keeping a distance while entertaining you with his patter. She tried to memorize him, memorize the moment. She might never see him again.

"Are you having a service?" he asked.

"We're going back east," Shannon said shyly, almost proud. "We haven't planned anything."

"You're going to New York?" Garbo asked.

"Massachusetts," Mara said. Her throat fluttered. She felt weightless, on the verge of tears, too many things. "We leave in a few weeks. We can do something before then."

"She admired Viking funerals," Garbo said. "Where you set the boat on fire."

"We can scatter her ashes in the ocean," Shannon said. "Like from the end of the pier."

"The pier," Mara said. "That's perfect." She squeezed Shannon's shoulder, surprised, again, at its heat under her hand. She turned to her mother's friend. "Tomorrow?"

"Tomorrow?" he guffawed. "I'ma need more time to prepare than twenty-four hours."

"No, no, you don't have to do anything," Mara said. "Just show up."

"Mary, I don't just *show up*," he told her, smoothing the faint hair on his head. "You have to understand something, girls: your mother was one of us. We need to mark her departure."

Was he angry with them? What was Linda to Garbo, to his community? Had she finally found her audience?

"How much time do you need?" Shannon asked.

"Gimme a week."

"How about next Tuesday?" Mara asked.

"Sure," he sniffed. "In the afternoon."

"Meet us at Denny's," Shannon told him. "We'll be there at one o'clock."

"Two o'clock."

"Two o'clock," Mara confirmed, chastened.

Mara made grilled cheese that evening. Shannon and Linda's dishes and utensils were the kind you bought at the grocery store when you were twenty and had roommates; Mara had spent a long evening scouring the crud from everything with powdered cleanser, and now the pan and the spatula had a cross-hatched, submissive blankness. She pressed the spatula into the bread, and the cheddar squeezed out and sizzled.

"So you draw a lot?" she asked Shannon, trying to sound casual.

"Yeah." Shannon scrolled through the Whately Community College fall course catalog on Mara's laptop. "But that's not, like, a job. Right?"

"Being an artist?"

"Drawing comics."

"I mean, it's somebody's job. I don't know how hard it is to get, or what it pays." She doubted it paid very much. "What about illustration? Or graphic design?" she asked, with no idea what they paid, but it had to be better than Rite Aid. She wanted Shannon to like her job, whatever it was.

"What's STEM?"

"Science, technology—"

"Oh, it says right here. Do engineers make a lot of money?"

"Yes. IT is part of that, too." Mara placed a pat of butter on the bread and flipped it. "Are you good at math?"

"I don't know. No." Shannon squinted into the screen. "Maybe you don't have to be. *I had written off science and math as something I couldn't do. Now, I see math and science as a major, or a career: they're attainable,*" Shannon read. "It's a program that starts in June."

Mara wanted Shannon enrolled sooner than a year from now, but she liked that Shannon was interested. "Start making a list," she said. "We can talk about all the options." She scooped the sandwiches from the pan onto two plates, tore some paper towels, and brought them to the kitchen table. She closed the laptop, and Shannon blinked, disoriented.

"So, like," Shannon said to her plate as Mara began to eat. "What are you, um. What are you gonna do? About the . . . ?"

Mara chewed slowly. She wasn't going to be alone much from now on, was she? Shannon sharing her apartment. If she stayed pregnant, she'd find a place with Nell. There would be three of them. Four, if Shannon stayed with them, which, maybe she should. Why didn't it fill her with the old panic?

"I talked to my girlfriend," Mara said.

"Is this mustard?" Shannon asked, alarmed.

"You don't like it?"

"I don't know." Shannon turned the sandwich over and took another bite. "What did she say?"

"She was mad."

"About the dude?"

Mara nodded. "But when I told her I was pregnant . . ." Mara could still hardly bring herself to say the word, especially in relation to herself. It was surreal, it grossed her out a little.

"What did she say?"

"She . . . wants to raise a child. With me." Mara found herself smiling in awe and bafflement. "She wants to meet you."

"See?" Shannon said, mouth half-full. "It's gonna be fine. It's gonna be great."

The following Tuesday, at five minutes to four, Mara looked up from her phone in the corner booth at Denny's to see a commotion in the near-empty dining room. She gasped. A statuesque, severe figure in black with white hair was ducking through the door, followed by five identically dressed mourners, in descending order by height. It was as if Garbo had shifted her immediate vicinity into black and white, like an old film. They progressed slowly to Mara's table, almost in sync, somber as a line of swans. One by one, they eased themselves into the booth. Garbo remained standing.

Her face was pale, with dark red lips, extravagantly dense lashes, and smoky eyes like Mae West's. Her wig, silvery platinum, was styled with gamine finger waves that fell to her chin and made her look twenty years younger. Her demeanor was ethereal, eerily calm, underpinned by the same steely confidence she'd shown on the pier.

Close up, she towered over Mara, who wondered whether to stand or remain seated. Garbo's dress, layers of black chiffon, had a high, straight neckline and long sleeves; the skirt clung to her hips and legs, with shimmery beaded details near the hem. Sculptural black-satin platform shoes, staggeringly high, peeked out from the bottom. She had long red nails and a starched white handkerchief in her fist.

"Sorry I'm late," Garbo said softly. "I was on a call with my astrologer." She leaned down and pecked Mara on the cheek.

Mara almost laughed, but she didn't want to disturb the five seated drag queens, who stared into the distance with expressions of quiet grief. They weren't dressed identically, she saw now, but wore variations on a narrow theme, kind of steampunk meets professional mourner, each one with a black satin pillbox hat and a little veil perched atop her head.

Garbo lowered herself into the booth as Shannon bumped through the glass door, butt first, hugging a grocery bag. Mara and

Shannon had not dressed for their mother's memorial, which, Mara now understood, was not going to be the brief, modest moment she'd imagined. Shannon beelined to the table, set the grocery bag down at the booth's edge, and scooted in next to Mara, smelling faintly of cigarettes.

"Ladies," Garbo announced. "Meet my regatta." She turned toward her companions. "Girls," she prompted, lifting her chin.

"Palm Stings," murmured the first, with a brief nod.

"Rancho Fantasé," the second declared.

"Venice," said the third.

"Legs Adagio," the fourth quipped, flipping her hair over her shoulder.

"Zenaida Macroura," announced the fifth, a lifetime of theater training in her voice.

They were decades younger than Garbo—younger, even, than Mara, possibly younger than Shannon. How did anyone so young figure out how to inhabit themselves with such confidence? How did they get their makeup to look so precise? How did they pay for everything?

"And this is Mara, Lindy's daughter from the east," Garbo said grandly, gesturing toward her. "And you all know Shannon, of course."

"Hey," the middle one offered. Shannon waved shyly. They sat for a while in silence, taking each other in. Finally, Garbo spoke.

"Lindy reminded me of my mother," she mused, playing with the handkerchief.

"Didn't your mother . . . ?" Zenaida asked, cocking an eyebrow.

"My mother was the Last Great Drunk of Tucson, Arizona," Garbo said, crossing herself. "She died when I was twenty-five, the night I came out to her. She went for a drive and ran the car into a department store window on Congress Street."

The others looked skeptically at Garbo, resenting, perhaps, the way she always made herself the star of the show.

"Was she drunk because of what I told her?" Garbo went on. "Was she always drunk? Was she *more* drunk? Did it matter, would she have driven through the dresses anyway?"

"How did she remind you of Lindy?" Zenaida asked pointedly.

Garbo smiled. "She had *style.* There was nothing ordinary about my mother—it didn't matter that we lived in a ranch house on a cul de sac in the desert, or that her misery was the same damn misery as everybody else's—she carried herself like she was somebody. Even walking through a department store, hunting for the sale rack, she had panache, you know what I mean? I'm still mad at her, but I miss her like hell. It hasn't sunk in yet that Lindy's gone, but I'ma miss her like hell too."

"Word," Fanta murmured. "She was funny as shit."

"Right?" cried Legs. "And you know what, mama? That bitch could dance. I know she was having a hard time at the end, like balance-wise, but I remember when I first started at Golden's, and there was this party or something, I can't remember, but all the tables were pushed out of the way, and we were all wildin' out, and there was Lindy, this old-ass, random-ass lady, and, like—you could tell she'd been a dancer. You could just tell." She sighed at the memory. "Did she send you guys to dance lessons? She must have."

"No," Mara told them.

"No?" Legs asked. "That's fucked up."

"Lindy looked good," Venice said, changing the subject.

"No, she didn't," Shannon replied. "Sorry," she added.

"That's not what she means," Garbo clarified. "She never lost it."

"Lost what?" Shannon asked.

"*It.* You know it when you see it."

This was true, Mara thought. Their mother *was* special—but being special, in itself, didn't save you from narcissism, from alcoholism, from the disaster of your life. It gave you a strange light that followed you around, flickering, never quite fading. Linda was special, and awful, and surprising, and dead.

Mara thought they'd turn heads on the boardwalk, their beautiful, spidery procession making its slow way to the pier. But they didn't. The drag queens from Golden's probably promoted the show out there all the time, and the funereal aspect probably just looked like another show, not an actual cortège. As they drew closer to the pier, Garbo signaled to the others, so subtly that Mara wasn't sure she'd seen it—a tiny motion of the hand, a flick of the handkerchief. After a moment, she thought she heard music, but it was so faint it could have been anything, maybe a car radio up on the boulevard. Then, slowly, the music began to fill the air around them, its volume increasing until it became their soundtrack: each of the drag queens was playing the same song from her cell phone. It was a dreamy song with a hypnotic beat, no vocals. It might have been an interlude between numbers at Golden's, a keyboard-driven EDM track that Mara and Nell had probably heard walking down Commercial Street in P-Town, but here, as accompaniment, it elevated the pathos of the moment to something cinematic. You only get a handful of moments in your life that feel like you're in a movie, and this was one of them.

Garbo snapped her fingers, and the ensemble paused for a breath. The music hastened its tempo, and they began a walking choreography, adding balletic arm flourishes, little crossover steps, head tosses, and even a three-step turn. The moves became more elaborate as they headed out along the pier toward the ocean. They were marvelously synchronized, despite their height and size differences; whoever directed them didn't brook mistakes. Mara stole a glance at Shannon and saw naked delight on her sister's face.

Would Linda have loved her daughters differently if they hadn't been so different from her?

Were they really so different?

The pier ended in a T-shape, fishing poles and fishermen leaning against the perimeter railing. The marine layer had burned off, and the sun was a bright, warm net over the shoreline. Garbo led the group to a corner between two coin-operated viewfinders. They gathered in a small circle, and she faced them like an officiant. The music had faded without Mara noticing the shift to silence.

"Where is she?" Garbo asked Shannon.

Shannon looked at Garbo, bewildered. "Who?"

"Your mother."

"Huh?"

"The *box*, Mary," Garbo implored.

"Oh," Shannon said, and she dug around in the grocery bag, which was full of random, nonessential items, like what you'd clean out of your desk at work. She pulled out a beige plastic container with a typed label on top.

A helicopter cruised overhead, making its way up the shore, but otherwise the pier was quiet: the water dipped and swelled, swallowing its own friction.

"It's heavier than I thought," Shannon said, weighing the box in her hands. Linda, who was so slight in life, finally dense with heft.

"I've never done this before," Mara said.

"I have," Garbo said, taking the box from Shannon. She held it gently atop her open palms, gazing down at it. She took one hand and smoothed her neckline. Finally, she spoke. "I want you all to think of a word," she commanded. "If you're feeling greedy, you can have two." She paused, then lifted her head and closed her eyes. "We are here to invoke and pay respects to our sister Linda Glory Meade, née Taggart, the misbegotten only child of the dear, departed Miss Audrey Draudt, may all of them rest in peace and strength," she said, projecting all the way to the fishermen.

Mara thought her grandmother's name was Gail, and that Linda had a brother, but the details of her mother's history had always been foggy.

"Linda Glory was born in Orange County, California, and to my knowledge she never set foot beyond Golden State lines. Her life was not a worldly, well-traveled life, but Miss Linda knew things. Understood things. Her immediate family did not understand her, didn't see in her what she saw in herself. A situation to which all of us can relate."

"Amen," someone said.

"She knew she was beautiful. She knew she was fabulous," Garbo said.

"*Yes*," Legs affirmed.

"Her life wasn't easy. She knew tragedy."

"Mm-hmm," Venice murmured.

"But Lindy—" Garbo faltered and glared at the sky. She shook her head, impatient with the threat of tears. "It's your turn, girls. Go." She turned to Zenaida, who was standing very still, her arms folded. "One word," Garbo prompted. Zenaida blinked and touched a gloved knuckle to her eye.

"Smart."

"Mm!" grunted Venice.

Zenaida turned to Legs, who offered, "*Port de bras*."

"Girl, what?"

"It's *French*, bitch. It's a ballet term, how you carry your arms." Zenaida rolled her eyes.

"Venice. Go," Garbo said.

"She was *funny*," Venice said. Garbo cackled briefly, and the others smiled.

Humor, as a quality in a friend, was something on which Mara placed an almost sacred importance. Her friend David was her funniest friend, but several of her friends had this gift. Nell, too. Would Mara have found her mother funny if she'd been a fly on the wall at Denny's, listening to Linda and Garbo and the whole clique jammed into the corner booth? How often had that happened, how enmeshed in their world was she? Did they all love her, or just the queens gathered here at the pier? Was there more than love—ambivalence, annoyance, repulsion?

She'd never know.

"Fanta. Go."

"Advice," Fanta said.

Shannon gaped at her.

"She'd be like, 'Darling, you know what the problem is?' Like I'd asked. She always had advice, she didn't care if you weren't asking. 'Darling,' she'd say, 'the problem is in the *rhythm*. You're cramming too many steps into each count, you're crowding the beats.' And I'd be, like, 'Bitch, what does that *mean*?' But you know what? She was fucking right."

"For real, though," Legs said. "You do crowd the beats." Fanta sliced her with her eyes.

"Sting," Garbo said.

The quietest of the group cleared her throat. "Family," she said.

Garbo waited, then slowly turned to Mara and Shannon, who stood to her left. "Go ahead, ladies."

"Um," Mara said. "Unforgettable." She hoped it would suffice, but it wasn't quite right; her memory of her mother was full of holes, shadows and blankness she couldn't explain.

Garbo turned to Shannon. "Now you, honey. Take your time."

"She was our mom," Shannon finally said. "She's going back to the water, back to Allison." Shannon folded her arms, hugging herself.

Garbo gestured with one hand, and the ensemble stepped forward to form a line at the railing, facing the ocean. Mara and

Shannon joined them, and Zenaida moved to the middle, where she lifted her face to the light and shook her shoulders back. She began to sing in a breathtaking tenor, the first note like a bell, clear as water. It was an old song, Mara guessed, its melody haunting, almost familiar. "In everything that's light and gay," Zenaida sang, drawing out each syllable as its own quivering moment, her voice carrying into the sun, "I'll always think of you that way . . ." When she finished, she bowed her head. Mara blinked, furious at her tears.

Garbo raised the little beige box high in the air.

"Lindy," she called out. "We'll be seeing you." Her voice gave way. "We're gonna miss you, girl." She lowered the box to her chest and fingered its lid open. Inside was another, smaller cardboard box; she handed the plastic box to Shannon. She opened the cardboard box, dropped it at her feet, and pulled out a densely packed little plastic bag, its contents fine and faded grey, like beach sand. It was closed tight with a twist tie, which Garbo unwound with weary expertise, flinging the tie onto the pier. She stepped to the rail, and Zenaida and Sting swiftly appeared on either side of her, placing their arms across her back for ballast. Garbo leaned out over the water. The ocean's surface was a blue that shifted from translucence to grey to green to something brighter, the foam swirling on top, the movement unhurried, unstoppable as the planet's gravity. Garbo upended the plastic bag, and they all inched forward, pressing themselves against the rail to watch the ashes float down to the water, a longer distance than you might think. Some seemed to disappear in the air; most of it settled weightlessly on the water's surface. The ocean inhaled, paused, and held Linda in its cupped throat. Then it rose and churned, and all they saw was foam.

Shannon took the week to clear her room. She lugged a garbage bag full of glass bottles to the curb, and Mara wanted to believe they were some kind of collection, the way people put green or blue bottles on their window sills to catch the light, but she figured Shannon had squirreled away a sizable portion of Linda's vodka stash, and she had her own stash, too. It would have been easy to conceal the extent of her drinking in those weird, silent weeks they spent in the apartment together. Plus, Shannon sometimes went on walks, and who knew who she hooked up with, what she smoked. Mara wasn't around drinkers and drug users enough to be able to discern from a brief glimpse what someone had been up to.

Well. This was why she was bringing Shannon to Massachusetts. They would take it one day at a time. When Mara thought about it, she came back to the same thing: if she left without Shannon, her sister wouldn't fend for herself, no matter what she said. Mara couldn't live with herself if she just went back to her life. Her old life wasn't there to go back to.

The twilit Friday before the Fourth of July, Shannon was out somewhere, and Mara peeked into her room. It was bare except for two duffel bags. She felt a pang for the crate of comic books; had Shannon thrown them out? The room still smelled skunky and fungal. The windows were open, and a balmy breeze fluttered the screens. Shannon must have slept on the carpet with the duffel for a pillow; the bed was gone, the furniture, the room empty, scoured of itself, no stray trash along the baseboards or in the closet. Mara wanted to dig through the duffels but didn't.

She thought of Shannon's comic, the notebook she filled. That was when Mara understood. The notebook sent roots into Mara, waking up the dormant knowledge that Shannon was real, she was alive, she was her sister. What if she hadn't shown her the notebook, hadn't drawn anything at all? Would Mara have pressed for a yes? Would it have made her so happy?

Everything in her life was conditional. She'd have loved her mother if Linda had been a better mother. She'd have been more generous toward Shannon if Shannon had been more—sympathetic? Say it: more like you.

If. If.

She'd have had an abortion if Nell and Shannon hadn't been so excited. If building a family didn't suddenly seem like a possible answer to the funnel of dark, empty air that howled at the center of herself. She pictured her sadness as the skinny tip of a tornado. Sometimes the bottom would vanish and it would seem to dance further away; then it bore down, pulling everything into its centrifuge.

Staying pregnant—raising a child—making a family with Nell, with Shannon—probably wasn't the answer. There was no answer, the cold funnel would always be there. But she supposed there were different ways to live with it.

She was relieved to see Shannon come through the screen door that night. She asked her if she was hungry, and Shannon said no. Mara tried to picture where she'd been, what she'd done, and couldn't do it. She didn't ask. It was Shannon's last evening of this particular autonomy, this life of hers in Silver Beach, this moment between being Linda's daughter and Mara's sister: it belonged to her.

Mara hoped Shannon wasn't that bad a drunk. She figured she probably was. Maybe she would be the sort of drunk who grew out of it, who didn't have to try rehab fifty times.

They'd decided to be a family.

They sat in the evening's blue silence at the kitchen table, the only light coming from a lamp Mara had saved and plugged in on the countertop. The cupboards and drawers were empty; the cord to the fridge snaked around its front, inert. The lamp cast a warm, quiet glow, transforming the kitchen into something softer. Mara wished they knew how to play cards. Nell's family played cards; Mara had gone with her to reunions in the Adirondacks, week-long stays at a big, rented old house on a lake, and the aunts, uncles, and grandparents passed the hours after dinner around a table playing pinochle, eating peanuts from a can. The easy companionability of it, the way it made you close without having to really talk about anything. Why didn't people play cards anymore?

They could learn. They could be a family that played cards. Her father and stepmother could move to Northampton, live down the street. They'd all play cards. The child would have grandparents.

A stab of sadness hit her then to realize the child would never know the drag queens who had befriended their mother or, for that matter, Linda herself, who would never have a chance to redeem herself, to be a grandmother when she couldn't bring herself to be a mother.

"Do you remember my father's parents? In Indio?" she asked Shannon.

"I never met them."

"You did," Mara told her. "Mom sent us to stay with them right after Allison died. We were there for weeks."

"I don't remember."

"You were basically still a baby. A toddler. You were incredibly fussy. Nobody could soothe you. I could, a little."

"You?"

Mara smiled. "Yep."

"What was the deal with Mom's parents?"

"She cut herself off from them. I don't know why. I asked my dad about it, and he didn't know either. He only met them once."

"I have, like, no family," Shannon said.

Mara sighed. "You have me."

"That's it. I have you."

The next morning, Mara woke before her alarm. Like Shannon, she slept on the carpet, using a towel as a pillow. Their flight was at noon, and Mara liked to get to an airport early, plus she had to return the car. She flinched at the thought of what the rental bill would be, but her father had offered to help her with it, and she'd relented. These were new times.

She was so fortunate.

Shannon's door was closed when Mara went into the hall. She washed her face, brushed her teeth, packed her toiletry kit and zipped it into her suitcase. In the kitchen, she unplugged the lamp and wound the cord around its base. She'd leave it for the landlord, plus the table and two chairs.

It was her last morning in California; she ought to go to the beach. Shannon wouldn't be up for another hour, at least, and they'd still have time to pick up coffee and pastries somewhere before heading to the airport, which was right there. The day you flew on a plane always felt like a hurry, but they didn't need to rush.

She pulled a sweatshirt over her head. It said *SILVER BEACH* across the front; she'd bought it at one of the tourist boutiques at the end of Obsidian. Not her style at all, but she liked how it made her blend in.

She'd miss the grey mornings. They were like a shawl, gentle and close, a whisper at your ear. A cool grey morning gave you room to think. If she lived here, she'd take this walk every day.

Diamond Street dead-ended at a vacant lot, but if you turned into the alley, there was a path between two buildings that led to a well-worn trail, which picked up where the boardwalk left off. On the ocean side, mounds of ice plant sloped down toward cliffs, which dropped to a hard, narrow beach. At low tide, it looked like you could walk across the sand, but you probably had to keep an eye on it and be careful not to get stranded. You couldn't see the sand from the path, only the grey water, the surfers bobbing, the white layer of moisture that hung over them.

She'd miss the smell of the air.

She had another month to decide if she wanted to stay pregnant. Technically. She didn't know the legal restrictions, but in her mind she wanted to terminate before there was a heartbeat. If that's what she wanted to do.

She was flying blind. She tried to find the panic this ought to have triggered, but couldn't.

She'd bring the child back to California, to Silver Beach, to this spot where you couldn't see the sand, and she'd say, "This is where you're from. I know it's weird, but we're from here."

In the apartment, she peeled off her sweatshirt and stepped out of her sandals. The apartment slept; in an hour, she'd wake Shannon. Everything was packed. They'd leave the key under the door. The landlord would love them for making his job so easy.

She sat at the kitchen table. She did not feel pregnant at all, whatever it was supposed to feel like. Nauseous? Fragile? Pained? Bountiful? She felt like her thin, hard self.

There was a note under the lamp she hadn't seen before, tucked beneath the cord. Notebook paper. Mara plucked it, unfolded it.

YOU GO AHEAD—IM GOOD, DONT LOOK FOR ME, ILL BE FINE—ILL TRY TO CALL. S.

Way down at the bottom, smaller: *SORRY ABOUT THE TICKET, ILL PAY U BACK IF I CAN*

Mara stared at it mutely. She went to Shannon's door and opened it: the room was empty. She walked out quickly, as though a malign spirit lingered there, and shut the door behind her. She wanted it to be an hour earlier, she wanted not to have gone to the water.

Had she been gone all morning? Had Shannon slipped out while Mara slept?

Mara hadn't thought to ask her sister about her car, whether she would sell it or what. A logistical item that had escaped her attention. Shannon would be in the car now, on her way.

Don't look for me. Did someone say this when she wanted to be looked for? Or the opposite? Where would she begin to look for Shannon?

They were strangers.

Mara locked the apartment behind her and slipped the key under the door, but she left a note tucked in the jamb with the landlord's number on it and the message that it was paid through July, if Shannon came back and wanted to stay longer. She wrote her cell number, her work number, her father's number, her address, her email. She knew it was pointless. She walked around to the carport, just in case, and the parking spot was empty. The damp oil spot looked fresh.

She felt a hollow, mean wind through her body. It started in her feet and pushed through her stomach, her limbs, her throat, and gathered in her head, where she felt a migraine coming on. She wished she was a crier; it might relieve some of the pressure. Her joints felt like screws.

Should she stay? That seemed stupid.

She drove to the airport, squeezing her fury into something small and dense. The grey moisture burned away, leaving a throbbing white sky. Everything happened too quickly: returning the car, catching the shuttle, checking in, finding a seat in the waiting area at the gate, the tarmac bright and unblinking. She was almost three hours early. She'd forgotten to get coffee, to eat.

Nell would understand. It was Mara's body, after all. She'd say she miscarried. It would be an easy secret to keep.

She could go somewhere else, release Nell from her bond, become the mysterious librarian in the little New England town, troubling no one. She'd be forgotten, eventually, by most of the people she'd known.

...

It was an escape route she kept tucked away through all their years together, a plan that became less plausible with time. The pregnancy was fraught, and it strained Mara's composure, her sense of herself. Her daughter, Lise, was born prematurely, but she was fine. Lise's life would go on to have its share of tragedy, no more than anyone else's.

All told, years and years later, of course Mara was glad. Nell was a more skilled parent than she was, but Mara was grateful for Lise and never stopped being a little in awe of her.

Mara hoped—more than she thought she could ever hope for anything—that Shannon might show up someday. She made sure she was always listed, easy to find. Maybe Garbo took her in; maybe her sister figured it out on her own. Mara would never know.

Acknowledgments

I am so grateful to the following people:

All the Hunters in the fiction program, 2011–2013, particularly Brad Fox, Dana Czapnik, Victoria Brown, Jesse Barron, Sadia Shepard, and Jane Breakell, and my Hunter elders, Kaitlyn Greenidge and Scott Cheshire, for advice and guidance. (Scott, you knew where the story needed to begin!) And, of course, Peter Carey, Colum McCann, and Claire Messud, for everything.

Sam Michel, for choosing this book. Sienna Baskin, for pointing out something important. Jeffy Hnilicka and Elliot Montague for helping me see Garbo. David McBean, for finding just the right song. My scientist neighbors in New England for their insight into bird, insect, and anuran sounds: Molly Hale, Charley Eiseman, David Spector, Bruce Byers, Paige Warren, and Lang Elliott. The generous social workers, doctors, and experts who helped me work out critical Linda details: Lisa Howe, Michael Eichler, Debbie Shriver, Andrea Glover, Pita Quintana, Dr. Mert Erogul, Dr. Ileana Benga, Elizabeth Pinedo, and Michael Manekin, who also gets credit for the phrase "in the irony-free zone, behind the Tofu Curtain."

My mother, Susan Cox; my family on both coasts; and the vital circle of my mother's friends. My mentor and friend Deb Salzer and the incredible people at Playwrights Project, who started treating me like a proper writer when I was seventeen. Len Berkman and Elly Donkin for their indefatigable encouragement. The indispensable QWG: may we someday meet around a table.

And of course: Carlos, my first, best reader. Thank you.

JUNIPER
JUNIPER PRIZE FOR FICTION

This volume is the twenty-first recipient
of the Juniper Prize for Fiction,
established in 2004 by the
University of Massachusetts Press
in collaboration with the
UMass Amherst MFA Program
for Poets and Writers, to be
presented annually for an outstanding
work of literary fiction. Like its sister award,
the Juniper Prize for Poetry established
in 1976, the prize is named in honor
of Robert Francis (1901–1987),
who lived for many years at
Fort Juniper, Amherst, Massachusetts.